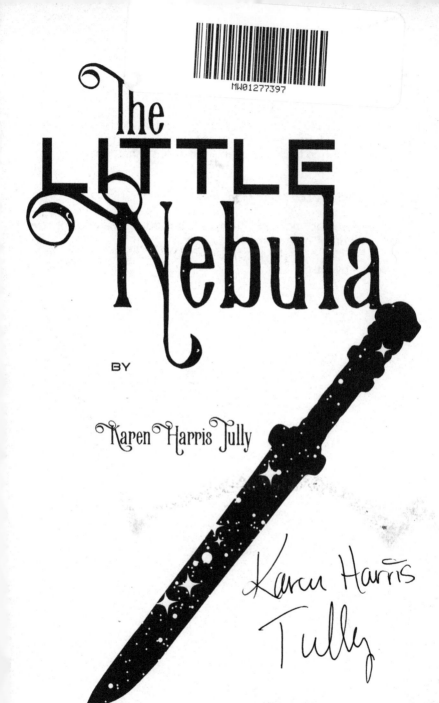

The LITTLE Nebula

BY

Karen Harris Tully

Karen Harris Tully

Blue Zephyr Press
2661 N. Pearl, #360
Tacoma WA 98407

This book is a work of fiction. Names, characters, and incidents are products of the author's imagination or are used fictiously. Any resemblance to actual events or persons living or dead is entirely coincidental.

Cover art by **LILT**.

ISBN-10: 1-7320863-8-9
ISBN-13: 978-1-7320863-8-8

Acknowledgments

First and always, thank you to my whole family for your constant love and support, especially my wonderful husband Mike, and our kiddos Gabe and Sasha. I don't know how I would do what I do without you.

Thanks to my proofreader, JoDean Jordan who helped me polish my work, and everyone who read my (not always stellar) early drafts. You're amazing! And a special, huge thanks to my brilliant, inspiring co-creators of this universe we call Galactic Dreams, JM Phillippe and Bethany Maines. Cheers, we did it!

Table of Contents

TIMELINE VI
INTRODUCTION VII

SOURCE CODE:
The Little Mermaid 1
CHAPTER 1: 2
CHAPTER 2: 11
CHAPTER 3: 16
CHAPTER 4: 20
CHAPTER 5: 27
CHAPTER 6: 32
CHAPTER 7: 38
CHAPTER 8: 48
CHAPTER 9: 51
CHAPTER 10: 58
CHAPTER 11: 63
CHAPTER 12: 65
CHAPTER 13: 80
CHAPTER 14: 89
CHAPTER 15: 101
CHAPTER 16: 109
CHAPTER 17: 112
CHAPTER 18: 123
CHAPTER 19: 137
CHAPTER 20: 144
CHAPTER 21: 157
CHAPTER 22: 165
CHAPTER 23: 173
CHAPTER 24: 182
CHAPTER 25: 197
CHAPTER 26: 211
CHAPTER 27: 215

CHAPTER 28: 235
CHAPTER 29: 242
CHAPTER 30: 252
CHAPTER 31: 255
CHAPTER 32: 258
CHAPTER 33: 264

DEAR READER 272
The Glitter of Gold 273
GALACTIC DREAMS 285
ABOUT THE AUTHOR 286
OTHER WORKS BY KAREN HARRIS TULLY 287

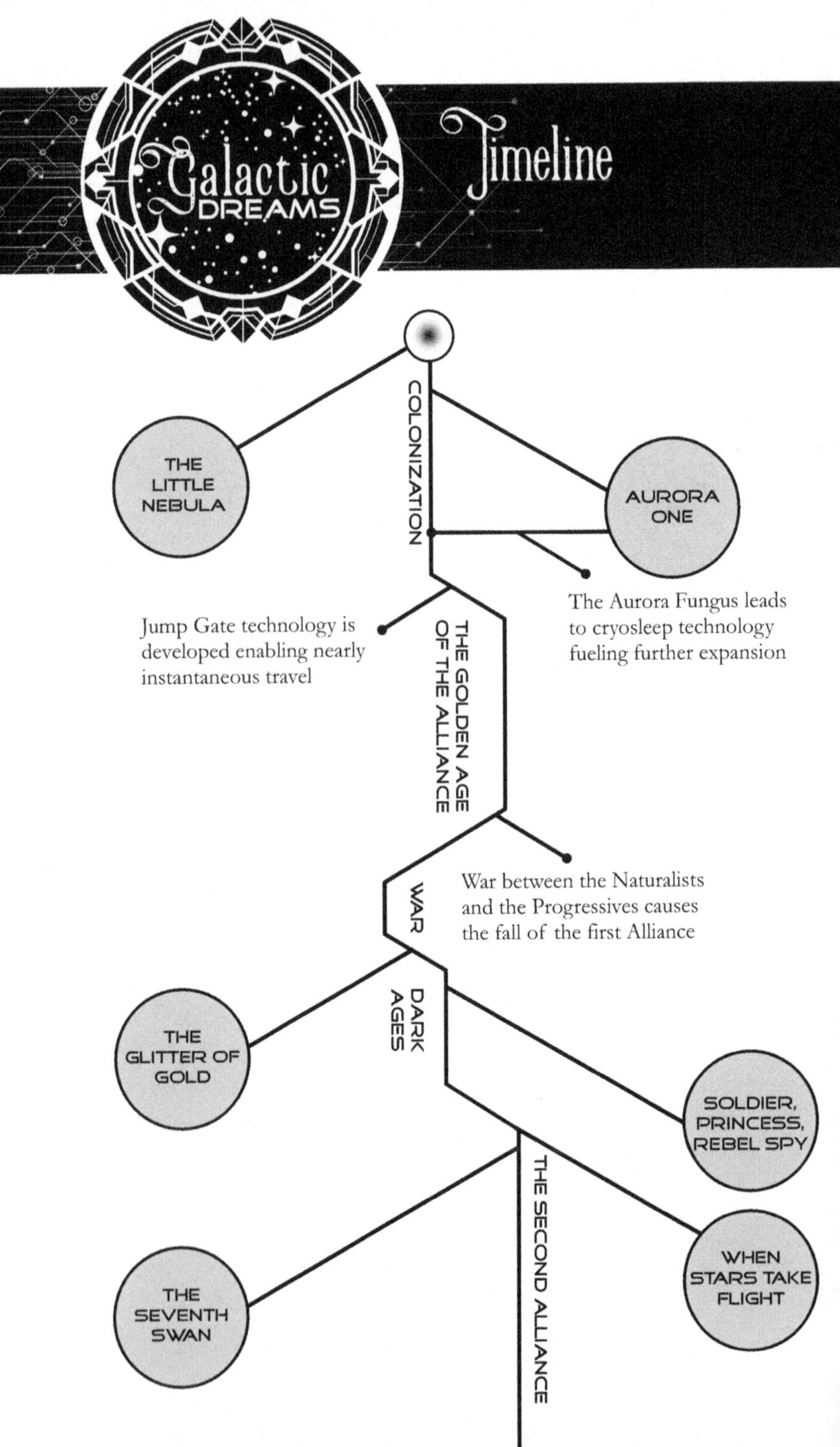
Galactic
DREAMS
Timeline
COLONIZATION
THE LITTLE NEBULA
AURORA ONE
The Aurora Fungus leads to cryosleep technology fueling further expansion
Jump Gate technology is developed enabling nearly instantaneous travel
THE GOLDEN AGE OF THE ALLIANCE
War between the Naturalists and the Progressives causes the fall of the first Alliance
WAR
DARK AGES
THE GLITTER OF GOLD
SOLDIER, PRINCESS, REBEL SPY
THE SECOND ALLIANCE
WHEN STARS TAKE FLIGHT
THE SEVENTH SWAN

Introduction

WHAT IF...

...in the future the stars must fight to save humanity?
...an algae farmer's daughter and a spy make a deadly bargain to save everything they both love?
...a silent engineer on an empty moon can save a prince from an ancient evil?

Welcome to the universe of Galactic Dreams, where fairy tales are reimagined for a new age—the future. In each Galactic Dreams Volume 2 novella you'll find an old tale reborn with a mixture of romance, technology, aliens and adventure. But this time, each Prince and Princess, each band of intrepid heroes, is fighting the same enemy — an entity so vast that he can span centuries and not everyone is guaranteed to survive.

Galactic Dreams is a unique series of science-fiction novellas from Blue Zephyr Press featuring retellings of classic tales from different authors, all sharing the same universe, technology, and history.

We hope you enjoy this adventure.

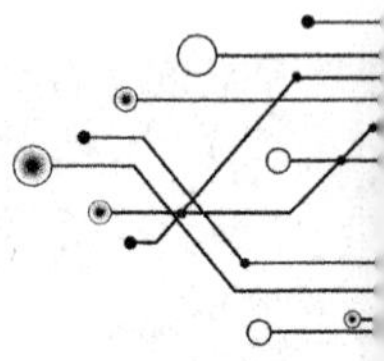

[T]he youngest was the prettiest of them all; her skin was as clear and delicate as a rose-leaf, and her eyes as blue as the deepest sea; but, like all the others, she had no feet, and her body ended in a fish's tail.

Hans Christian Andersen, The Little Mermaid (1836)

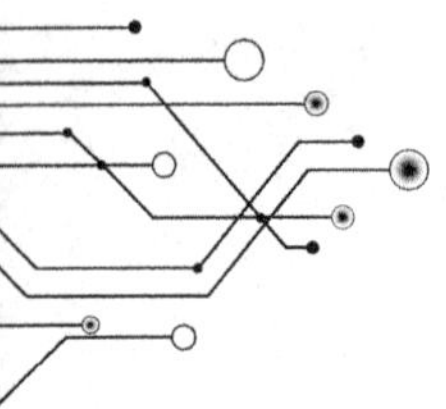

Chapter 1:

SATELLITE SURFING

—Luminous—

Luminous was an energetic nebula, as far as nebulae go. Living in the cold, near-vacuum of space, made up of energy, gas, and dust, she refused to settle for the gravitational pull of any of the larger celestial bodies, like her siblings kept advising her. Why would she want that? Her surfing verged on art, creating beautiful aurora borealis above Earth. Plus, she loved to watch the fast-paced, short-lived people on its surface, both from above and through their holo-vision signals.

The humans were so full of life and noise, growth and emotion, as they floated through space on their blue-green planet. They were fascinating. They were also dirty, careless, and wasteful.

Look out below! Luminous crashed through a snarl of broken satellites and defunct space junk, surfing her once-favorite atmosphere: Earth's. The debris spiraled out of orbit in her wake to burn up on re-entry.

For many hundreds of Earth's orbits, the people had been extracting Earth's resources and turning it into trash. The space around the planet was now so full of human-made debris she could barely even surf her favorite spots. And now they'd turned to mining nearby asteroids to get more resources to create more short-lived junk for an ever-growing population. They could not seem to control themselves in creating either more garbage, or more people creating more garbage.

She'd tried talking to them, but communicating with humans was hard. She'd come to the conclusion that their attention spans were too short for meaningful conversation. Also, they didn't seem able to see her as anything other than random gas and dust. And so, she'd had to watch while they junked up the Earth's oceans, land, and her orbit. She'd had to devise a more direct way of communicating the problem to them.

Bombs away! she called in the universal language of radiation, though humans did not seem to recognize it in the least. Undeterred, she gathered up some junk in her gaseous dust cloud and released it toward a newly-launched satellite. Pieces ricocheted off its solar panels and it fired boosters to right its course. But she couldn't have that. For humans to take action, she had to hit them where it hurt: in their brand new technology.

She stretched herself out and tumbled the satellite into her gaseous tentacles, swung it around, aimed and released it to enter Earth's atmosphere, burning toward the giant island of trash stuck in the swirl of the ocean's currents. She followed it up with a whole swath of debris and felt a deep satisfaction in returning some of the humans' litter to them. She knew aiming at cities would garner more attention to her cause, but she drew the line at terrorism.

Recently, over the last two hundred orbits or so, humans had actually been trying to deal with their discarded resources on Earth's surface and oceans. Skeptically she'd watched them build something they called the Elevator. It was a moving platform that rose from one of the land masses in the northern hemisphere up into space to a well-fortified satellite tethered in geo-synchronous orbit. She'd heard the excited chatter on the radio waves when it began working, and ever since, over the course of many orbits, humans had used it to shuttle large, compact trash cubes from the Earth's land and oceans up into space. Weak ion pulses set them on a long trail to their fiery demise in the Sun. But humans hadn't yet addressed the junk they'd left adrift above Luminous's favorite planetary atmosphere.

It hurt to see the Earth this way. But without being able to talk with humans, satellite destruction was her best—her only—method of communication.

As for the overcrowding, humans seemed to be trying out several solutions, none of which had even made a dent. They had placed surface domes on the moon and planet Mars, but hadn't yet seemed to figure out how to create an atmosphere like Earth's in either place. And, they had built an enormous space station currently out near Luminous's home planet Neptune, which used thrusters to keep itself in a strange, unnatural non-orbit. She supposed they must have a reason, but stars if she could figure out what it was. They called it the Tersa Tellus Space Port.

So many ships had puttered their way out to the silver, double-ring port, including recently, the three biggest space ships yet. Though she couldn't talk with the humans, she could hear their excitement and knew this was a big deal for them. She kept hearing one word: colonies.

And then, the excitement spiked, with a strong added emotion: fear. She heard a mass of radio waves projected all around the Earth and saw more frenzied activity than any human event she'd ever witnessed. She had no idea what was causing it, except she kept hearing the same word over and over, in every language: Pangaloid.

She had no idea what a Pangaloid was, and the signals from the satellites she hadn't destroyed had been no help. She needed to consult her sister and best friend Astri, who liked to stay close to Neptune, but first she turned to look out at the distant, prophetic stars. What she saw there made her stop in her orbit. Any thoughts about chucking another satellite back to its makers died a fiery death. Could she be reading that right? Now she really needed to talk with Astri.

A ship came to the space platform and she moved in to see if she could find out more about what could be causing this fervor on Earth. But as usual, the people aboard paid her no attention, launching and burning a highly inefficient, fiery tail from the rear end of the ship. She followed and stuck with them as they came up to what appeared to be max speed. For such a fast-lived species, even their fastest space travel was glacial. She checked their trajectory and was fairly certain they were headed toward Neptune and the space port.

She tried to signal to the people on the ship that she wanted to talk, to warn them, and finally got their attention with a series of energetic flashes that brought them to their windows. But all they did was stare at her for a while. They pointed, their energies showing awe and wonder at the nebula somehow stuck in the wake beside them, like that was even possible. But they didn't seem to understand anything she radiated at them. She tried again and again, but it was almost like they couldn't see more than a tiny range of the entire radiation spectrum with those round, frontal sensors attached to their bulbous heads. In frustration and as a last-ditch effort, she tried making shapes at them, imitating with her gaseous cloud the shape of their own ship. They'd have to recognize that, right? But though one or two watched her for a while, their attention was short. They soon wandered off, and Luminous had to admit defeat.

She sped ahead of them to talk it all over with Astri. Luminous found her lazing around in one of Neptune's rings, absorbing the minimal sunshine that made it out this far.

She watched as Astri ricocheted off a meteoroid and spun off in a new direction. Sometimes Luminous thought Astri had forgotten she was a nebula. Or, maybe she simply preferred being solid.

Lu! Are you finally giving up on the blue-green monster? Come to relax with me?

Earth is not a monster, Astri. It's exciting. You should really come with me next time, for the people watching if nothing else.

They blew up Callisto! Just a few cycles ago!

True, which I'm sure was an accident. Luminous had thought they'd finally gotten to the point in their evolution that they weren't going to destroy themselves. And then they'd blown up one of Jupiter's moons. It wasn't very reassuring. *You're the one who retaliated by chucking satellite parts down on areas of dense human activity.* She reminded Astri. *Don't you think you can let it go and move on?*

We've seen their ships, Lu. They open up their maws and pull us out of orbit and then, she whispered dramatically, *they* eat *us.*

Astri, you're an energy being. Get off your rock and avoid them!

Luminous, you're a nebula. If you want them to understand you, you've got to be solid with them. Send their satellites back to the inhabited areas that sent them in the first place, I say. Now, that's a message they would hear.

Oh, but they're not as bad as you think, Astri! I mean, yes, they're capable of destruction, but also love, and kindness, and creativity, and problem-solving. Remember when they were heating the planet so much it was killing them? They solved that.

Halfway, Astri conceded. *They may have stopped the Earth from warming further, but they never did slow the great storms, or their consumption of every Earth resource.*

But they took the first step. They're making progress! Except, Astri, there's something new going on right now, and I need your help to figure what it is.

Astri expelled an exasperated puff of gas and spun away from Luminous. *You need help alright. Here's some advice: Stop surfing Earth. Stop watching them! Stop trying to get those tiny humans to do the right thing. You work too hard and they're going to do what they want no matter how much you try because they can barely see past their own puny lifetimes. Earth is a lost cause, Lu, and you won't be radiant forever. Stay and have some fun with me. You can surf right here!*

But surfing Earth made her feel like she was experiencing something bigger than herself. There was nothing else like it. She wished she could make Astri understand.

Instead, she gestured at the stars with her shifting extremities.

Astri, look at the stars. What do you see? Her own change in perspective hadn't made any difference. Astri was silent for a long moment, observing the prophetic stars, twinkling in their usual soundless song through space.

War, said Astri at last. *War is coming. War and destruction.*

Another Earth ship passed by and she followed them, towing Astri along despite her protests, still not knowing how to engage humans in a way they would listen. She trailed them a short way to that giant, gleaming ring in space, Tersa Tellus. It was slowly spinning, usually with some ships docked around its shell and humans working and frolicking in space vehicles nearby. Every once in a while, blue and red laser blasts slashed through space, reducing rogue meteors and comets to dust before they could impact the port.

But it wasn't the light show that caught her attention. One look at that silvery, spinning ring and all thoughts of trying to talk with the humans again stopped. It was now clear why there was all the excitement and fear on Earth. A very strange, unknown type of ship, white and softly glowing, was docked at the port.

Humans were getting their first official alien visitors. But, Luminous sensed something much bigger than one alien ship docked at port. There was an energy shift in the solar system. She felt its incoming waves. And, a few stretching hops away, she found the source.

The ship was merely the tip of the alien iceberg. An entire new *planet* was now parked outside the Kuiper Belt, orbiting the ninth and farthest planet from the Sun, enormous, dark Planet IX. No matter that planets did not travel, not that she'd ever heard of, but this one was here, now. And its radiation signature was the same as the alien ship at port.

Planet IX was the one planet that Luminous, Astri, and their nebula siblings stayed away from, for it housed an energy being like them, and also, not like them. This one was older, old as the solar system, old as the galaxy. This one they knew simply as Ix, and they studiously avoided his creepy, extremely elliptical orbit, which would soon cross into the Kuiper Belt and come the closest to Neptune it had been in thousands of solar orbits. Did these aliens, on their strange lush planet, know about Ix? About the energy beings who quietly, sparsely inhabited the galaxy? What was the reason for their visit—Ix or the humans?

The traveling planet wasn't large by any means, only about half the size of Earth, but for a planet to travel, and to stay warm in the far reaches of space where everything else was ice—how was that accomplished? Had the humans noticed? More importantly, how would they react?

This last question was vital, because of the humans' star weapons. The time was long past when they could only blow up their own planet. She had seen the weapon they'd launched at poor Callisto, and she'd watched them unload multiple identical weapons at their space port. She hadn't worried much about it at the time. Ice moons couldn't shoot back, but now, well, she supposed it all depended on how their first alien encounter was going.

She felt worry build in her greater than she'd ever felt before. She tried to calm herself. Energy beings had been here long before biologicals, and would be here long after, she reminded herself. Energy beings did not interfere with the short lives of humans. But this? She looked at the verdant Traveler planet, in a place where no such planet had any right to be, and back toward Earth. It was not even a speck in the distance, but she could picture the beautiful, blue-green planet clearly. Humans had made terrible choices with their home, but they and the Earth were hers. This solar system was her home. There had to be some way she could help humanity avoid war with these Travelers. If she could only talk with them.

She tried at the port's great silver ring, but the humans were in too much of a frenzy with the alien ship being there to pay attention to a nebula out the windows. So, she headed back toward Earth to find another ship, on its long, slow jog to the space port, and hopefully someone who would pay attention to her warnings. Astri, curious, tagged along and they soon found what they were looking for. A human ship had recently launched from the Earth Elevator platform, and an unusual one. This one was super shiny, slightly faster than usual, and it held only one person: a pleasantly symmetrical young man.

Chapter 2:

DOUBLE-OH PRINCE

The mermaid kissed his high, smooth forehead, and stroked back his wet hair; he seemed to her like the marble statue in her little garden, and she kissed him again, and wished that he might live.

Hans Christian Andersen, The Little Mermaid (1836)

—Nik—

"Your mission, should you choose to accept it," Prince Nikolas III of the Greater British Commonwealth intoned upon taxiing from the Elevator, "is to shag the alien princess into giving us their best technology. Use your most charming pillow talk. Eh-eh?" He mimed elbowing a non-existent co-pilot, purely for his own amusement. "She's quite fetching for someone covered in scales." He dropped the voice. "Shite, this gives a whole new meaning to chasing tail." In his flashy racecar of a space ship, flying the British colors as any good head of state vehicle would, he felt like a strange combination of James Bond, superspy, and the first sacrifice to new alien overlords. But that's what those two weeks of espionage boot camp were for, right?

The Elevator had taken him up out of the Earth's atmosphere and the ship's Super-Shine, New-Lar sail unfurled like a ball in front of the ship. The high-powered cold lasers mounted on the Elevator platform shot five brilliant green beams onto the sail-ball, four keeping the ball on course, and one, more powerful, center laser thrusting him forward like a great blast of wind, throwing him back in his specially designed seat. After the lasers could no longer accurately target his sail, the ship would reel it back in and the on-board thrusters would further his acceleration across the solar system toward the space port, Tersa Tellus.

The enormous double-ring space port was named for "dry land," the last island of humanity at the edge of deep space. Its mission was to be a supply port and jumping off point for interstellar travel, one last touch of Earth for those 15,000 brave souls preparing to board the first colony ships to the new world, the Alpha Centauri tri-star system. Probes had brought back viability reports for three planets, one in each goldilocks zone, the closest being Proxima Centauri b. It was about forty years away at humanity's fastest achieved space flight. The other two would take a good ten years longer, as long as everything went well.

They'd learned a lot about space travel ever since those first, tiny probes were launched over two hundred and fifty years ago. But, fifty years was an awfully long time to be stuck on a space ship, even one with simulated gravity and every convenience they could find space for. Nik would be stuck on this ship for a week out to Neptune and that was plenty for him. Still, someone had to do it, and millions of people had volunteered for the coveted spots.

Climate change had wreaked havoc on Earth. Whole historical coastlines and hundreds of cities were underwater, millions were dead, and the storms that had swallowed them kept on coming. The melting of the polar ice caps had irrevocably altered the ocean currents that had kept the land temperate, making storms more severe and more common, while the interior was prone to drought, fires, and famine. He could understand why people were anxious to leave.

The current space race—before these Pangaloid, er, Travelers arrived—was to find and colonize new, habitable land. Terraforming Mars had been put on hold after the test trial to jump-start a planet's core had resulted in blowing up the moon, Callisto. That method would need a redesign prior to use on Mars with its domed colonies.

Earth's other neighbor, Venus, had the opposite problem. They still did not have the technology to cool a planet covered in lakes of lava.

That left traveling to and colonizing worlds outside their own solar system. The newly built Navigator, Prospector, and Stalwart Mariner were ready and awaiting their crews and supplies at Tersa Tellus. He hoped they would find a habitable world before their supplies ran out, and that it would not already have sentient beings.

Nik had a theory that the reason so many horror streams involved aliens coming to Earth to enslave, exploit, and exterminate humans was because humans knew, deep down inside, given very little prompting they would do the same. And it would be really nice not to do that, again.

But before the Settlers' historic voyage could begin, a surprise ship had arrived at port: aliens. They had come slowly, flown up and docked in full view, seemingly unarmed and not making any sudden moves. And in trying not to spook the humans, they'd spooked the bloody hell out of everyone.

Humans began calling them Pangaloids because of their uncanny resemblance to pangolins, the near-extinct, scaled mammals of Earth. However, now that they had found a human who could translate, people were supposed to call them Travelers. The sight-based nickname was hard to break though. They were humanoid in shape, left-right symmetrical with two arms, legs, eyes, and ear holes, one snout-like nose and mouth, a powerful tail, and were covered in glossy, brown scales. And they were entirely cold and emotionless. They were worse than the palace guards back in New London.

And now, Nik was supposed to marry their princess, appropriate their travel technology, and never once reveal how truly unimportant he was on Earth. Fourth in line for a throne he'd never sit on, in a country where the monarchy was a figurehead anyhow, a career as an engineer for the Royal British Astro-Force had seemed like a good choice. Conducting travel research in space was certainly more exciting than dedicating new buildings and posing for publicity holos. And then these Pangaloid Travelers had shown up.

To say communications weren't going well was an understatement. Their only translator was a telepathic scientist named Cassandra Stillwell. She'd used herself as a lab rat a few years back and had such highly enhanced telepathic abilities that she'd shut herself away in a remote satellite as far from people as she could get. But now they'd called her in to translate to a space port teeming with people. *That* was bound to go well.

And someone, on which side he didn't know, had suggested that marriage between royal families was traditional for cementing a shaky peace treaty. Never mind that Earth hadn't worked that way in centuries. And so, he'd been recruited by the oft speculated, though never confirmed, interstellar intelligence agency, MI-7. A crash course in espionage and here he was.

He'd seen holographs of his "bride-to-be" as she arrived with her envoy at the space port. She was certainly elegant. Pretty, he guessed, as far as a girl covered in scales with a tail could be. He wondered what kissing her would be like, and if she was a better spy than him. His handlers had to realize she was probably a spy too, right?

Nik sighed. He was a scientist. What had he gotten himself into? Still, he was glad their first aliens hadn't turned out to be squid people.

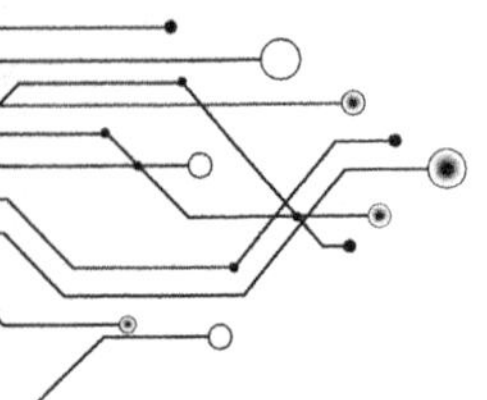

Chapter 3:

THE WOW MOMENT

—Luminous—

Despite his solid shape and complete lack of diffusivity, he was a fine creature to look at, Luminous thought. She watched him function gracefully in zero gravity in a way humans seldom could, through the windows of his ship as he went about his days. He tended small, green biologicals, singing and talking to them with the orifice on his bulbous head. She wondered what their names were, what his name was.

He used a hand-held, glowing screen to project and interact with images, either of other humans, or words and numbers. Often, he seemed tired of floating and moved down a tunnel into the wide wheel that rotated around the center ship. It was in this wheel where he seemed to sink, feet first to the wall. He ran on a machine that made his upper body and face glisten. And he gave his body biological inputs.

The skin of human ships never allowed her inside, and this one was no different, but something about *this man* was different. She wondered if he looked hard enough out his window would he, could he see her sparkle hello to him? But he kept busy and only looked when he passed a large celestial body like Jupiter. He never saw her, though she tried everything she could think of to get his attention, short of making herself dense and bashing his ship. That probably wouldn't work out well for him.

On his third day in space, one of the thin lines connecting his ship to its shiny ball sail let go, and the ship began to drag off course. This seemed to cause the man great anxiety and he came out of his ship, covered in some sort of protective outer shell. He banged on a panel on the skin of his ship that seemed to be stuck. If he looked her way, could he possibly see her now? She was careful to match his velocity alongside his ship, so that her diffuse atoms did not pose a threat to him. She went up to him, waving an arm of dust and gas in front of him to say hello. Again he didn't notice her. But even in that funny, metallic shell that protected his frail body, there was something about him. She reached out and surrounded him, certain he had to notice her.

Then the panel popped open under his hands. A little metal creature scuttled out and down the body of the ship to fix the fluttering, detached line, and the man stopped working for a moment. He looked around himself and brushed a gloved hand in front of his visor, as if trying to clear his vision. Her fine particles swirled in response and gently flowed in the direction he sent them. She felt electrified at his touch, and she wondered if any of her kind had ever experienced anything half as new.

He seemed alarmed at first. Then, slowly, amazement took over his features as she twinkled as hard as she could at him in hello. Realization stole over his expression in layers. He looked quickly back at his ship.

Yes, she thought at him. *We are still traveling through space at the speed of your ship. Of course, I matched your speed. I'm not a complete muscovite.*

His mouth formed a word, "Wow," and though she didn't speak his language, she thought she knew what he meant. They were sharing a definite *wow* moment.

Uh, Lu? What are you doing? Astri whispered behind her. She saw the man's eyes go wide with fear, looking beyond her diffuse, sparkling curtain.

Shhh. It's all right, she tried to twinkle reassuringly. Astri was the least threatening asteroid she knew. Luminous looked back at her sister, who was not even traveling toward the man and his ship, but then looked beyond her. A comet with a rogue band of icy bits was hurtling toward them.

The man gazed on them with abject terror, swung the panel shut, and tried to get back to the door of his ship as fast as possible. He pushed off with his solid appendages and jetted quickly toward the portal, but in his haste, he fumbled and kept floating on by. His tether was attached, but it was long, making complicated serpentine shapes through her dust cloud, and he tried to quickly reel himself in, hand over hand. But he wasn't going to make it to the door in time.

She could see the comet and debris would go straight through his protective outer shell, and it would mean certain death for her human. As many humans as she'd seen from afar over the entirety of human history, she'd never been this close to one, had never had a *wow* moment. She concentrated on becoming a dense, flat sheet, and impenetrable. She stretched herself into a shield, covering the man and his ship. He watched, his frontal orb sensors becoming huge and his internal fluid pumping erratically.

The comet and icy bits hit Luminous and she made herself like iron. They bounced and deflected, spitting debris on their way past. She checked to make sure they had all gone before relaxing and becoming diffuse once more. The man quickly slipped inside his ship's hatch, closing the door and staring back out at her through the window.

The large orifice on his face moved briefly and the energy layers around his body seemed to express dazed gratitude. She understood his meaning, if not his human words.

She drifted away from the human's ship and let it fly on without her.

Astri was excited. *How did you know you could do that—stretch yourself into a solid shield?*

Luminous looked absently out at the stars all around them. *I didn't.*

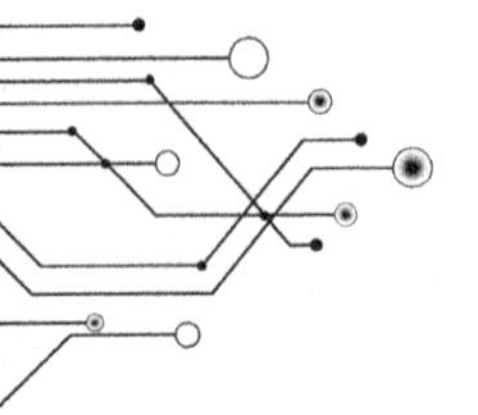

Chapter 4:

THE MATRIARCH

—Luminous—

When a star goes supernova, it leaves an imprint on not only space, but time as well. The stars Luminous looked to told of multiple coming mini supernovas. And the imprint pointed at her solar system as the location. She'd seen related signs before, most recently before the destruction of Jupiter's moon, Callisto. Then, it had not been a star exploding, but the humans' star weapon. With the arrival of the first aliens to human space, she had no choice but to read this as war, right?

There weren't many energy beings around to ask. Luminous, Astri, and their siblings had all come into existence at the same time, as far as any of them knew. Many had ridden the interstellar currents to bigger and better things, to galaxies unknown, never to be heard from again. Only seven, including Luminous and Astri, remained in their home solar system. Now, they searched out their five siblings in their favorite places and asked them: *what do you see in the stars?* But they could only confirm that she had read their prediction correctly.

There was one more local energy being she could ask. Ix of Planet IX inhabited the furthest planet from their brilliant, life-giving Sun. Past icy Pluto, past the Kuiper Belt, Planet IX was a dark gas giant in such a huge, unusual elliptical orbit that he'd been all but invisible to Earth for centuries. And he was the last being she wanted to talk with. She shuddered.

Of the few energy beings scattered across this galaxy, Ix was much older than Luminous and her siblings, not merely as old as humankind like Luminous and her siblings, but as old as the Sun. He had been attached to the dark Planet IX as long as anyone could remember, so long that they were now one and the same. It had been speculated that he was there in exile, The Matriarch having put him there herself. But all that Luminous's siblings knew for sure was that every energy being they'd ever heard of making a deal with Ix never returned, like Corhalae. The loss of her sister, the only one who had appreciated Earth with her, still hurt Luminous. Corhalae had been lured by the rumors that impossible desires became possible, for a while at least, after a visit with Ix.

That left Luminous with only one other energy being to ask, one far more powerful than any of them, even Ix. One who could change the course of the solar system, with the wave of one star-strewn arm—The Matriarch, Sagita.

She is wondrous, one of Luminous's siblings said, who had been to visit the Matriarch many cycles ago, *yet her pull is inevitable. If you go, you must stay well outside her event horizon or you will be lost to her embrace.* Luminous decided, for Earth, for her beloved solar system, and her human, she had to try.

Be careful, both of you! their siblings called after her, and she realized Astri was beside her.

What are you doing? Luminous asked Astri.

I'm coming with you. Someone needs to keep you out of trouble.

Luminous felt a small sense of relief and glowed at her in

thanks. The Matriarch was not, it was said, the beginning and end of the entire *universe*, which was so vast that Luminous could barely comprehend it. But if anyone remembered the beginning and contained the end of their *galaxy*, it was The Matriarch, Sagita.

She lived far, far away, at the very center of the galaxy, so far that Luminous had only ever dreamed of visiting. But if anyone held magic enough to save her humans from a coming war, it was The Matriarch.

Determined, Luminous stretched herself into a two-dimensional ribbon, as thin as a single atom, toward Sagita's kingdom at the center of the Milky Way, before contracting all her mass into a tiny, radiant pebble at the farthest tip of her reach. Then she spread herself forward again. In this way, she sped across the cosmos, Astri hanging on for fear of being left behind. She was scared at the same time that she was hopeful, for it was said that Sagita ate entire solar systems that strayed too close. But it was also said that when pleased, she held sway over time, space, and the very essence of matter itself.

Luminous pushed herself to a speed faster than she had ever flown before, passing whole solar systems by the thousands until they looked like the blur of an Earthen blizzard. She didn't stop to explore. They were in a hurry.

When she arrived at the edge of The Matriarch's voluminous, starry kingdom, she saw lonely stars and entire solar systems, all powerless in Sagita's enormous gravitational pull. Sagita herself was entirely dark, but surrounded by a glorious swirl of stars as her followers orbited closer and closer, caught up in her radiant skirts, and Sagita welcomed each one graciously into her embrace.

Come tired ones, she whispered. *Rest and I shall make you anew.* Her voice was an angelic echo, soothing and beautiful. It at once spoke of acceptance and love, power and truth. Only if Luminous strained to listen past her voice, could she make out the screams of worlds torn apart, crushed in Sagita's cavernous depths. But that was easily ignored in the presence of Sagita's glory.

Luminous pretended not to hear the moan of indecision from Astri as they fell into orbit around The Matriarch. It was only then that she felt the icy heat of Sagita's embrace. She focused on the image of beautiful planet Earth, and unintentionally, the handsome man's face, and continued forward.

Matriarch! she called, flaring her radiance to catch Sagita's attention. She and Astri bowed. *May we please request an audience with you?*

Approach, young ones. The other stars and planets seemed to fade as they were wrapped in Sagita's loving voice of radiance. *Your presence here is curious. What is it that you seek?*

Astri stayed back, but Luminous approached as far as she could, careful to keep herself outside Sagita's event horizon. A trip into her massive black hole was not in Luminous's schedule. For one thing, she had no idea what lay on the other side. For another, she didn't know if there *was* another side. Carefully, she explained her desire to know what could be done to save Earth and its solar system.

Ah, the Terran system. Even I cannot change the stars of the universe, young one. A battle is coming to the Terrans, possibly war. It is the outcome that has yet to be decided. Planets and their biologicals come and go, though I can see the tiny humans' emotional energy from here. They may be miniscule, but their passions shine brightly, do they not? Even across the depths of space. Love and hate are merely different kinds of burning. Yet, like everything else, nothing is forever.

But, is the outcome set? Is there nothing that can be done to save them? Our home?

Your home system will be… merely altered. Change is the one constant of the universe.

But—

Humans could change their course if they wanted, but most are blind to the warnings of the stars. If they remain on their current path, it will alter the Earth to the point where humanity will not survive, but who knows? Biologicals may be short-lived, but they are highly changeable. That's what makes them so interesting.

Interesting enough to help them? Luminous asked hopefully.

Sagita laughed, a warm rumble, followed by a horrible gnawing sound issued from her gut. She waved an arm around at her spiral kingdom, hundreds of thousands of stars and solar systems within her galactic realm. *There are always others, young one, equally interesting. Only energy beings can change the course of their own actions.*

Wait, are you saying that humans, and these new Travelers, are energy beings?

Sagita laughed. *We differ in size and mass, yet in the end, we are all interconnected.*

So, destruction is not inevitable?

Sagita sighed. *The outcome is not yet written, merely the collision of energies, multiple goals in opposition. I am interested to see what happens, yet it has nothing to do with me. Now, it is time for you to go. Unless, you wish to stay?*

If you can't do anything, then who can? Luminous yelled over the rushing tide of Sagita's gravity that was pulling entire solar systems into her depths, ignoring her warning. Luminous contracted her gas and dust in tight to keep from getting caught in Sagita's pull, the galactic winds buffeting her on all sides at the edge of great hurricane Sagita. But all she heard in reply was sucking and pulling, tearing and grinding. She hadn't realized how close she'd gotten, too close, and she tried to propel herself back and away from Sagita's event horizon. She tottered on the edge, backpedaling for all she was worth.

Luminous! She realized that Astri was yelling and grabbing at her to pull her back to safe space. They had almost made it when a large star, many times larger than their own Sun, sped by on its own collision course with Sagita's dark maw. Its gravity pulled Luminous farther in, over the event horizon, past the point of no return. She and Astri screamed in terror. And then… a sigh from Sagita, a tiny flick of her mighty skirt hem and they bounced. She and Astri both scrambled backward, no graceful undulation now until they were back in sure, safe space. Deflated, yet still determined, Luminous pulled Astri along and they hurried on their way home.

Energy beings can change their own course. She repeated Sagita's words as she made her way back across the galaxy. *Humans and these new Travelers are energy, we are energy. So how can I communicate with them? How can I get them to change course? To not fire their star weapons at each other? What could go so terribly wrong in their meeting that they would want to destroy each other, and risk altering the entire solar system?*

She was concentrating so hard on these unanswerable

questions that she didn't realize they were traveling straight for the territory of Planet IX now. They were back at the far edge of the Terran system.

Luminous, Astri twinkled warningly when she paused, looking at the dark Planet IX. Its only sources of radiation were flashes of lightning across its atmosphere. *You're not really thinking…*

Yes, Astri. I am.

Astri expanded a bit and wrapped the edge of her own nebula around Luminous to pull her to a stop. *Beings go to him and never return! I know you had a special moment with that human, but it was only a moment. You heard The Matriarch. They can change their own path. Nothing is set.*

Luminous looked out at the stars again. *But they won't,* she predicted. *It's obvious they can't see where this is heading. And that's where I come in.*

Ah, that's what I like to hear! Radiation rumbled at them impressively from Planet IX, making both of them jump. Lightning lit up the atmosphere in a coordinated fanfare. *Welcome to all those who would change the stars! Welcome!*

Um, Luminous, Astri mumbled from behind as Luminous moved forward. *This is not a good idea. Just look at those energies. Look!*

But Luminous was focused on making the impossible possible. And she felt as she went forward, the stars did change slightly, etching her name and her human's on a new path. It was only later that she saw, it was a path still heading toward human destruction.

Chapter 5:

IX OF PLANET IX

I would give gladly all the hundreds of years that I have to live, to be a human being only for one day, and to have the hope of knowing the happiness of that glorious world above the stars.

Hans Christian Andersen, The Little Mermaid (1836)

—Luminous—

Come closer, come closer! I hardly ever get visitors out here, and despite the rumors, I don't eat my own kind, even if your emotions do look delectable. He laughed. *Tell me, my dear,* he said and Luminous looked around to see that Astri was hiding behind the nearest object, which oddly enough, appeared to be a human satellite in orbit around the dark planet. *These emotions are so new and vibrant on you. Protective too. What have you been up to?* He seemed surprised but then continued on without giving her even a moment to answer.

Let me guess. You've seen the signs written in the stars, and know this solar system is on the road to war. Can't those miniscule humans keep their peace together for two measly centuries? Am I right? But, at least watching them keeps things interesting. You have been watching them, haven't you? He pinned her with a radiation probe before continuing.

You're too young, but I remember what the Earth was like before humans. Other biological creatures' drama was always limited to who was eating whom. Then humans came along and it's been war and destruction ever since. They are entertaining creatures. I can see why you might like to save them. Maybe even keep one, a special one? Mmm-hmm. I can see there is a certain male you fancy. But I'm not sure they would make good pets. So many bodily functions, he said with an air of disgust.

I don't want him for a pet! she broke in, aghast, finally managing to get a word in.

What else would you want him for?

I want to be able to communicate with him! To warn him what's coming. So he can change their course!

Ix's energy twinkled with humor. *Like he would listen to a nebula, nor would any of the humans for that matter. Humans don't communicate with energy beings like us, believe me, I've tried everything. Haven't you?*

Well, yes, but there must be—

A way? Yes, there is one way that I know of, and it is open to you.

What is it? she asked eagerly.

You could become human, of course, as others have before you. Your sister Corhalae most recently.

What? Corhalae became human? But how? This was not any magic she had ever heard of.

It's a simple matter of having access to enough energy to convert your nebula self into human mass. Energy that I happen to have stored for a special occasion. If, hypothetically, you did want to become human.

She paused, considering this. *Can you really do it? Can you make me human?*

Planet IX, the entire planet, stopped turning. The moment stretched with anticipation before he sprang back to his normal rotation. Mumbles of lightning and thunder rippled across his dark atmosphere. *Hmmm. Are you making the request? A gambler's request?*

I thought you said it was simple.

I said the energy conversion was simple, not that changing the humans' stars would be easy. Even if you are able to communicate, I still don't think your prince will listen.

He's a prince? She paused. Of course, he would have to be someone important, to be voyaging to meet the Travelers. They wouldn't send just anyone. But why was he alone? There were still so many unanswered questions.

Oh yes, and if you want the chance to communicate with him, I can make you human, for the length of one human lifetime. Do we have a deal?

She watched his signals closely. That much energy this far from the Sun could not come cheap. *What would you ask in return?*

Oh, you know, nothing too terribly difficult. When your hopefully long, happy human life is over, you will turn back into a nebula and return to me. Share with me all those lovely human emotions you will experience. You see? Nothing much at all.

The energy signatures in Ix's atmosphere seemed to yell out all at once, but he quickly silenced them.

Luminous, no! Astri yelled coming out from her hiding place.

But Luminous was decided. Ix didn't think she could change the stars, but she'd take that bet. She remembered how the prince had looked at her. With his help, together they could do anything. *Deal.*

Ix spun excitedly and his energy sparked and crashed into a storm to rival the great red eye of Jupiter. She could have sworn his gravity increased, if that was even possible, and she began to realize she was being pulled in.

I almost forgot, there is the small matter of your radiance, required in the conversion of course, he said.

Luminous tried to stop moving forward. *My radiance?* she backpedaled. *But how will I…?* But she was farther into Ix's orbit than she had known. She felt the pull increase on her nebula extremities and pulled them in tight.

Well you certainly can't keep it, child. Humans do not radiate, you know. But mortality does come with benefits. A lovely human body, female I presume?

Luminous nodded.

Yes, and all the working parts of course.

A voice to talk and sing? She thought of the prince singing to himself aboard his ship. Singing must be important.

Of course. Ix plucked out a few more ingredients and tossed them in. *Everything a human body does. Though I cannot give you skill,* he warned. *That you must do for yourself.*

She felt the tiniest unease now as Ix plucked flashes of light, gas and dust, and an entire small moon from his orbit and sucked them all into the swirling tempest of his atmosphere. There were so many variables. She hoped they had thought of everything. Luminous felt herself drawn in and she did not resist. She could do this. She would make this gamble for her solar system and win.

But, how will I get to him in his ship? she asked in the few moments before getting sucked in.

Ah, time and space my child, yes, I'm glad you reminded me. I usually deposit my clients on Earth, as human babies. But no, that won't do in this case. You do not wish to be a baby, do you?

No! The same age as the prince, please!

Of course, no problem my dear. Ix plucked a few more flashes from his now roiling clouds and tossed them in. Luminous felt briefly guilty as the energy hissed and screamed, but then fell silent. It had to be done. And Luminous concentrated on her own goal—to save humanity and the solar system. She focused on the image of her prince's face.

Yes, think of him as you go. Hold his image tightly!

Luminous held *herself* tightly, in the smallest sphere she could manage so as not to be torn apart in the vicious, freezing tornado in which she found herself as she swirled down, down into Ix's atmosphere. The forces she felt now were like those she imagined in The Matriarch's core, ripping and tearing her cosmic body apart. She screamed and wondered briefly if she'd done the right thing. It was agony. She felt part of her very essence, her radiance, torn out into the crushing swirl. And then it all turned black.

Chapter 6:

KNOCK, KNOCK

Then the little mermaid drank the magic draught, and it seemed as if a two-edged sword went through her delicate body: she fell into a swoon, and lay like one dead. When the sun arose and shone over the sea, she recovered, and felt a sharp pain; but just before her stood the handsome young prince.

Hans Christian Andersen, The Little Mermaid (1836)

—Luminous—

When she awoke, she felt herself drifting and coming back together, bit by bit. Her matter re-firmed in a new, more delicate way. She saw out of new, literally new, eyes that she was back home, near Neptune, and she felt the burning cold of space in a way she never had before. Her new body was surrounded as it formed by a bubble of Ix's dark power, but the bubble was thinning. She could see the human prince's ship, so close she could almost reach out and touch it. But she wasn't going the correct speed. She waved new arms frantically, trying to get his attention as he passed her by.

Here, I'm here! She tried to say. But her new lungs started to do, something: a gasping motion she was unfamiliar with, and the dark bubble broke. In a flash of realization, she knew something had gone terribly wrong. She was human, yes, but adrift in the cold of space. She could feel her new skin start to freeze and shut her eyes against the lack of air pressure that threatened to pull them from her skull. Oh, what had she done?

Luminous! she heard a yell. Oh Astri, she wished she could tell her sister that she'd been right, and ask her to say goodbye to their siblings for her.

But then she felt herself wrapped in a warm bubble, the pressure around her delicate body stabilizing. Was this what it felt like, to die? Luminous opened her eyes again and realized that the warmth she felt were her nebulae siblings surrounding her, protecting her frail, new body. But her lungs still gasped awkwardly for air they couldn't find.

Oh Luminous, what have you done? they asked as they whisked her to the human ship. They brought her to the man's window and tapped gently on it with a few pebbles, while she flailed awkwardly at it with her new fists.

He jerked his head up and yelped at the sight of a woman outside his spacecraft, knocking frantically. He stared for what seemed like an eternity with his mouth open as she coughed and gasped. She put her hand out on the cold surface of the window, protected by her nebulae siblings, and he snapped out of it. He propelled himself away and she felt her heart drop. Was he leaving her?

A minute later, though it felt like an eternity, the door opened and her heart started beating again when he floated out in his protective covering. Her siblings floated her to him and through the door of the ship. Astri stayed around her new body protectively while their other siblings quickly released and left them both inside. The man closed the airlock door, still looking astounded, and pushed some nearby buttons to equalize the pressure with the rest of the ship. He moved away to take off his helmet and Astri collapsed under the new air pressure into a dense, oblong rock and floated off to the side. Luminous found her body curing into a ball, gasping the glorious air into her aching, painfully new lungs.

The man caught her as she floated into him and she looked up into dark eyes that were like coming home.

"Luminous," he said in awe, staring at her face.

Unfortunately, that was the only word she understood as he kept talking, saying something and pausing expectantly. He seemed to be waiting for her response and she shook her head, then stopped, touching the bulbous, bumpy thing atop her thin, bendy neck. She had a head. She started to laugh, and then, surprised at the raspy sound she was making, she laughed some more. The rough sound quickly turned melodious and she felt amazed at this delightful noise. Sound waves didn't travel in space.

When she stopped laughing, she ran her hands over her arms and her new skin was miraculous, smooth and dark brown and subtly glowing, though she couldn't help but miss her inner radiance. She ought to have shined so brightly that he would have known immediately what she was from the light she emanated. But, when he looked at her and touched the skin of her face and arm with awe and said, "Luminous," well, she felt more beautiful than she ever had.

He let her go and turned his head away, the skin on his face glowing slightly red.

"Are you all right?" she tried to ask, but what came out were strange, unused sounds that apparently didn't make any sense to either of them. He looked back at her uncomprehendingly, seeming to make sure that he kept his eyes above her neck.

He said something, and though she couldn't understand, his voice made nice vibrations in her ears. He took off his shirt and held it out to her.

Oooh. She ignored the proffered shirt and reached a hand out to touch the smooth, tawny skin of his nicely muscled chest. He sucked in a breath. She looked down at her new body, nice too, but different. Both of them were symmetrical and well-formed, but, hmmm.... She cupped one of her female chestial lumps and one of his male ones and squeezed.

He yelped, gripped her wrist, and gently pulled her hand away, an expression of surprise on his handsome face. He shook his head and said something again. Oops, she guessed that squeezing those was not an approved human activity. But conversely, the subtle energy field surrounding him seemed to be telling her that he *did* like it.

He held the shirt out to her, with emphasis this time, interrupting her perusal of this energy around him. It was so interesting having skin and hands to feel and touch, but apparently, he was telling her not to. He said something she again didn't understand, but he gestured from the shirt to her and she realized he wanted her to cover her beautiful new skin.

She raised her shoulders a bit, the gesture feeling natural, and accepted the shirt, trying to figure out how to put it on. It was harder than expected as the material floated around uncooperatively. He had to help her, holding the bottom of the shirt open and jabbering at her the whole time.

With no air in space to carry sound waves, and no eardrums either, she'd never truly *heard* anything before, in the human way. She reached up to put her hands over her new ears, testing. These sensory organs were outstanding, and at the same time, all of them together were overwhelming. Brightness and movement, and all the things in the room came through her eyes. So many things to look at and decipher. So much to hear in the timbre of his voice and in the smooth hum of the ship.

She felt her hair floating against her face, neck and shoulders like a puffy cloud, tickling, getting in her eyes and mouth. Why was there so much of it, and why did it have a mind of its own? Had Ix been *trying* to drive her crazy? She pushed it back, clamping her hands over her ears and squeezed her eyes shut for a moment of relief. But she could still feel the gentle rumble of his voice through her body, feel the air currents blowing her skin and hair. She could still smell the sharpness of the new ship all around her, and a nicer, warm smell coming off his golden-brown skin and short, dark hair.

She opened her eyes to see him looking at her strangely. She dropped her hands to her sides and pulled the shirt down that was floating around her on its own. He was used to all of this. She must seem so strange to him. He asked her something she was sure was a question. But even after all these years of watching

Earth, she'd never experienced all these details of human interaction up close. It was all confusing now, speech most of all.

When he'd said, "Luminous," she'd known that was her name. Unfortunately, they couldn't agree on the sound of anything else.

Chapter 7:

MUTE

The prince asked her who she was, and where she came from, and she looked at him mildly and sorrowfully with her deep blue eyes; but she could not speak. Every step she took was as the witch had said it would be, she felt as if treading upon the points of needles or sharp knives; but she bore it willingly, and stepped as lightly by the prince's side as a soap-bubble, so that he and all who saw her wondered at her graceful-swaying movements. She was very soon arrayed in costly robes of silk and muslin, and was the most beautiful creature in the palace; but she was dumb, and could neither speak nor sing.

Hans Christian Andersen, The Little Mermaid (1836)

—Luminous—

After a few moments of staring at each other, stymied, the prince looked behind her ear and comprehension dawned across his handsome face. He held up his hands as if telling her to keep her body where it was, and left the room, opening the door and floating through. What was she supposed to do now?

Oh, Lu, Astri's mental voice came to her, filled with regret. She turned her head and spotted her sister floating nearby, a small, rocky body inside the ship. Astri had always liked being dense. She'd chosen an oblong shape, like one they'd both often seen humans play with on the satellite images. It took effort for

Luminous to turn her new body, finally having to push against a wall, but when she did, she grabbed her sister and hugged her rockiness to her own soft chest.

Astri! You stayed!

Of course. Someone has to look after you. I can't believe you made a deal with that trickster, Lu. First, he let you go adrift in space to die, and second, he said you would have everything you needed as a human. And yet you can't even talk to this man, the one thing you did all of this for.

But Luminous looked down at herself and had to smile. She was alive, in this wondrous new body, and that had to count for something. She tested its stretchiness and twistiness. It did some of each, in most directions, but of course, not nearly what she was used to. It was so… solid feeling, even air did not penetrate her new skin covering, yet it felt soft too.

She was hit with another smell through the door he'd left through, something rich and bright at the same time. She took Astri with her and followed her nose, pushing herself through the door.

Unfortunately, she pushed too hard and her new body zoomed through the next room. She tried to stop, but couldn't stretch her arms enough to reach anything to grab onto. She let go of Astri and they crashed, hands and arms first, into the wall of plants that was making that pleasant, bright smell. Leaves and aquaculture matter floated all around her.

What'd you do that for? Astri asked, bumping into the wall to ricochet off in another direction. Luminous didn't answer, but frantically tried to catch each leaf and plant and pot to put it all back on the wall before he saw the mess she'd made. But it was no use, and she realized, her hand hurt. She had to laugh at herself. She'd been weightless all her life, but almost never solid, and never with a delicate, sensitive shell. She obviously did not know how to handle this new body.

Shhh. He's coming! Astri warned and Luminous caught her sister.

She heard his voice come close and he gently turned her toward him, looking down at her hands. Little pokey black things stuck out of one of them, all the way up to her elbow. She touched one and jerked her hand back. She laughed again. What a strange, unpleasant sensation.

She looked up and he was giving her that look again. That wow look. He seemed to remember what he was doing and said something sharp, like a command. A small metal non-person of the sort she'd seen in Earth's orbit from time to time came into the room, opened up a vent on its belly and began sucking all the leaves and particles out of the air. Which was good, because the little bits bumping into her face from every direction were really annoying.

The prince then showed her a band on his wrist that blended into his golden tawny flesh, and then held out to her a similar white one and helped her put it on. Next, he showed her a matching, tiny—thing. He mimed placing it inside his ear and handed it to her. She quizzically did as he'd shown her, pushing it into her ear. When both were in place, they adhered with a *shoop* that probably signified something, but she didn't know what, and the band changed to match the cool brown of her wrist.

He had another shirt on, sadly, and he took something else

from the robot, something long and flowy. Leg coverings. He held them out to her. She sighed. When human, do as the humans do. Without his help this time, but not without a struggle, she got them over her feet and up over her hips. All the while, the prince turned away and kept talking, looking at a flat egg-shaped thing with multicolored blinky lights in his hand.

Whew, leg covering success! She waved to get his attention, and realized she was starting to understand a little of what he was saying. He began running the egg device up and down her body, a few inches away from her skin, saying something about checking to see if she was injured, and then something about her hand and arm, which really did hurt whenever she inadvertently bumped the tiny stickers. He finished the scan with a puzzled look. She took the scanner from his hand and pointed it at him instead, hoping it would tell her why he seemed uncomfortable with her staring at the gold star flecks in his dark, galaxy eyes. She wished she could explain to him that she felt at home in his eyes. That would surely make him more comfortable.

The scanner didn't tell her anything, but it gave her an excuse to examine his very nice body. He took it back with a smirk and a finger wag that made her insides squeeze interestingly, before trading it for a little silver thing from the robot. He kept talking, his meaning becoming clearer as he pulled each of the little stickers out of her hand and arm. The device on her wrist *dinged.*

"Huh, it usually doesn't take that long," he said and she felt her eyes widen. She could understand him. "I'm Nik. Prince Nikolas III," he rolled his eyes, "but call me Nik. Welcome aboard.

That was quite an arrival you made. Your scans were clear for injuries, but are you feeling alright?"

She found herself nodding, and the motion seemed a natural affirmation. "I'm fine, I think. I'm Luminous," she tried to say, but the sounds that came out of her mouth did not sound like anything that came out of his. He looked at her strangely, took his earpiece off, inspected and replaced it, then did the same with hers. She could see when he had it in his hand that it had changed from white to the color of her skin.

"Come again?" he said.

She tried some more words, but nothing came out how she meant it to sound. She sighed and he looked confused.

"You can understand me?" he asked and she nodded. "Well, I don't know what could be wrong with these things. They've never worked in only one direction before that I know of." He sighed, "I guess we'll have to wait until we get to Tersa Tellus, the Port, to get them properly inspected. Until then, I wish I knew what to call you at least."

Oh! She waved back at the room where she'd entered the ship.

"You want me to call you Airlock?" Somehow his confusion was adorable. She shook her head and tried to mime to him when she had come in the door from space and he had said—

"Uh, Doorway?"

No, no. She shook her head.

This guy is cute, but slow, Lu. Astri said. *You'll have to show him.*

That seemed a good suggestion. *Astri, wait here.* Luminous

let Astri go adrift and grabbed his arm to tow him back to the airlock.

"Whoa! Whoa, easy! Fingertip pushes!" he said as she banged them into walls and doorjambs as they went. "It's like you've never traveled in zero grav before." More like in a human body before. "Alright, we're here. Window? Door? Spacesuit?" he asked pointing to one after the other.

She turned and put her finger to his soft lips like she'd seen humans do over the centuries in their holo-vision shows, then quickly pulled back. She hadn't known that simple movement was so tingly.

She more carefully positioned them both in front of the door. She mimed coming in with him and pointed at him as if to say, *then you said…*

"You want me to call you Luminous?" he asked, finally getting it. She nodded vigorously. "You're sure?"

She nodded even more decisively.

"OK then. But how did you get here? Where did you come from? How exactly did you not freeze to death out there, among other worse things that should have happened?"

She gestured out the window, wanting to tell him all of it. But how could she make him understand? She sighed. Human vocal chords were hard.

"Have you always been mute?" Nik, asked. She shook her head, no. But then, she'd never actually had vocal chords, so then she had to nod yes also.

"No, and yes?" he asked. She shrugged. He sighed.

"Do you know sign language then?" His eyes looked up and

to the left and he began making clumsy movements with his hands, but she shook her head. His hand gestures reminded her of some of the holo-vid signals she'd intercepted from Earth satellites. Sign language, yes, that was what she needed.

He waited, then prompted, "You're going to have to ask your Deb for it then, so we can talk. International sign would be best at the port I think, don't you?"

Ask it? How? She raised her hands at Nik, but at the same time thought, maybe radiance speak.

Uh, Deb? She radiated at the band on her wrist.

Your new Data Emission Band is ready and waiting instruction, an androgynous voice said in her earpiece. She started in surprise.

"You've never had a Deb before?" His look plainly said, where did you *come* from? She shook her head. "Wow. I thought these were standard equipment on every continent these days, even the subterranean Antarctic."

She gestured out the window at the starry surroundings, trying to tell him again, *but I come from space.* But humans didn't communicate with radiation, and he looked like he couldn't even see that she was saying anything at all.

"Okaaay, a Deb is an information database and universal translator," he explained, then stopped as if a new thought had occurred to him. "Well, I guess it's not universal, is it? Because it doesn't work at all with the Pangaloids, er Travelers, I mean. Not even halfway." He gave her a speculative look. "Anyway, you tell it what you want and it will bring up the most relevant search results to your holo-emitter." He pointed to her wristband. "Anything you want to learn about, simply type it in, or press the symbol for the category you want. Oh, see? It's already started up." Both sides of the band were now blinking green. He touched it and a funny lot of square buttons were projected onto her forearm. She tentatively pressed one and a group of symbols popped up, hovering above. But she had no idea what any of the simple pictures meant.

He waited a few beats. "No?" he asked when she didn't select one. She shook her head. She wanted to simply radiate to the Deb again, but he took her wrist in his hand and it made her body do a funny shiver. He swiped some buttons in succession on her forearm, then pressed another projected button and all the projections disappeared. "Out here in space, it may take a minute or two for the signal to reach a data beacon. While we wait, let's give you a tour, hm?"

She nodded emphatically. That's exactly what she would have asked for if she could. She hadn't seen any farther than this room and the airlock, and she wanted to see the rest before they got into the big questions. Besides, she had a big question for this Deb first, and she was going to need some time apart from Nik to ask it.

They floated, slowly this time, through the ship. She scooped up Astri on her way and admired the shiny, sometimes fuzzy leaves on his plants, touching the broken stems and giving them a bit of extra energy for growth and healing. She leaned forward to smell their wonderful, sometimes pungent smells.

He briefly showed her the pilot's chair and controls, across from the plants, but didn't seem to want to linger there. He mentioned getting her food and water, but she declined. Having never eaten or drank anything before, she didn't want to mess it up in front of him yet.

They moved on to a hatch and tunnel leading to what he called the "grav wheel." This new part of the ship was in the large, turning wheel she'd seen from space. They floated inside a long, curved room and he helped her orient the correct way before he instructed the ship to begin artificial gravity. Her feet were slowly pulled to the floor, her whole body experiencing a heavy sensation she had rarely felt before as a nebula.

Well, this is strange, Astri said. Luminous agreed but had to focus on stiffening her legs and body to hold herself up.

Clench your butt muscles, Astri suggested.

She took a wobbly step, almost dropping her sister. Geez this was harder than it looked.

Coordinate, Lu. Work your muscles together! Coordinate! Astri shouted mentally.

Why don't you try it, Astri? she snapped, and then she fell, wind milling her free arm in vain. Nik grabbed her and held her against him until she regained her feet, Astri digging uncomfortably into her side and arm. She looked up into eyes so dark she got lost for a moment, until he cleared his throat.

"Disorienting, isn't it?" he said, his voice for some reason lower than it had been, and gruff. She glanced back the way they'd come and saw the hatch was shut. Out the window, she could see the par0t of the ship they'd been in, and it appeared to be slowly turning, or they were turning. Her head tried to follow of its own accord and she fell toward the floor again. She caught herself on his arms, studiously not looking out the window any more. She took a few steps, feeling awkward, heavy, and gangly.

That's it! Astri cheered supportively, and she wished she would stop. Even breathing seemed harder now.

Is this what gravity feels like all the time? I feel so heavy. I mean, not like it's terrible, if you like that sort of thing. Propulsion might be a problem though, Astri said. *Hey, drop me. Let's see if I could go straight through this floor, huh?*

Luminous ignored her and took a few more shaky steps.

"Do you want to sit down?" Nik pointed over to a kitchenette with a counter and chairs that looked like it was attached halfway up the curved wall from where they were. She shook her head, concentrating on the floor. "Have you not been in space before? Or, have you been in space a long time?" He seemed confused by what he probably thought were conflicting actions on her part.

She nodded to the second question, nearly bumping into a small room attached to one side of the grav wheel. She looked inside, curiously.

"The water closet," he said. She felt confused. Before she remembered to ask the definition from Deb, he elaborated, "For your, ah, personal business," he said. He seemed startled as she rushed inside and closed the door. "Uh, okay, I'll just, be out here then," he called.

And Luminous asked Deb her first of many questions: *how to be human?*

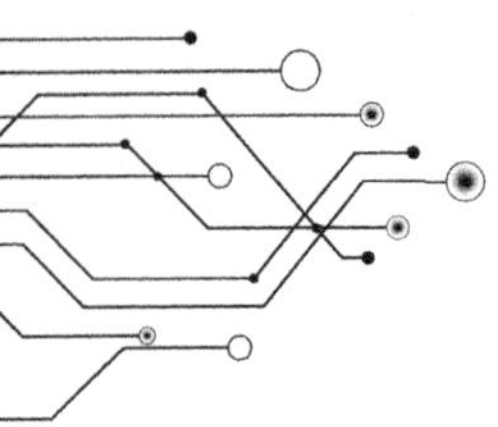

Chapter 8:

THEORIES

—Nik—

What was she *doing* in there, Nik wondered. It was going on five hours now and he needed to use the lav soon. There was only one on board, of course. Where did she think she was?

He knew she'd been through a terrifying ordeal of some sort, but this was getting bloody ridiculous. His previous attempts to check on her had resulted in the door opening a crack, enough to smile at him, sign that she was okay, and close the door again in his ruddy face. Could she really not speak? That had seemed a surprise to her as well, so he had to assume she could speak before her time in space. What had happened to her? He'd come up with a few possible theories, none of them good.

One, she'd been kidnapped by pirates or slave traders. With the domed colonies on the moon and Mars, and the new space port up and running near Neptune, piracy was a reality that was bloody hard to police in the vastness of space. She could have displeased her captors and been chucked out, he supposed. Considering what torture she could have endured first, this was his least favorite option.

Two, she'd been kidnapped by the Pangaloid Travelers and chucked out into space as an experiment. Whether to see what the human body could withstand, or to see if he'd open his ship for her, he didn't know. Could they be kidnapping humans from Earth or from the port somehow? Was she the tip of the iceberg? Okay, now *that* was his least favorite option.

Three, she *was* a Pangaloid, they could shape-shift, and she was here to check him out before he showed up to marry their princess. He realized that true shape-shifting was impossible within all known laws of physics, but he also had a strong feeling that a beautiful woman showing up floating in space at the same time they were having their first official encounter with extra-terrestrials would be one helluva coincidence. However, his scanner had said she was human. Without being able to question her, he had no idea which theory was more likely. And blimey. Now they were all his least favorite.

He had already sent messages to Earth and to Tersa Tellus with the scans he'd taken, informing them of his new passenger and asking them to advise him on these possibilities. Now he had to wait the hours it would take for the message to get to each place and to receive a response. They were still after all, constrained by the speed of light. But, were the Pangaloids? It seemed they were not. They had traveled after all, not just with a ship, but also a *planet*, from another solar system, if not much farther. Which would take humans forty years in a ship, at best, to their *nearest* neighboring system. He knocked on the lav door again.

She again cracked it open with a surprised look on her face. It was really remarkable. He would have expected some severe frostbite at least, eye trauma too, but her skin was completely unmarred, dewy and glowing like the finest brown pearls. Perfect. He cleared his throat.

"I, uh, need to use the, uh…" he stammered to a stop, pointing at the lavatory. Why was he feeling so awkward with her?

Her eyes went wide with realization and she stepped out. *Sorry,* she signed.

"It's okay. I know what you went through must have been terrifying. We'll get some food when I get out and talk."

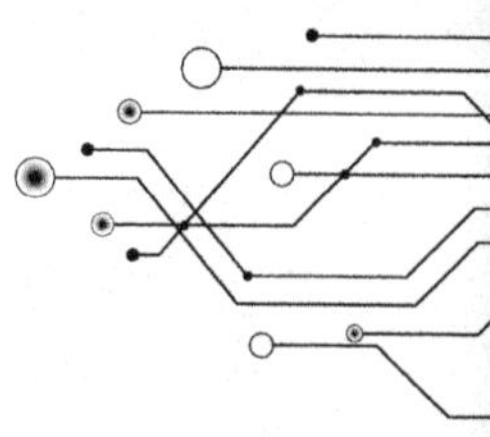

Chapter 9:

MEANT TO MOVE

—Luminous—

She had absorbed as much information about being human as possible. Now she had to hope it was enough. She'd come out of the little room when Nik had said he needed to use the lavatory. She'd been able to ask Deb everything with her radiance, the same way she spoke with Astri, thank goodness, because the whole typing and symbols button language was murky at best. And now she asked one more question, exactly what "using the lavatory" meant. She was promptly bombarded by more info about the human body's excretory system than she'd ever really wanted to know. Stars, she was really going to have to do *that?* Astri laughed.

A few minutes later, he emerged and helped her walk up the sloping floor until they stood before a small kitchenette that had previously looked to be on the opposite wall. This curved grav wheel made the entire curved walkway into flooring, depending on where one stood. He helped her into a chair.

"Here, what are you carrying this asteroid around for?" He tried to take Astri from her and she hugged her sister to her chest, shaking her head, and holding out a hand to stop him.

That's right, meat sack. Back off, Astri blustered. Thankfully, again he didn't seem to be able to hear her. He stared at Luminous clutching the football-shaped Astri to her chest. It had been one of the first things Astri had wanted to look up, the popular Earth game with the oblong-shaped ball. She was a fan, and had so far been disappointed that Luminous wouldn't throw her.

"O-kaaay. Uh, let's just get you some water and food. You must be starved."

She realized that her new body did seem to be signaling something to her. She didn't know what this new sensation was, but she suspected it was requesting biological inputs.

She'd never actually eaten, besides absorbing occasional gas or dust clouds in space. She was nervous, but knew she had to do it sometime. She hoped he didn't give her something difficult the first time out of the gate, like hot soup, or anything requiring what they called utensils or chopsticks, which all seemed to be popular on Earth according to Deb.

The stubby robot that had helped clean up her earlier plant snafu trundled up as they sat at the counter, a white towel over its metal arm and a tray holding cups of hydrogen and oxygen molecules. They each took one. She put Astri down on the counter.

"Thank you," she signed, and Nik gave her another strange look.

"Please do not take the water outside this room for gravitational reasons," the robot intoned in an artificial, calm voice and rolled into the kitchenette. She saluted in understanding and Nik laughed. She took her first sip of water and it slid cool and wet down her throat. She guzzled the whole thing.

"You should have told me you were so thirsty." Nik looked concerned.

"I didn't know," she signed back. He watched her hands, and seemed to accept her answer. The robot delivered two white plates, each with a pressed bar neatly presented atop it. She tried a nibble of the food and it burst in her mouth with flavor. She took a big bite and closed her eyes to savor the salty sweet flavor and texture that Deb told her was ground fruit, vegetables, and nuts.

"Mmmm," she made the sound without meaning to and was surprised that it sounded correct. Deb had said that human babies often took one whole Earth orbit around the Sun to say their first words. She hoped it wouldn't take her that long, but she also had to wonder if Ix had played a nasty trick on her. He had said though that she had to learn skills for herself. At least the rest of her body worked so far as advertised, and the sign language was helping with communication.

She chewed the delightful combination of tastes, swallowed, and took another bite before putting the rest of the bar down to sign while her mouth was busy enjoying. "This is wonderful! What is it called?" Her belly rumbled and she quickly ate the whole thing.

He laughed again at her delight. "It's only a foobar. You must be starved, you're acting like you've never tasted one before."

"More?" she signed, sighing with her last swallow.

"Um, maybe wait a bit. They tend to expand in your stomach, you know."

She nodded as if she knew this, sipping more water and realizing how quiet it was. She'd been watching Earth holo-recordings from Deb for hours. At first the silence was nice, but now there was nothing except the hum of the ship and his chewing.

His mouth noises are really annoying, Astri said.

Shh, Astri. Again, she was happy he didn't seem to be able to hear Astri's mental speech.

What? They are. Maybe we could do something with him. Like whack him over the head and stuff him in a cabinet.

Astri!

What? Humans on their satellite images are always bonking other people over the head. I mean, I know you like the guy and all, but he's loud. Everything here is loud! Did you know loud was a thing?

I guess their moving mouths on the satellite vids had to do something, only we couldn't tell what without air to carry the sound. She smiled at Nik and awkwardly put her finger to her ear and jiggled it to alleviate the buzz from the ship's engines.

"Music?" he asked, thankfully unaware of Luminous and Astri's mental communications. She nodded. "Music," he ordered the ship and on came a slow, relaxing instrumental piece. It was pleasant, but suddenly her mouth did a strange motion all on its own.

Deb, what was that? She asked, trying not to appear alarmed.

A yawn, Deb informed her, and gave a physiological explanation. How strange.

He laughed. "Tell me how you really feel."

He changed the selection and the music picked up, with vocals and a driving beat. She didn't always know what they said, but her head started bopping along and soon she got up, her body demanding she move. He laughed as she shimmied around, moving to the rhythm. She'd seen people dancing in several vids, and sure there were more complicated forms, but this seemed easy enough. This body was meant to move.

Yeah, woo! I'm dancing too, can you tell? Astri's football form rocked the tiniest bit back and forth on the counter.

And, for some reason, Nik was still sitting on his stool. She went back and held out her hands to him, but he hesitated, seeming shy.

"I don't know how to dance to this," he said finally.

"What?" She moved side to side to the beat and her signs became part of the dance. "It's easy." He still hesitated. She grabbed his hand and pulled him to his feet. "Come on. Who's going to see?"

He began moving awkwardly with his arms held stiffly in L's at his waist. Still, it was a start. She was surprised. He'd been human all his life, but he'd never learned to dance? It was in at least half of the vids she'd zoomed through with Deb, trying to absorb what it was to be human. She took his hands and shook them out, trying to get him to loosen up. He sighed in resignation and suddenly pulled her close with one of her hands in his, the other around her back. Her breath caught in her chest.

"Ship, play Blue Danube Waltz," he said. The music changed and he began to glide, leading her along with him. He looked down at her and winked before spinning them around and around until she laughed. He certainly did know how to dance.

"You think that's funny, do you?" he asked with a twinkle in his eye. The protective, prickly layers around his heart faded and his energy opened up to meld with hers. Dancing, it appeared, was some kind of magic.

"Ship, moon gravity, please," he said and the tube gradually slowed its rotation until they were bounding around the room in great spinning leaps, laughing to the playful orchestral music. In her mind's eye, they together were a glorious swirl of red and yellow, other colors coming out to play as well until they were engulfed in a cacophonous rainbow of emotion. When that piece was over, another began. And despite the change in gravity, despite being in gravity period, she felt secure in his arms.

She looked up into his face and saw the light there, the joy in his smile. He held her close and leaped into the air in a spin, but she kept her eyes on his face and found he was looking at her too. Like she, with her curly hair floating around them wildly, was the most beautiful girl he'd ever seen up close. Which surely couldn't be, with all the women on Earth, but without words he made her feel that it was. As they spun, drifting back down to the turning hull of the ship, the music slowing to a close, she just wanted to feel one more human thing. And if this was her chance, she was going to take it.

As his feet touched down, she pulled herself up and placed her lips to his, softly, sweetly, partly in thanks for this beautiful human moment, and partly because she wanted to feel what a kiss felt like, to give in to the magnetic draw of his lips. It was soft and exciting and unsure all at once. He tasted of foobar and sunlight, as if he held it within himself, an energy being for sure, even if he didn't know it. She pulled away with a sigh and a smile, her eyes still closed, savoring.

As if he were out of breath and she was his air supply, he pulled her back in and kissed her again. His hands drew tingles on her skin, and she knew then, this feeling, *this* was why energy beings would give up their freedom to Ix, to experience one lifetime, short though it was, as a human.

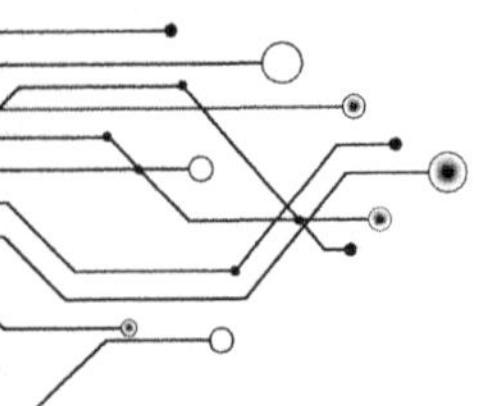

Chapter 10:

QUESTIONS AND ANSWERS

—Luminous—

After too few, short moments, he pulled away.

Ewww! What was that? Astri shrieked mentally across the room from her spot on the counter. *Did you try to eat his face?*

Luminous ignored her and tried to move back in, but he stopped her with his hands on her arms. His eyes were closed, his face looked calm, but the energies she could see around him were anxious, jagged. He held her by the arms and opened his bottomless black eyes and managed a smile.

"I—I can't," he said. "That was lovely, you're lovely, but I," his Adam's apple bobbed as he swallowed hard and his energies spiked. "I am to marry another," he said in a rush. "I've never even met her, and now you're here, and I—"

She could see how unsure of everything he was feeling and wanted to reassure him. Romance was not her mission.

"It's fine." She used the signs Deb suggested. "Calm down." He stopped, surprised, and she continued. "I only wanted to know what it was like."

"What what was like?"

"Kissing." She loved that sign. He seemed even more surprised. "You," she added hastily. "Kissing you."

His eyebrows smoothed a bit, along with the energy he was exuding.

Deb, what is this energy around him?

It is called an "aura", Deb replied, pulling some information to project from her wristband onto her forearm. She quickly turned her arm and the holo-emitter thankfully shut off. An aura. For some reason, that seemed like a silly name for the depth of emotional energy she could see like a cloud all around him.

Is it normal for me to see it? she asked Deb, who informed her that most humans did not have the ability to see auras. Luminous internally winced at the inadequacy of that ridiculous sounding word.

Unaware of her inner dialogue, Nik took a deep, calming breath. "You have to stop being so tempting, all right? We have to talk. I have questions."

"Fine. I guess," she signed with a scowl before she remembered she was not supposed to care about the ceasing of the kissing. It was pleasant but highly unnecessary, she reminded herself sternly.

He laughed. "I'll take that as a compliment. Now, we've been fed and watered, and thankfully we can communicate. So, first question. Where in the hell did you *come* from?"

It was Luminous's turn to laugh and she gestured to the window and signed, "Space."

Luminous, Astri broke in warningly, *are you sure you want to tell him what you are? You have no way of knowing how he'll react.*

Meanwhile, Nik was asking, "Uh, would you care to elaborate?

How did you—Did someone throw you out an airlock?" Concern etched his features.

"No! Not that!" Luminous signed emphatically, wanting to reassure him.

"Are you sure?" he asked, clearly not believing her.

"Yes." She paused to ask Deb for the right signs again. "I come from space."

Luminous… Astri warned.

But Luminous looked over at Astri and replied, *He deserves the truth, Astri. This is why I came after all.* And she turned back to sign to Nik.

"I am the nebula. I stopped the comet," she kept having to pause to ask Deb for signs and how to accurately locate them in front of her to describe the event in time and space, "when you were outside the ship." Signing was harder than it looked in the videos.

He looked at her hesitantly, "You're the what?"

She took a big breath and checked the next signs with Deb, wondering if Astri was right. She continued anyway. "I was the nebula. But I asked Ix, who inhabits Planet Nine, to make me human, and whoosh!" She made a big flying movement. That one was fun. "There I was, outside your door."

His energies and facial expression left a lot to be desired. "What?"

Luminous sighed. Of course, he wouldn't believe her right away, she reasoned with her disappointment. All of this was completely outside of human experience.

She tried again, this time more slowly. "I. Was. A. Nebula. I," she hesitated between the signs for 'turned' and 'became'—there was no right sign for this, "turned human, to warn you."

"Warn me of what?" Nik looked totally confused.

Astri was probably right. She really should have eased him into this. She plunged ahead. Slowly. Learning many of the signs along the way.

"The stars say that war is coming," Luminous signed to Nik. "I think it must be the Travelers. They arrive and then the stars say mini supernovas—here! I can't think of an explanation other than humans firing their star weapons on the Travelers, and them firing back. This is a very bad plan for Earth, and maybe even this solar system, to pick a fight with beings who can make their whole *planet* travel."

"Uh…" Nik had begun inching backward while she described this important information.

She watched him hopefully. This was it, the reason she'd come. To warn the humans of the coming war and convince them that they needed to change their actions toward the Travelers to maintain peace in the solar system and protect the future of Earth.

Look at his energy, Lu, Astri said. *This isn't working. You can see his energy, right? He's throwing up wall after wall around himself.* She was right. Luminous focused on the energy he was exuding around him and she could actually see him shutting her out, see his previous warmth turning cold.

"I've, uh, got to go check the, uh…. Yes, I need to make sure we're on course and everything." His eyes were huge, surprised, and even scared as he backed toward the door. "Just, ah, stay here, okay?" He held his hand emphatically out in the symbol for stop, and his energies echoed his desire for distance. She wondered if maybe she'd overloaded his brain.

"I need some time to, ah—" and he bounced for the door, as fast as he could in moon gravity. She stared with her mouth open as he closed her in. How rude.

Well, Astri said. *That could have gone better.*

You think? Luminous grumbled and bounded to the small kitchen to find another foobar. She found one labeled Chocolate.

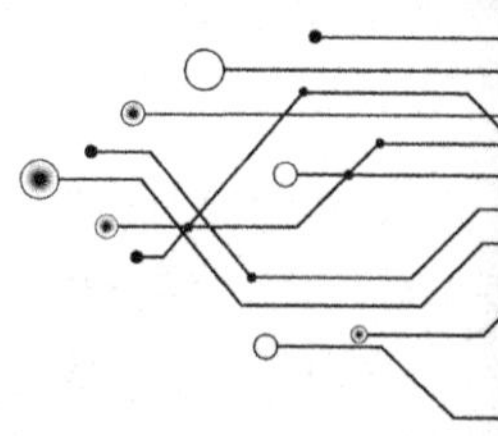

HANDS OFF

"Oh good Lord, I'm hot for a nutjob," Nik said to himself as he floated, back in zero-G, into the pilot's seat and strapped himself in. The girl thought she was a nebula turned human. That was not… normal, or even possible. He shook his head. Could their translation have failed? Could she have meant something else?

Thankfully she hadn't followed him, as he hadn't thought to lock her in the grav wheel. Could she have been sent—by who?—to harm him or his mission?

No. However deluded she was, she wasn't dangerous. He was certain of that. How could anyone dance and laugh with such delight, look into his eyes as though she was as sucked in by him as he was by her, and be dangerous? He'd never shared a kiss like that with anyone before in his life. It was full of energy, had made him feel alive, while being completely open and honest. She didn't seem like she was hiding anything. She didn't seem like a spy. Or, was she merely very good at it?

His Deb chimed and he saw an answer to his earlier messages had arrived. He held his breath as he opened it and gave it a quick scan. Nothing. He released his breath. Her scans were completely normal, showing her in perfect health, and her DNA had zero matches. That in itself was bizarre. Everyone, as far as he knew, was entered into the database at birth. Additionally, no known person with her fingerprints or retinal scans had gone missing. There were no reports of anyone else being found floating in space. And, they had no indication that the Travelers could shapeshift in any way.

He was sure his handlers would insist on thorough re-testing and vetting when they reached the space port. Until then, they advised that he be careful. *Something* had to have happened to her. There was no best scenario there. And, how had she survived in space? He could have sworn he'd seen some kind of shimmering forcefield around her, floating her inside. Was it a new technology he'd never heard of? Since the building of the port, space tech and safety were growing exponentially. It was impossible for anyone to keep up with all of it.

"OK, I mean, there has to be a logical explanation for all of this. Amnesia, PTSD. She's undergone something hugely traumatic and her brain is blocking, coming up with an alternate reality to protect itself. That can happen, right?" He thought it could. He tasked his Deb with research regarding that question and his brain continued speculating.

She is probably suffering from PTSD or something. Who knows what her captors, human or alien, did to her? But a few things were certain. One: the girl needed help, and he was going to make sure she got it. Two: as a scientist, he knew there had to be logical answers to all of these questions, and he was going to find out what they were. And three: from now on, he absolutely had to keep his hands off the mental patient. He'd get them to port, get her to medical, and they would help her with her delusions. Maybe then he'd get to meet the real Luminous.

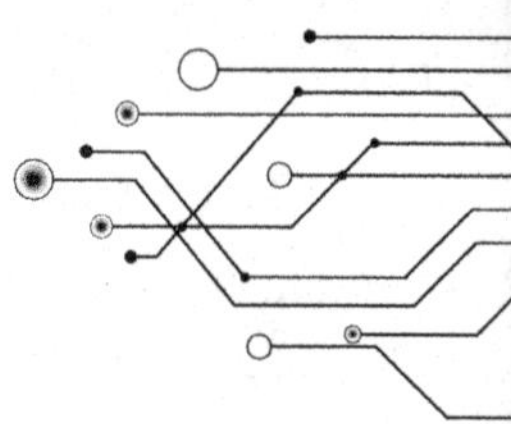

Chapter 12:

ARRIVAL AND TESTING

—Luminous—

Luminous spent much of her time during their glacial trip across the solar system learning international sign language, researching and *absorbing* humanity, and wondering what she'd gotten herself into. Now, after five days as a human, she hoped she was getting the hang of it. At least she now knew what she'd done wrong with Nik. In sharing the truth about herself, she'd overshared. According to her research, they didn't know each other well enough for that level of honesty.

Throughout the trip, he'd been friendly, but had kept his walls up and Luminous at arm's distance, which was too bad. She'd found out that there were definitely more interesting ways they could have spent five days alone together in a spaceship. Not that their time hadn't been enjoyable. Each day had passed with new discoveries about Nik and Earth.

She finally got to watch the Earthen holo-vids the way they were intended—through eyes, and ears. Some even included smells, through something he called an olfactory emitter. She hoped that wasn't what Earth *really* smelled like below the atmosphere.

He laughed when she wrinkled her nose at those horrid smells and she decided she could listen to his laugh all day every day. She asked for comedy after that, and loved hearing and feeling him laugh beside her, seeing the lightness in his energy and on his face. And she decided she loved her own laugh too. It was smooth and warm and conveyed happiness in a way she never could in space. Laughter was her new favorite sound.

She found a favorite show too, a late twenty-first century vid about a surfer and her quest to clean the ocean. But it made Nik sad, and he said it was a warning not taken soon enough. He'd watched it with her all the same and that had made her feel good in a different way.

He showed her holos of the palace where he'd grown up, in New London, in south central Alberta, Canada, and talked about discovering an old telescope, his grandfather's, and deciding he wanted to travel the stars in search of new planets. And he described his favorite evenings, watching the aurora borealis dance across the heavens, even taking trips north for more spectacular views.

The way he spoke of her beauty in the night sky made her blush. She wanted to tell him again that he was talking about her, but kept away from the topic for fear of making him run away again. At least she was able to agree with him that it was someone up there's best form of art. He'd nodded, satisfied with that description.

She asked him to tell her about the port, but he did better than that. For days on end, he was a most dedicated teacher, showing her vids and answering every question she could think to ask, and more. He projected a moving holograph of the great double-ring space port while he talked about it.

The small inner ring was a military base, and docked around it were a few matching military ships of various sizes. The larger outer ring was for civilian use and docked all around it—inside and out—were ships of every known type, make and model. Dozens of dirty, matte gray, ice-mining vessels of every shape and size lined the outside, unloading cargo, rotating crews, and getting a quick solar panel and window cleaning before going out again.

They mined, Nik said, from comets, moons, and large rocky bodies of the outer solar system, often traveling deep into the Kuiper Belt for the precious ice, so necessary for human life in space. They mined not only for water to drink, but also to split the H_2O molecules into oxygen to breathe and hydrogen to power laser defense cannons, for secondary propulsion, and for emergency energy reserves. Ice jockeys were well-paid for their dangerous work, and treated like rock stars, both demanding and enabling all other jobs, at the port.

But, *why* was it built, she had to ask, so far from Earth? It was something she'd wondered ever since the humans built it. The Port of Tersa Tellus, he explained, was named for "dry land" like the island it was in space. It would soon be the launching point for colony ships like the three enormous, brand new ones, tethered next to each other on the protected inside of the large ring. These ships, The Navigator, The Prospector, and the *Stalwart Mariner* were the first of their kind, colony ships that would soon carry 5000 Settlers each toward the new world, Proxima Centauri b.

Their historic flight to the nearest, supposedly habitable exoplanet would be powered by the newest, top of the line forward sails and precision laser cannons mounted on the port until they were out of range. Then, they would continue drifting at speed until they passed strategically placed laser buoys designed to blast their mammoth light sails even faster across the cosmos, which for Luminous was still ludicrously slow. At best, it would take forty years for those intrepid colonists to travel to ProxB, as people had taken to calling it. They'd given up their lives on Earth for the chance to claim a piece of the new territory for themselves and their children. But first, they had an entire generation of space travel ahead. And now they were delayed at port, by the arrival of another ship, this one docked alone on the exposed outside, reflectively white and literally alien.

Nik filled her in on what they knew about the Travelers, also known as the Pangaloids, and showed her holo-vids of their arrival. There were so many unanswered questions about them. What did they want? What would they do? And would they, could they, teach humans technology that would allow the colonists to shave years or more off their trip? It was worth the colonists waiting around to find out.

They finally arrived at the gleaming silver Port of Tersa Tellus after their week-long crawl across the solar system. Nik seemed to think traveling 2.7 billion Earth miles in a week was fast. He burned thrusters to slow their approach, and Luminous saw it with new eyes, and this time, a human perspective. The great, double-ring fired lasers into space, targeting and pulverizing meteoroids to dust that had the temerity to get too close. It also used sporadic thrusters to keep it at the shortest distance to Proxima Centauri b, explaining its strange non-orbit.

The Traveler ship, still docked in the same location, had a wide, flat oval front with seemingly no windows anywhere on its perfectly smooth hull. It tapered quickly from that large head into a long body, resembling a hammerhead shark. It was currently joined to the port with a glowing white docking bridge that was merely another difference from the dingy, stiff, warped, and often shared tunnels of the docked human craft.

Nik steered them toward a section of shiny new ships on the inside of the large ring, each embossed with diplomatic flags on their sides. As they slowed down to dock where Nik's royal advisor, already at port, had indicated, a half-dozen small, dirty mining tractors flew crazily toward them, chasing each other around the curve of the port, directly in their path.

"Fek!" Nik shouted and jerked the ship to dodge, Luminous's Deb defining the word for her with eye opening clarity. The tiny, single person tractors scattered out of their way like flies before resuming their race, and Nik docked as quickly as he could. The woman on flight control cursed and called for a status update.

"We're fine," Nik said. "They just… surprised me."

"Blaster brains," she said. "Unfortunately, you're now out of rotation. You can stay where you are for now. We can get you redocked later."

Nik agreed and directed the ship to extend its docking tunnel from the airlock. Nik checked to make sure all lights were green before opening the hull door and leading the way into the port's gravity matrix. Luminous followed, making sure to grab Astri on her way and tuck her sister's rocky body securely under her arm.

It was strange. One minute they floated down the docking

tunnel, and the next they entered a port hatch and gradually fell sideways to change their entire perspective on which way was up. Luminous felt a fluttery nervousness and a tightness in her chest.

Breathe, Astri reminded her. *Humans need to do that.*

Luminous nodded, but had trouble complying. This was it. She was going to have to convince humans not to go to war, when she'd never been able to even convince them not to litter. She almost stumbled and fell, but Nik held her till she caught her bearings in the giant donut of simulated gravity.

"Uh, I should warn you. This is going to be loud, in every way possible." Nik looked chagrined as they walked into a vibrant world of people, action, and noise.

Everywhere she looked, on every surface, everything was new, and bright, and yes, loud. People, so many people, every kind of people, from every country on Earth, hurried by on foot or hover transport, many talking with full-size holograms that appeared to walk along with them. That is, until a speeding hover-cycle cut right through a hologram, narrowly avoiding the pedestrians. But no one seemed to notice or care. This was apparently normal in this cacophonous world.

Shops lined either side of the thoroughfare, curtained doorways and proper storefronts all vying for space two and three stories high, right up to the port ring's curved ceiling. Human hawkers and holograms alike yelled out come-ons for food, products, and services.

Nik looked around for something, appearing mildly annoyed. "I guess they didn't get the message about the new docking location. I would've expected someone here to meet us."

Luminous shrugged to say that she didn't know the protocols.

"Well," he said, shouldering his bag, "I know where I'm going. We don't need to wait for anyone. I know you must hate all this loud noise, so I'll try and get us to the suite quickly."

He gave her an encouraging smile and they set off into the mainstream of foot traffic.

Glowing ceiling and wall advertisements in every language, flipped, switched, rotated, and moved to catch the eye, and when Luminous focused on one, it descended to hover right in front of her.

Intrepid Settler Festival ~ Fashion Show starting now on Promenade F! Showcasing the newest in efficiency wear and stylish impact helmets for the high winds of ProxB! It showed a 3-D rotating picture of a silver helmet with front horns that to Luminous's untrained eye was the last thing she would call stylish.

Nik swiped the ad impatiently away and it zoomed back up to drift flashily near the ceiling among a bevy of glowing ads and tiny mechanicals.

Drones, Deb defined for her when she asked. They flew in all directions, some with insect-like legs carrying packages, others sporting one or more glowing eye that seemed to look everywhere at once. Some were a bit larger, sporting red and blue flashing lights, and small holes on the sides that Deb told her were stun blasters. Sheriff's drones.

Mobile, hovering carts made their way up and down the market walkway too, selling food and drinks, herbs and remedies, crystals and trinkets, and all kinds of devices. It seemed anything anyone could want could be found right here. Luminous looked wide-eyed up at the scantily clad young women and men on balconies above. Anything.

Luminous looked here, there and everywhere, clutching Astri to her side. It was all too much. She tried to block it out, and backed into a hover-cart selling oranges, tumbling a few of the bright, globe fruits across the promenade just as a hover-cycle zipped by on the other side. The orange seller barely avoided being creamed as he swerved, and the spilled fruit was quickly scooped up by random hands and disappeared.

"Hey! Watch it!" The seller yelled, calling her a name Deb said was medium-high on the rude spectrum.

Deb, proper response?

The Insult Etiquette Manual says the proper response is at least one middle finger, two if you're feeling sassy, Deb said. Luminous didn't get even one up in time, but Nik did. As she watched him yell in her defense, she focused on him and oddly, everything else faded to a manageable background level.

"You okay?" he asked. She swallowed and nodded, keeping her focus on him and his calming, dark eyes. "I would've paid for the oranges if that arse wasn't such a bloody wanker." He kept her close to his side as they made their way through the market.

As they walked, a scantily clad couple greeted them, beckoning them into a curtained doorway for a drink or a game of something called Durongo. Though they couldn't see in, raucous music blared and a din of voices could be heard.

"Come on in, loves. We've got anything you might want after your long journey." One of the hawkers, a pretty, highly-groomed young man in an open vest, tight pants, and high boots swept open one side of a velvet curtain invitingly. From the other side of the doorway, a young woman with lots of wild hair and large, painted breasts proudly on display in her own tight vest winked one over-large eye at them and blew a kiss with shiny purple lips.

Luminous curiously took a step toward them, looking inside, but Nik pulled her back.

"No thank you! No thank you!" A voice yelled above the din, and she spotted a man in a fancy striped suit and fluffy neck scarf hurrying toward them. The woman pouted and swung the curtain shut, but not before Luminous caught a glimpse inside and a couple at the back table caught her eye, cozily enjoying a drink. This woman had shiny brown scales and a tail curled somehow demurely around her chair legs. A Traveler.

"Your Majesty!" the man called with arms out wide and a large, toothy smile. He slowed to a more dignified walk, straightening his suit and fluffing his silk scarf. He smoothed his full, unnaturally dark hair before bowing to Nik—and then smoothed it again. "Prince Nikolas, I am terribly sorry for those mining misfits racing out there. We shall have someone redock your ship immediately." He steered Nik away, completely ignoring the showy couple in the tavern doorway.

Luminous waved goodbye to the friendly, scantily clad folk, and walked with Nik who kept one hand behind her back. She didn't mind him leading her. It felt nice, even a little shivery when he touched her.

"Lucky girl," she heard the painted woman say behind her as they walked away.

"And this must be the young lady you messaged us about.

Miss Luminous, it is an honor to meet you, my dear. I am the prince's Royal Advisor, *and* the official European Union Delegate for the first ever interplanetary trade talks." He puffed up with self-importance. "But you may call me Maximilian." He rolled his own name with flair and somehow managed a half bow toward her while continuing his brisk walk.

"I hear you have had quite the mysterious ordeal and I am so glad Prince Nikolas was able to save you! Stories of your heroics, Majesty, have already spread round the port and back again." As if on cue, a group of a dozen people and robots came hurrying up, bowing and curtsying to Nik. He nodded to each human in turn. A few bustled off to where they'd docked the ship, presumably to move it and unload the luggage.

"It is a bit of a walk from here, but we have a lovely suite prepared for you, Highness, and a room nearby for your guest, after she is checked over by the medics, of course."

A woman wearing what Luminous recognized as a medic's uniform from the holo-vids unexpectedly took Luminous's arm on her other side and pulled her gently away from Nik to steer her into a hover-chair, though Luminous didn't want to let him go. Hardly breaking stride, the medic pressed a device to the inside of Luminous's elbow, right next to Astri.

"Your oxygen levels and blood pressure are within normal ranges. That's good news," she announced after a moment and began steering Luminous away down a hall toward what the woman said was Medical. Luminous felt her heart rate speed up in alarm and reached back for Nik.

"It's alright Luminous," he said, walking to keep up with

them and putting his hand on the arm of the chair. "I'm here. They're merely going to run some tests to make sure you're in good health. You're in good hands, I promise, and I'll be here for you when you're done."

Though still alarmed, she allowed herself to be comforted. Nik wouldn't send her someplace dangerous.

She found Medical to be cold and sterile, but blissfully quiet after the market and corridors, with no advertisements or holograms popping up on every surface. But it still had too many unknowns going on for her to be comfortable without Nik. She forced herself not to freak out. He'd said he would be right there when she was done. She wished she knew how long that would be.

The next several hours were filled with doctors, nurses, machines, robots, and equipment, beeping, blinking, poking, prodding and squeezing, running every test imaginable. Go here. Sit there. Drink this disgusting goop for something called "every immunization known to man." She tried to cooperate with their demands but Luminous wanted out of there. Besides, she was sure Nik had already done much of the same testing aboard the ship. They took fingerprints and eye scans and DNA swipes and sent the results immediately off to Earth to search every database for who she might be. She tried to leave, but they steered her back in for "only a little while longer."

The doctors inspected and tested her mouth, vocal chords, throat, tongue, and every bit of her skin with scanners, especially her extremities. They said they were looking for signs of frostbite, but she thought they were also looking for something else as well.

Something they wouldn't say. Evidence of shape-shifting, perhaps? And she loved her new skin, but she found that showing all of it to these impersonal doctors was uncomfortable. And when they wanted to put something they called a "probe" *inside* her to take pictures in what they said was a "standard *pap smear* exam" she looked that up with Deb on her arm and signed, "No," and put her clothes back on.

After that, she tried to take Astri leave again to go find Nik. She was so done. Where was he anyway? But again, they steered her to another room and two more doctors sat with her for what seemed like hours, asking every question they could think of until she wanted to scream with frustration.

She knew the answers to their questions, but not *how* to answer them in any way they'd believe. At least Astri was there with her, though she wasn't any help. Luminous had already seen how Nik had reacted when she'd told him she was a nebula. She wasn't going to make that mistake again. As much as she appreciated honesty, that kind of disbelief wasn't helpful to saving the solar system.

The doctors finally had no choice but to come to a similar conclusion that Nik had, that she was blocking whatever trauma she'd experienced. They stopped short of calling it PTSD, but said that was a possibility. However, her vocal chords, throat, and tongue all appeared normal and undamaged. And more than once a doctor commented that her cells looked brand new, with no signs of damage anywhere on her body, not even a scar, or a blemish. Like *she* was brand new.

Yet she still had to wait in her exam room for permission

to leave! These people were very confining. She tapped her foot impatiently. She had things to do, and sitting here waiting wasn't accomplishing anything. She finally heard Nik's voice outside in the hall, apparently arguing with the doctors. At least she'd managed to pass the sanity portion of the questionnaires, and that was definitely worth something.

She went over to the door to look for him through the little window and found him within view down the hall with his advisor Maximillian and the lead doctor on her case, a short, middle aged woman in a white coat. Just the sight of him made her feel better, that he had come back as promised.

"Look, don't you think you've poked and prodded the poor girl enough? If you haven't come up with anything by now, maybe there's nothing abnormal to find," he said.

"I didn't say there was nothing abnormal," the head doctor blustered. "Her tests may not have shown anything wrong, but there's definitely something odd about her, Prince. It's like she only came into existence a week ago."

At this, she saw Nik's head jerk up and he turned to look at her. She waved adamantly through the window. *Get me out of here!* she signed. He held up a finger for another minute and turned back to the doctor.

"What do you mean by that?" he asked more quietly but the soundwaves seemed to echo down the hall toward her.

"Her cells look brand new. She can't tell us anything about her parents or family or where she came from. She never had any immunizations, not one. She knows more about the debris field around Earth than which continent she grew up on. We almost have to wonder if she's ever actually been on Earth. If I had to speculate, I'd think she was part of some secret cloning program or something."

Even as Maximillian nodded thoughtfully, but Nik was skeptical.

"A secret cloning program?" Nik asked. "Don't you think you're reaching there?"

The doctor bristled. "Maybe. I'd keep her here overnight, to run some more tests, but until the results come back from Earth, I don't have any more tests to run. It's obvious to me that yes, she has been traumatized by something, and she's not able to talk about it. The best I can recommend is to get her into some healthy daily routines, including counseling sessions, and give her some time. She may remember everything, eventually."

Maximilian spoke up for the first time. "Does she seem entirely sane? She's not a danger to the prince, or anyone else, is she?"

The doctor frowned and shook her head seriously. "We have no indication that she's a danger to herself or others. She's quite odd, with her insistence on her therapy rock especially, but she seems perfectly sane."

"Well, that's good news, then." Nik didn't wait for an answer but strode to her exam room and opened the door. "You're all ready to go." He smiled at her though his energy was unconvincing. "Here." He handed her a large shopping bag full of clothes. "I thought you might like something of your own to wear out of here."

At that, she jumped up and gave him a hug in relief that she wasn't going to have to stay in that place any longer. She pulled out several outfits, holding them up and spinning around to see how the fabric floated and draped in the Earth-like gravity of the port. There were loose pants and tops in soft, rich fabrics and colors that were so much more interesting than Nik's shirt and pants from the ship.

As soon as she started getting dressed, Nik spun away, his cheeks red, and scooted out of the room. She'd made him uncomfortable again. She wanted to remind him it was just a body, everyone had one, and she was much more comfortable with him than with all the doctors, but suddenly she felt flustered and flushed as well. Why was he able to do this to her?

Chapter 13:

TACOS

The prince said she should remain with him always, and she received permission to sleep at his door, on a velvet cushion. He had a page's dress made for her, that she might accompany him on horseback.

Hans Christian Andersen, The Little Mermaid (1836)

—Luminous—

When she was dressed in pants and a top in a lovely blue and white pattern and had put on shoes that somehow stretched to the perfect size, a woman Luminous guess to be in her forties entered and introduced herself as Sarah, another royal advisor.

"I've served the prince and the royal family my entire career in New London. Though until this trip, I've never had cause to leave the planet!" She laughed and held up a second shopping bag full of what she called "basic toiletries" from which she pulled out a bag with a strap that was perfect for Astri.

"Thank you, this is wonderful!" Luminous signed and slid her sister's dense rocky body into the velvet purse and arranged the strap more or less comfortably across her body.

This is alright. I can get used to this, Astri said.

"I'm glad you like it," Sarah said. Luminous looked quickly at her, but saw she was responding to her comment, not Astri's.

"Now, we have lots to do before the Royal Delegate dinner celebrating the prince's arrival. We need to drop off these bags in your new room and get you situated. The prince is waiting for us out there, but first," she pulled what Luminous recognized as a comb out of the bag she'd brought, and a bottle of some kind of hair styling goo she called *The Magic*. "Your new outfit is lovely, but your hair is, well let's just say it looks like you've been traveling for a week without an ion-comb. May I help you with it?"

Luminous nodded, and sat down on the doctor's stool while Sarah called up a mirror on the nearest wall. Her hair *was* rather a wild nest after a week aboard the ship with no idea how to manage it. Sarah had a lot of curly hair too, and though she was ruthless with a wide-toothed comb, the ionic waves it emitted made quick work of detangling. She added a liberal amount of *The Magic*, combed it through, and it made her tight curls defined and glossy.

"Thank goodness you didn't get your period aboard that ship, eh?" Sarah asked as she worked. "It seems it was poorly stocked for a second person, especially a woman." Luminous nodded, though she had no idea what Sarah was talking about. Deb heard her mentally question that term "period" and projected some explanatory info on her forearm which Luminous quickly hid against her side. She'd look that up later.

Sarah didn't seem to notice and quickly swept Luminous's hair back into a large clip. While it looked nice, Luminous somehow didn't really think it looked like *her*. But she didn't know how to tell Sarah that, and so she kept her hands quiet in her lap.

"Ah, that's better. You look lovely." Sarah smiled at her, and her energy seemed genuine. "Now, let's not make the prince wait any longer, shall we?" They left the exam room finally and Luminous was glad Sarah had suggested they do her hair first when Nik's energy lit up at the sight of her. Maximilian stood next to him, looking at the device on his arm.

"You look great," Nik said with a smile that made his eyes crinkle. "Let's get out of here. Now that you've got a clean bill of health, we've got a whole port to explore." He held out his arm to her and she took it, allowing Sarah to carry her bags so she could sign, though she didn't want to have to let go of Nik to do so. Sarah led them out of Medical, and Maximilian's Deb chimed immediately. He looked at his arm device.

"Your Highness, I'm afraid we must take our leave. We are being summoned for you to meet the delegates in charge of negotiations with the Travelers."

Nik stiffened. "Will I be meeting the Travelers—and their princess—immediately as well?"

"No, Your Highness. You will need to be briefed before that meeting takes place. This is a simple meet and greet with the regional delegates and then we will all go to dinner. Miss Luminous can meet us there."

He sighed in relief. "Very well." He looked at Luminous and patted her hand on his arm before pulling away. "I have to go, but you're in good hands with Sarah, and I will see you soon at dinner." He followed Maximilian in the opposite direction that Sarah led her.

"We have a room all lined up for you, Miss Luminous," Sarah said. "We'll go there first to drop off your new things and get you settled before dinner. It's not big or fancy, but it's serviceable, and I've outfitted it with everything a girl could need." But Sarah's energy didn't match her smile as she walked. Like Maximilian, she seemed highly reserved and cautious.

"Thank you," Luminous signed.

"You're welcome. And, so you know, the prince has also set you up with a small spending account. It's not a lot, but it should get you by until you find some kind of job here at the port," Sarah said.

A job? Luminous considered and nodded. Yes, that was what humans did to earn their way, though when she'd find the time, she didn't know. She couldn't exactly tell them that she'd already chosen the job of preventing nuclear war. From her research it appeared there was no one specifically in charge of that, but it definitely seemed like there should be. They walked down corridor after corridor, each one narrowing and having fewer people than the last. There was no way she was going to remember all of this. A few taps on Deb's projection on her arm and she was able to bring up a map of the port with their location.

Satisfied she could find her way if she had to, she looked at Sarah to find her energy had clouded and she was wringing her hands together. She looked from their path to Luminous and back, as though she was hesitant about saying something.

"Luminous, I feel like someone needs to tell you something important, and I think it has to be me. After your time together aboard the prince's ship, it seems… You may have developed feelings for the prince. I mean, he is very handsome, and he saved you. Who wouldn't fall for that? But you know the Royal Diplomats are arranging his marriage to the Traveler princess, right? He did tell you, didn't he?" She looked very unsure of herself and Luminous had to feel sorry for her, being the one to bring up this awkward subject. Luminous nodded.

Sarah radiated relief at that. "It's important that he concentrate on what he has to do. If circumstances were different… but they're not. You understand what I'm trying to say, don't you?" Luminous nodded again. They were now walking down narrow corridors with doors closely spaced on either side and marked with numbers and letters.

She's saying, Astri interjected, *anyone can see you like the guy, but he's marrying a scaly alien, so suck that dust back in, huh?*

Yes Astri, I get it. Luminous blew a puff of annoyed radiation at her.

Several minutes later, they stopped at a door in a narrow residential hall. "Here we—" Sarah cut off abruptly as she tried and failed to open it. She checked the number with her Deb and, confirming it was the right door, tried again. It was locked from the inside. After a few moments, the lock clicked and the door cracked open enough for an eye to peer out at them.

"Who is it?" a suspicious voice said.

"It's Royal Advisor Sarah Quinn. This room was designated for the prince's guest. Who is *this*?"

But the voice didn't answer that question. "This is my room now. Go away." And the door was shut in their faces.

Sarah pressed the buzzer again and rapped on the door insistently, but whoever was inside didn't open it again. Finally, Sarah gave up, with much swearing under her breath.

"Well, we shall see about this," Sarah said, leading the way again, tapping constantly at her Deb projection on her arm while they walked. Luminous had to adjust Astri's bag several times to find the most comfortable position where she didn't bang against Luminous's side. Astri was getting heavy. When they arrived at the Port Housing Office several minutes later, there was a line of people out the door and snaking down the hallway, sitting or leaning against the walls and entertaining themselves with projected holograms.

As they walked to the end of the line, Luminous heard several people muttering among themselves about 'getting Mafia Don to take care of this.'

Deb, define Mafia Don please.

Mafia Don, Deb replied into her earpiece. *In the context of the port, Mafia Don is an unknown, shady entity who is said to be able to get things done when no one else can. They are also said to have been indispensable in bypassing bureaucratic red tape to get the port constructed.*

That sounds useful. How do I get ahold of this person?

Unfortunately, no record exists for contact information for Mafia Don.

Sarah told Luminous to wait at the end of the line and bypassed everyone to walk into the office. It wasn't long before she returned with a sour expression on her face. "We've been given a number and told to wait," she said. A few people in line snickered, but stopped when she glared at them. She spent some time sending messages through her Deb before turning to Luminous.

"I will wait and get this taken care of Miss Luminous. Maximilian is on his way to get you for dinner." Sarah's smile seemed forced.

"Are you sure?" Luminous signed.

"I'll be fine," Sarah reassured her. "Enjoy your evening."

Luminous was delighted to see Nik with Maximilian speed up a few minutes later on a hover-transport. Everyone in line watched in awe as the prince held out his hand to her and helped her step aboard.

"Will you be able to join us soon?" Luminous signed to Sarah from her perch next to Nik.

"Don't worry, Miss Luminous," Maximilian said. "Sarah will get this taken care of. It's an attaché's job after all." Sarah smiled, but didn't answer her question.

Chaperoned by Maximilian, Nik escorted Luminous to dinner to celebrate their arrival at port and Luminous's release from Medical with her clean (though strange) bill of health. They entered a beautiful dining room which seemed to cater to well-dressed royal dignitaries from every region of Earth. It was so redolent of spices and good food smells all mixing together that her mouth began to salivate excessively, excited for her first meal that was not a processed foobar. They were seated right away, at a reserved table, and immediately people started coming over to introduce themselves to Nik, shake his hand, and thank him for coming, giving her the side-eye, but otherwise ignoring Luminous.

Their waiter had to wedge himself in between Nik's admirers to take their order, though Luminous had no idea what kind of food to ask for. She was about to give up and order a foobar when Nik ordered for them both, something called tacos. The people had finally gone back to their own tables by the time the food came, and they were wonderfully delicious and messy, soft and crunchy at the same time, with a spicy sauce that lit her mouth on fire. She closed her eyes to better savor the glorious mixture of textures and tastes. Nik laughed and she opened her eyes to see him watching her with delight.

Maximilian watched them both, squinting with disapproval. He proceeded to talk the entire time about nothing and Luminous stopped listening. If she had to guess, she'd bet he was making it clear to any observer that she and the prince were not on a date. After eating all the food, she felt heavy, warm and satisfied, and was sure she would not be able to move again. Nik assured Maximilian that he was not ready to turn in to his room for the night yet and tasked his Deb to search port activities and nightlife. Immediately, colorful holographic fliers advertising events descended from where they had been hovering more or less discreetly in one corner of the ceiling.

"Fortunately for us, the Intrepid Settler Festival is just beginning. Starting soon, there are mining speeder races," he told Luminous, then shook his head with her as they both remembered having had enough of those for one day. He caught that holographic flier as it zoomed around their table and crushed it in his fist. She laughed as it sparked and disintegrated into holo-dust and disappeared. "There's the ProxB fashion show, hmmm?" He pointed at a flier strutting across the table in the shape of a person, stripping off outfit after outfit, each one listing info about the fashion show. But she shook her head again and crushed that flier in *her* fist, watching it dissolve into showy fireworks. All around her was a fashion show. It was all new.

"Whew! Thank goodness for that." He smiled at her and she

felt her insides go mush. Seriously, he had to stop that. "Let's see, there's a holo-cabaret showing. That should be interesting. If we hurry-" But Luminous brushed that dancing flier away, spotting and expanding the plain flier for the event she really wanted. "The Town Hall Meeting for new Settlers?" he asked skeptically. "Um, you know that's going to be boring as dirt, right?"

But Luminous tapped insistently on the flier for the town hall meeting. She had a mission, and she had to start by getting familiar with the local issues.

Nik shrugged. "OK, Settler Town Hall it is."

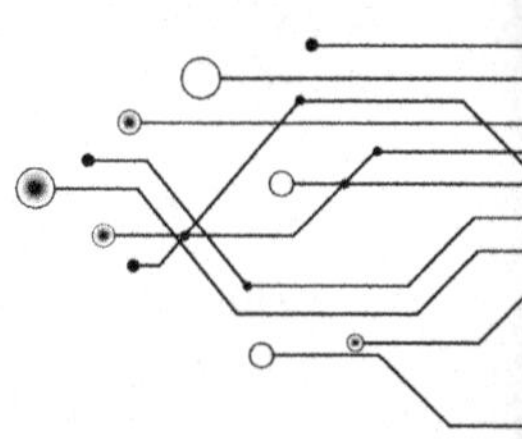

Chapter 14:

CROSSED SIGNALS

—Luminous—

They arrived at the meeting as it was ready to begin to find a full house and a restless crowd of young, early twenty-something Settlers, slated to leave soon on the three colony ships. And, Luminous was surprised to see a group of ten scale-covered Travelers sitting awkwardly due to their tails in the back of the auditorium.

The Travelers silently observed the proceedings, with very little in the way of expressions on their shiny, scale-covered faces, or body language giving away their thoughts. The feel Luminous got from them though was one of curiosity. The dark flower-like mark on their foreheads, above and between their eyes, seemed to open and shut little by little, like breathing. The reports she'd seen on the Travelers had mentioned and speculated on the purpose of the marks. Most experts thought they were decorative. But Luminous wondered if they were taking in sensory information.

Hmmm, the humans sure are ruffled right about now. Astri observed the energy in the room. *I'm glad you and Nik stopped stuffing your biological bellies in time for this.*

"Why are *they* allowed to be here?" a woman asked, gesturing toward the Travelers at the back of the room. Luminous thought she recognized her as a nurse from the hospital wing, but now she had a completely different, darkly manipulative energy swirling around her. Humans couldn't see that?

"Yeah!" several people shouted.

"People! People!" A middle-aged woman in a suit who Deb said was the port mayor was up on stage, trying to calm the crowd, and obviously already sweating under the lights. Over her left shoulder stood a man in a brown uniform with blasters visible on his hips. They both stood in front of a table where five older military types sat silently observing the crowd and the Travelers. "The Travelers are our honored guests." She made a small bow to them. "They are allowed, like everyone, at all public events." The crowd grumbled.

"The man behind the mayor is the port sheriff," Nik whispered to Luminous. "And behind him, the five Generals in charge of solar system security, the military base here at the port, and the colonization mission."

"Five?" she signed.

"I know, you'd think one would be enough, right? But the five regions on Earth each insisted on having a General here, on account of the nuclear arsenal."

She felt her head jerk up. That was what she needed to know about! She nodded at Nik encouragingly to go on.

"Don't worry. If it ever came to that, it takes three of the five generals to fire the weapons. And the military base and arsenal are protected by military androids. There are a few back there, see?" He pointed to the back of the room where five thin, humanoid robots stood silently. "They stay on base or with the generals because folks were worried about a large number of troops turning the port into a de facto military state. So, the port sheriff and his deputies are the ones in charge of port security. But mostly, I hear folks out here like to take care of things themselves." Meanwhile, the debate between the audience and the mayor continued.

"This is a resettlement meeting! Are they somehow part of resettlement now? Well, are you?" the same nurse asked the Travelers belligerently from the back. Her energy seemed off somehow Luminous thought, but she couldn't pinpoint it exactly. The Travelers didn't answer in words, but together they bowed and left the hall. The mayor ran after them, apologizing profusely. No one else seemed to notice, but as soon as the nurse was done speaking, she shook herself and seemed confused, and the darkness in her energy field faded. But the room's focus had already shifted away from her.

"You don't have to go! This is an open meeting!" the mayor said, but the Travelers filed out the door. The last Traveler out took the mayor's hand for a moment and patted it reassuringly before leaving. The mayor slumped for a moment before again taking her place on stage. Luminous could hear her mutter to the sheriff and generals, "Thanks for the help."

But the generals were all focused on the group of silver military droids that immediately swept the back area where the Travelers had been. Luminous and the crowd watched them carefully search for something with scanners, and when they were through the lead droid, denoted by its red-painted face, shook its head at the generals on stage and the team silently returned to their stations around the perimeter of the auditorium.

Meanwhile, the sheriff had stepped forward to reason with

the crowd. "Folks, that was not only incredibly rude, it was also stupid. As I'm sure our military presence would tell you, the last thing we need is to offend the Travelers. Don't you realize the power they wield?"

"We don't know that! We've never even seen them use a weapon!"

"We saw them absorb cannon blaster fire when they first arrived, remember? They did it on purpose, with not even a scorch mark to their ship." Agreement rumbled through the audience. "If they know how to make a whole planet travel in the darkest reaches of space—travel farther than we can even dream—don't you think they can certainly blast us out of existence easier than sneezing? Our laser defense cannons would be no match for whatever they've got if we anger them."

"Then we have to attack first! Blast them out of existence with the planet killers!" someone yelled.

"Are you insane?" someone else yelled back and the entire auditorium was awash in people yelling back and forth.

"Do you want to piss them off? Do you want to find out what kind of nukes *they* have, or worse?"

"What could be worse?"

"I don't know! But I do know that we don't want to find out!" A fist fight broke out in one corner and uniformed sheriff's deputies had to go break it up when the combatants started waving around blasters. Fear was thick around the room, and many people had pulled their own weapons. Nik made her crouch on the floor to avoid stray blaster fire and Luminous had to wonder, what was she *doing* there. How could she ever convince these blaster-happy humans to avoid their own downfall?

"All right, settle down everyone, settle down," the sheriff called from the stage as his deputies disarmed and led the two fighters from the room, amazingly without a shot fired.

"That was close," Nik muttered, standing back up. His energy was excited and wary at the same time.

Everyone seemed to be watching each other and slowly holstered their blasters, while Maximilian urged Nik and Luminous to leave. Luminous ignored him, feeling drawn to where the Travelers had been. There was something there, an energy signature, or more like an echo. Something the military droids with their scanners hadn't picked up.

Astri, are you seeing this? She asked her sister silently.

Yes, something. Can you get closer?

She made her way quietly over to investigate, pretending to take a seat in the empty row. Nik and Maximilian followed along after her. She looked and didn't *see* anything with her eyes, but she was sure there was something.... She ran her hands over the chair backs in front of her.

"Luminous, what is it?" Nik whispered, looking at her with confusion. She held up a finger for him to wait. There was something there, a faint shimmer.

Meanwhile, the mayor, the sheriff, and the generals seated at the table on stage were trying to get the crowd to calm down and take their seats. Each general had a hologram placard hovering in front of them with their name and which region on Earth they represented. General Ngata from Oceania, seated on the far right, pounded a meaty fist against the table. Even seated, he was easily the biggest human Luminous had ever seen in person, large muscles clearly defined through his uniform, which held three stars on the collar. The other generals were, from the left, General Garcia of the Americas, a hard-looking, stocky man with a face like tree bark and thin, wispy hair falling over his forehead. General Okafor of the African Alliance was a tall, thin woman with smooth skin of the darkest brown covering long, muscular limbs. General Varma of the Asian Unified Coalition was more of a reddish brown and surveyed the crowd from the center of the table with steely eyes. Next to the others, General Martine of the European Union was pale as the moon with spiky white hair, bright blue eyes, and an aura that said she didn't miss a thing. The only sign of a difference in rank was that General Varma at center had four stars on her collar to the other generals' two or three.

The sheer variety in looks of the people on stage made Luminous look around at the hundreds of Settlers in the auditorium. Humans came in a range of neutral skin colors, from cream to darkest brown, but the majority of people at the port were somewhere in the range of medium. The Settlers were all young and in shape, an equal number of women to men. They also looked impatient and ready to get on with their next adventure.

Ngata pounded on the table again for attention. Once the Settlers were again in their seats, Generals Okafor and Martine stood, left and right of center, to address the crowd.

"Prospective Settlers," General Okafor began. "We have called this meeting to address some issues of which we have become aware. There were selection standards in place on Earth, as you all know. We were promised, we *need*, fifteen thousand Settlers with real-world survival and engineering skills *and* who are best suited to working *together*. However, we've since found out that at times selection criteria were bypassed, and a few world regions may have inadvertently sent along candidates who don't play well with others." Okafor nodded to General Martine to continue. Luminous listened while continuing to search for the source of the shimmer with her other senses. She felt a small bump, and her energy pulled into it when she covered it with her fingertips. She pulled away in surprise.

"We've been hearing a lot of placement feedback." Martine waved a notepad device in the air before putting it down on the table with a final-sounding *thunk*. "Much of it to do with the progressive genome movement vs. the naturalists. Each of you were recruited for necessary skill-sets, some of which you arrive at naturally, and some of which are enhanced abilities. It is not possible to put together comprehensive teams that have only naturalists or progressives.

"In addition to that rift there are others." She began ticking issues off on her fingers. "Socialists don't want to be with capitalists, and vice versa. Atheist scientists don't want to be with God-fearing folk. Fundamentalist Christians only want to be with those who share their restrictive views on Christianity and, quote," she read from one of the cards, "no Muslims, Jews, atheists, or so called 'economic refugees' who can't pay their own way, end quote.

"Muslims don't want to be with other types of Muslims. Indigenous peoples don't want to be with any of the descendants of their historic oppressors, while those descendants just want to forget any oppression ever happened. The few elites who chose to leave Earth seem to expect first class quarters apart from the 'unwashed masses,' while also expecting to be in charge. Economic refugees, that's pretty much all of you, don't want to be with politicians, bankers, or any type of law enforcement." She took a breath having long since run out of fingers.

"Environmentalists don't want anything to do with miners, somehow thinking they'll conserve water so well that they won't need ice jockeys aboard in the next forty plus years." She cleared her throat while most of the crowd sniggered. "And those who are vegan don't want even synth-meat or growing facilities taking up space on their ship.

"Oh, and no one wants anything to do with the Neo-Fascists who seem to think they are somehow superior to everyone else. Did I cover everything?"

General Varma, in the middle, rubbed her forehead. "So, we have three ships, fifteen thousand Settlers, and everyone wants their own ship." Even seated, Luminous could feel the vibrancy of Varma's energy, but when she spoke, it expanded to draw all attention in the room to her. Luminous had no choice but to look up and give her full attention.

"Yes," Martine confirmed and sat down, the strength of her own energy overshadowed by the woman next to her. Varma placed her fists on the table, stood, and slowly walked around it. She was a human Sun, drawing the entire crowd into her gaze. It was only then that Luminous noticed that she had what Deb called active blade prosthetics in place of where human legs and feet normally would be. Deb informed her that Varma had lost both legs in her youth in the Great Civil War that had proceeded the current Asian Unified Coalition. She was one of the first to receive this type of prosthetic that allowed her to do much more than un-enhanced humans. Somehow, this only served to amplify her will to the room at large.

"Prospective Settlers, let me tell you what will happen now. We will run the cooperative compatibility tests again." She continued despite audible groans around the room. "Anyone who refuses, cheats, or fails will be sent back to Earth. Fascist ideology is an auto-fail. Would that we had a separate planet to send fascists off by themselves, but we don't. And yes, we have ways of scanning for invisi-tattoos. Any whiff of *mafia* intervention will also result in disqualification for all involved. We will mix everyone else up randomly and assign you to ships." At this, people in the crowd began shouting. She held up her hand. "We will do our best to keep family members together. We have only three ships, people. Either you want to go on this mission, or you don't. The time for your final decision is now. Let me remind you that you have all volunteered for this *military-led* operation, and each of you has signed a contract to follow orders. No Settler is above any other. Is that understood?"

The room was, for once, silent.

"Is that understood?" General Varma's voice boomed through the auditorium, projected with the very energy that pushed out from her body in a brilliant shock-wave. Humans must truly be blind, Luminous thought, to have not seen that with their minds' eyes.

"Yes, General," the majority of people present said together, as if compelled.

"And one more thing. Only military personnel will have access to lethal weapons aboard ship. Anyone caught waving around a blaster for any reason, whether here at port or after launch, will be court-martialed. You are dismissed," she said and people filed out, many looking dazed. Luminous shook off the effect and refocused on the small, energy-sucking bump.

"Luminous, what are you doing?" Nik asked, looking concerned again for her sanity. It was time for the moment of truth. Could he feel it? Would he believe her? She took Nik's fingers and guided them over the anomaly. He pulled back with a confused look.

"There's something there, isn't there?" he whispered, getting down in front of it to peer at the tiny bump. She nodded. Though almost entirely invisible, it had a slight shimmer. She wanted to pry it off with her handy dandy fingernails to get a better look, but what if it stopped working? While Nik inspected the spot, she caught the attention of the head soldier droid and waved it over.

"There's an energy absorption signature here. Bring your scanner," she signed. But the droid merely looked at her until Nik issued the command verbally. She sighed and got out of the way as the soldiers took Nik's word and came over to scan the shimmer.

Take heart. You're making progress. Astri gave her a mental hug while the soldiers confirmed something was there and had to call in a team of scientists to remove what she suspected was a tiny listening device of non-human origin.

Nik looked at her, exuding awe. "How did you know that was there?"

"I felt it."

"Felt it? From over there?" He gestured to where they had originally been standing and shook his head. "You're coming with me to the trade talk meetings. I'll get you in somehow."

As they were about to leave, Luminous noticed someone new arriving, skirting the still departing Settlers as if she strongly did not want to touch anyone. She wore a flowy knit caftan and layers of colorful cotton skirts, her wrists and neck dripping with stone and crystal jewelry. She seemed tense, her energy field weak, and threaded through with the same faint dark lines that the nurse had earlier. The mayor and sheriff summoned her over to them, and immediately began berating her.

"Where were you?" The mayor's energy was red, jagged, and uneven around her. "Travelers were here and we couldn't communicate with them."

Luminous watched the woman bristle. "At last count, there are at least thirty of them, coming and going from their ship at all hours. I have been running all over this port night and day for weeks now. I can't possibly be everywhere at once, you know."

"Well, what if they had something important to say?"

"Yes, it's a problem," she nodded as if they were idiots to only see the issue now. "I suggest you emphasize the importance of an alternative translation method to those in charge of the linguistics team. Until they come up with a reliable way to communicate with the Travelers, well, I'm only one person, and I need sleep. Goodnight."

Luminous nudged Maximilian and gestured to the exhausted looking woman who was now walking out. "Who's that?"

He took his time answering, apparently not appreciating being nudged. "That, Miss Luminous, was Cassandra Stillwell, the renowned telepath, and the only one who can communicate with the Travelers presently."

"They only speak telepathically?"

"Apparently, Miss. Are you ready to retire to your quarters now, Prince Nikolas?" He turned pointedly away from Luminous.

Astri made her own rude radiation gesture at his back. Of course, he couldn't see her passing gas at him.

"No thanks, Max. I've one more stop for Luminous." He sidestepped Maximilian to take her arm. "A little shop I think you'll like."

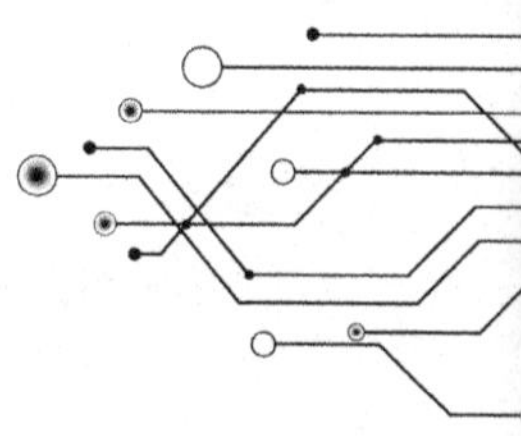

Chapter 15:

IMPERATIVES

—Luminous—

He wouldn't tell her any more until they got there, ushering her aboard a two-person hover-transport. Maximilian had to follow by himself. They arrived a few minutes later at a small, sparkling shop called *Imperatives* in a nice section of the market district that was filled with upscale shops, salons, and an insurance company. All of them had a sunrise design peeking out of their signs and logos in different ways, which was interesting in a place so far from the Sun. The only business that didn't sport a sunrise on the signage was a large shop down the way called The Self Defense Emporium, with glowing signs in the window reading *Dojo* and *Classes Available.*

But this cozy little shop, *Imperatives*, to which Nik opened the door for her, was filled with exotic things from Earth that Deb informed her were *delicacies.* Most of it though, was chocolate. Thankfully Maximilian and his grumpity energy stayed outside.

"Samples? Handmade here by yours truly," the middle-aged shop lady called to them over the tall, glass case with a smile between helping other customers. "Milk or dark, white or clear?" She had dark, wavy hair streaked with grey in a braid over one shoulder and her voice was a song.

Luminous liked her energy immediately, but she had no way of knowing the answer, and her mouth was already watering.

You're going to feed your face, again, *aren't you?* Astri said.

The smell in here alone is amazing, Astri. You don't even know what you're missing.

"All it is, then," the lady laughed when Luminous and Nik didn't answer and handed a small plate with teasing bits of dark, light brown, and white chocolate, and also some clear confection over the display case. She tapped away with a thin white cane to help the next person, which Deb informed Luminous that meant the chocolatier was blind. Luminous and Nik tried each piece while she observed the woman's sureness with her space and everything in it.

"What do you think?" the shop lady asked, tapping back to them when Luminous had tried the pieces, dark to light. She made a face. The white and clear bits tasted like sweet nothing.

"That's not even chocolate," she signed. Nik laughed and translated for her, since the woman couldn't see her signs. Well, that was going to need some thought, since this was sure to be her favorite place, and she definitely wanted to be able to talk with the woman who made such deliciousness.

Plus, her energy was like chocolate itself. Rich and dark, mysterious. Every time she turned, Luminous saw something new in her–power, grace, decisiveness. But there were also layers of her kept well-hidden. She was an enigma, Luminous decided.

"Luminous?" Nik prodded her when she didn't order right away. "Do you know what you want?" She looked at the case and saw fifty, maybe a hundred different varieties of chocolate, with every possible filling and coating.

She held up her hands in a shrug to the old lady. "Help? Which is your favorite? But not the white or clear." She made a face and waited for Nik to translate.

"Ah, a woman who knows when to ask for help. I like that. Shall I make you up a sampler of my favorites?"

"Yes please." She nodded enthusiastically and watched while the woman made up a large mixed box, at least twenty different varieties. Luminous accepted it with glee, and Nik put his palm on the counter to pay, while Luminous immediately opened the box and selected one. She bit through a decadent dark shell, into a bright berry center. "Mmmmm." Her eyes rolled back in her head and she realized, at least that one noise came out right. She savored the smooth, bright taste, wanting to tell Nik that *this* was her favorite, but couldn't with her hands full.

Nik laughed again and the sound was like music. She'd only been human a few days and already she didn't know how she'd gone so long out in space without knowing the sound of his laugh. She reached the second half of the sweet up for him to taste, not thinking about it until his lips touched her fingertips and his eyes met hers for a long moment. He cleared his throat as he chewed and opened the shop door for her.

"Thank you, Prince. Miss Luminous," the shopkeeper called quietly after them. She must have gotten Nik's name when he paid.

Luminous signed goodbye to the enigma of a woman, though she was not quite able to take her eyes off Nik. She barely even noticed Maximilian hiding his scowl as they left the shop and she took the arm Nik offered.

Luminous and Nik shared half the luxurious box and a leisurely stroll around the high-end shopping district while waiting for news that Sarah had found her a room. They looked in shops, and watched the laser show outside the large port windows that seemed just for them on this magical evening. Red and blue lasers pulverized any meteors that dared come close in a silent, dazzling display. And Luminous found that for a little while, she wasn't worried about the stars and their portents, but was merely happy, being human with Nik.

Not long later, Sarah pinged Nik to let them know that she had summoned a servant droid to continue standing in line overnight for the Port Housing office. After hours waiting, she was not even inside the door, and Luminous felt bad that she had lost her entire evening. It looked like Luminous's room situation would not be resolved anytime soon.

"I suppose she can bunk with me until we get this straightened out," Sarah said, but it was clear she did not want an extra person sharing her quarters.

"Don't be ridiculous," Nik said. "You have only a single room while I have a whole suite with a second bedroom that would otherwise go to waste. Luminous can take that room."

"Your Highness!" Maximilian protested. "How will that look to the Travelers, sharing your suite with an unknown young woman?"

"Come on, Max. If anyone asks, you'll explain to them there were no available rooms with the influx of Settlers. It's not like we're sharing a bedroom." Nik didn't look at Luminous while he said this. Was it her imagination, or did the tips of his ears turn pink? Perhaps it wasn't only her bodily thermostat that failed at moments like these.

Hours later, Luminous lay in bed and thought about Nik's words. It was quiet in the guest room, too quiet. She was used to hearing Nik's breathing while he slept, as she had every night of her human life in the zero gravity sleep sacks. Here, her body felt heavy on the soft mattress and if they had been sharing a bedroom… She felt her body heat up at the wayward thought. No, that wasn't going to happen. He'd made it clear he didn't want that. Pity, she sighed.

Astri? She mentally whispered to her sister, sitting on the other pillow. *I can't sleep. Can you make some breathing noises for me?*

First you want me to be quiet all night while you recharge your human body. Now you want noise. Would you make up your mind? Astri griped. Nevertheless, she began sucking in air and expelling it rhythmically, unfortunately sounding more like an asthmatic bag pipe than the sleeping prince.

"No, no, stop. That's not right," Luminous said. She tossed and turned, freeing her arm that kept getting trapped under her own weight. How did people sleep in gravity like this? She sighed again and got up, walking to the door and opening it quietly.

Where are you going? To listen to the man breathe? You've got to be kidding.

No! And would you quit calling him 'the man'? He has a name, you know.

Fine, Nik, the one who didn't believe the truth when he heard it.

I'm only getting some water, Astri. She probably wouldn't even be able to hear him through his door. She got herself a glass of water from the robot attendant in the kitchenette and looked longingly from Nik's bedroom door to the nearest chair. Maybe if she just scooted the chair a little closer she could… She took a step.

If my prediction algorithm is correct, I must highly recommend against that course of action, Deb said into her earpiece, making her jump. *If the prince awakens to find you in a chair next to his door it will be…*

I know, I know. Awkward, Luminous finished for her with a sigh. It was a warning Deb had given her a lot aboard the ship while Luminous was learning to be human. The database assistant seemed to have taken it upon herself to save Luminous from embarrassing social faux pas. Luminous had thought she was doing better.

Awkward, Deb agreed.

"Luminous?" Though she'd barely taken a step toward it, Nik's door opened and he stuck his head out. His hair was adorably rumpled as he stepped out, looking concerned. "Are you okay?"

She nodded, gesturing to her water glass, her eyes straying to his bare chest. She quickly looked up and away.

"What's wrong?" Nik stepped closer and she felt herself drawn to him like he was magnetized.

She found herself reaching toward his bare skin with her free hand. He sucked in a breath as if he felt it too.

Awkward, Deb warned and Luminous curled her hand back in, and then felt a flash of anger.

Be quiet, Deb!

Powering down now, Deb said.

"What is it?" Nik whispered, taking that last step between them. She looked up into his eyes and cleared her throat, though why she couldn't say. She waved her free hand vaguely.

He took her glass from her hand and set it down, as if that was why she couldn't say what was bothering her. "Tell me."

"I couldn't hear you breathing," she signed with small movements, like a whisper. She bit her lip and looked away. If she looked at him, she was going to touch him. She curled both hands in.

And then miraculously, she felt his fingertips caress her cheek lightly. She closed her eyes and leaned into his touch. She looked up and found him staring at her mouth.

"I couldn't hear you either," he whispered. And then his lips were on hers, pulling her to him like he couldn't help it, and something like an electric current ran through them both.

She uncurled her hands to feel the smooth, warm skin of his chest, and slid them up to play with the soft hair at the nape of his neck. After several long moments he pulled back, but only enough to put his forehead to hers.

"This is complicated," he said.

Though she didn't want to, she had to pull away to sign. "Why? Because Maximilian and Sarah say…?"

"Because I'm supposed to marry an alien," he laughed derisively. "This is crazy. She and I are not at all compatible!" He ran a hand roughly through his hair. "And you—" He took a step back toward her. "What happened to you Luminous?" he whispered. "Out there in space, I mean. Do you remember now?"

But she took a step back, shaking her head. She'd already told him, and now he wanted a different story. She fled back to her room.

she'd had no idea how much. Ix must have really blown through his stockpile for her. Of course, he'd been betting that she would die right away, and all that energy plus her own would revert to him. But she couldn't dwell on that now.

"How much exactly, I couldn't tell you. I was being pulled into Planet Nine's gravity well at high speed at the time, fast enough to strip away my radiance."

He looked at her as if he couldn't understand the words she'd just said. "I didn't say the process had to occur at light speed. It's merely a mathematical constant," Nik finally said. His energy was jagged, frustrated. Luminous knew hers was probably no better.

"I'm not telling you how it has to happen either. I'm telling you how it *did* happen. There's a difference."

She could see him grit his teeth. "I'm sorry, Luminous. It's not a reasonable hypothesis."

"I'm not asking you to understand the science behind it. I'm asking you to believe me."

"I can't," he said quietly, shaking his head. "I'm a scientist, Luminous." His energies were regretful, but closed and prickly. They were at an impasse.

She picked up Astri and gathered her things, leaving for.... Sarah's? No, for Maximilian's room. He'd be so happy to switch with her, she'd bet he wouldn't even complain.

Do you want me to eat him? Astri asked, while she stuffed what few belongings she had back into the shopping bags.

Luminous sighed. *No.* She walked out past Nik, not looking at him.

Are you sure? I mean, I'm full, but I could make room.

"Astri!" She must have signed it without thinking because Deb's voice broke the silence. Luminous put her hand out to open the suite door.

"What—" Nik began. She looked back and he looked conflicted. "What do you think the rock said?"

"Oh, nothing. It's all in my imagination anyway, right?" She didn't wait for his reply, but walked out the door, shutting it behind her.

Deb, you know where Maximilian's room is, right?

It is nearby. She popped up a corridor map and immediately Luminous knew where to go. As she'd thought, Maximilian was delighted to switch rooms with her. He ordered a robot maid service, quickly packed his many, many things, and was out the door.

"If I've left anything," he began, standing outside the door.

"I'll have Sarah bring it by," she signed and shut the door in his grinning face.

She put Astri down on the one cushioned chair in the utilitarian room. Astri let out another belch, this one smelling like brimstone. In the small space, the stench immediately filled the air and Luminous's nose wrinkled of its own accord.

You should've left me over at Nik's to off-gas tonight. Astri said. *It would serve that know-it-all idiot right.* Luminous had to agree.

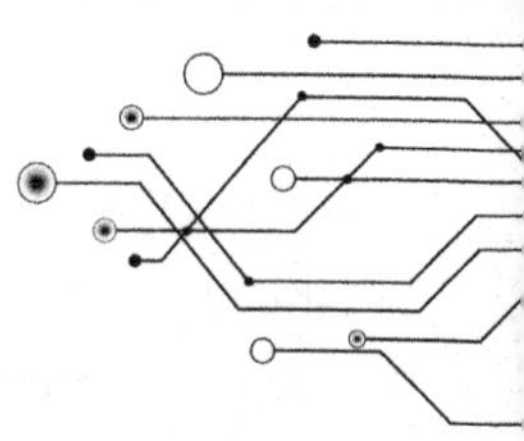

Chapter 19:

SELF DEFENSE

—Luminous—

The next morning Luminous and Astri were up and out early for breakfast. They had things to do and a new strategy to plan. Plus, the talks had been erased from her daily schedule, which she took to mean she'd been uninvited. In a way it was good because Luminous wasn't ready to see Nik yet. It was also bad, because she had no faith that the humans wouldn't horribly offend the Travelers without her and cause interstellar nuclear war.

She was trying not to think about Nik. She'd done enough of that the night before and it had only made her unhappy, her stomach hurt, and her chest ache. She'd had to ask Deb what was wrong with her, and had not liked the answer that she was suffering a broken heart.

My heart is broken? she'd asked in alarm. She knew the heart organ was important for her body to function, but that *was* where she ached when she thought about Nik. *Is my heart muscle in danger? Should I go to Medical?*

No. It is merely a figure of speech to describe the hurt that is felt when a romantic relationship ends, Deb replied.

So, it's truly over, she'd thought to herself and felt her body slump. She'd sunk to the bed and cried, even as the android maid had cleaned around her. This morning, she only felt marginally better, like she'd lost something important, in a way that she was hopeless to fix. But she had to carry on and complete her mission. Then she could return to space, even if she did have to serve Ix, and leave this awful human feeling behind. She forced her head up and marched herself to breakfast.

I still say you should've let me eat him, Astri said. Luminous had to laugh a bit at her attempt to cheer her up. A message came in from Nik, but she decided that was not a high priority at the moment.

They went to a nearby Settler dining hall. It wasn't nearly as fancy as the Royal Delegate banquets she had grown accustomed to, but it was time for a reality check. The place was crowded and noisy, the food mediocre, either reheated or reconstituted, and there were as many drones in the air as at the port market. Some delivered morning packages, some projected posters and banners for the upcoming Intrepid Settler Festival, and some merely loitered annoyingly overhead. But Luminous got through the eatery line and figured out how to pay for her own meal—with credits Nik had supplied her.

During her largely sleepless night, it had become glaringly obvious that she needed to get some kind of job to support herself. What if Nik decided to cut her off now? What would she do? Where would she stay? She couldn't let anyone hold that kind of power over her.

And, even more apparent after last evening's attack, was that Luminous needed to be able to protect herself. Being attacked had highlighted the stark reality that if she couldn't protect herself, she couldn't count on someone else to do it for her.

With Deb and Astri's help, she researched self-defense classes while working on a list of who else she could talk to about preventing nuclear war. She was pretty sure after their reactions the day before that none of the delegates would give her the time of day, especially without Nik by her side. And the generals, who were the only ones who could order a nuclear strike, were either in meetings or holed up in the Tersa Tellus central military ring, to which she did not have access. And besides, she was sure they wouldn't believe her either. She had a list of folks that possibly *could* help, if only she could get them to listen.

Someone sat down across from her and she looked up to see who was interrupting her think session. It was Sarah. She seemed relieved to have found Luminous, but didn't make any comment about the prince or their argument. She merely informed Luminous that she was supposed to be in the medical labs, and to bring her rock.

Out of habit, Luminous got up to do what she was asked, but then stopped, and sat back down.

"Why? What tests do they still have to run?"

Sarah's eyebrows rose in surprise. "Though we haven't yet figured out where you come from, or why you can't seem to remember your past, that is of less importance now. The delegates would like you to focus on proving your hypothesis, that the Travelers communicate not only telepathically, but also through their so-called 'auras.'" It was clear that Sarah thought the idea was ridiculous. "While remote, it's a possibility that no one had thought of, not even our linguists. And, Prince Nik has also requested that we thoroughly test your rock for any unique properties."

"I see." Luminous motioned to the chair opposite her for Sarah to take a seat. "You know, you were right when you suggested that I ought to get a job. I can't count on the generosity of others forever, can I?"

Sarah gave her a look that seemed to say, *where did you come from?* But Luminous continued.

"Astri and I are unique, and as I'm sure you understand, we can't work for free." Once she'd started talking about a job, Deb began suggesting things to say in a negotiation. Luminous plunged ahead.

"You're asking me to solve your translation problem with the Travelers. Humans communicate not just verbally, but with body language and facial expressions. Likewise, Travelers communicate only partly through telepathy. Though you don't understand it, you realize you're missing a big piece. That's where we come in. We're ready to hear your best offer."

"Well, I—" Sarah seemed flabbergasted. "I need to consult with my bosses."

"Of course. We'll be at the," Luminous checked back to the info she'd been looking up, "Self-Defense Emporium. You may find us there."

∞

Many people carried blasters around the port, like Nik, but Deb informed her that took special permits and training to do so legally, and port authorities were always trying to take away that right out of fear that some idiot would shoot a hole in the port hull. Luminous didn't have time for permits and training, but she also didn't have time for this amazing, yet delicate, body to be injured. Thankfully, Deb had found her a self-defense class starting soon using something called an energy whip. Luminous didn't know what that was, but she was anxious to get started.

The Self Defense Emporium was clear on the other side of the port and she and Astri barely made it in time. Nik had sent her two more messages in the meantime. She felt a pang where her heart was that told her she was not ready to talk, plus she had equipment to purchase and a class to get to. She decided he would have to wait.

Luminous saw about twenty students as she slid into the back of the large practice room. Most were young, she guessed newly arrived Settlers, many wearing traditional clothing and head coverings that marked them as one religious sect or another, gathered in clusters. They glanced at her and moved away, avoiding eye contact, and Luminous had to wonder if she was putting off some kind of stink vibe.

The dojo had padded mats on the floor and was lined with hover-dummies, with one in the center of the room. She looked at the energy whip she'd purchased for the class. It was a meter of springy, black-coated wire, with a handle at one end and a shiny metal tip at the other. They were quite flexible and were meant to be worn around the waist like a belt, expanding in size to each individual. There was an instruction download to her Deb, but she didn't have time to look it over before their instructor arrived.

To Luminous's surprise, it was General Varma who strode out of a nearby office, slightly bouncing on her blade prostheses. Her energy was still bigger than herself and all eyes were immediately on her. She whipped the energy belt off her waist and began flicking it, first with her wrist only, then with her whole arm against a hover dummy. It made a satisfying cracking noise with each flick and energy sparked out the end on each contact, leaving brown scorch marks on the dummy's self-healing skin.

General Varma stopped and turned to the class, looking them over like new recruits and pausing briefly on Luminous in recognition before continuing.

"Welcome," she said. "You are all proud new owners of an energy whip 6000. It is more versatile than its predecessors and, with three power settings, it's one of the easiest to use, non-lethal self-defense weapons on the market. In its default length, it is more flexible than an old-time rapier sword and more easily carried while giving approximately the same reach. Its handprint sensor is now attuned to you and you alone. Someone else could use it to hit." She put a glove on and whacked the dummy with no spark. "But, it won't taze for anyone else." She stripped off the glove and hit the dummy again, this time with the accompanying electric *zap*. She backed up ten paces and pushed some buttons on the handle. "And you can easily lengthen it to a classic bullwhip, though it obviously takes more practice to use." She demonstrated from the farther distance, cracking the tazing tip precisely against the dummy.

"Now, I know you all have your reasons for a non-lethal weapon. Doesn't take a special permit, for instance, and they will be allowed in private possession on the Settler ships, unlike blasters which will be locked for the duration of the journey. Or, perhaps

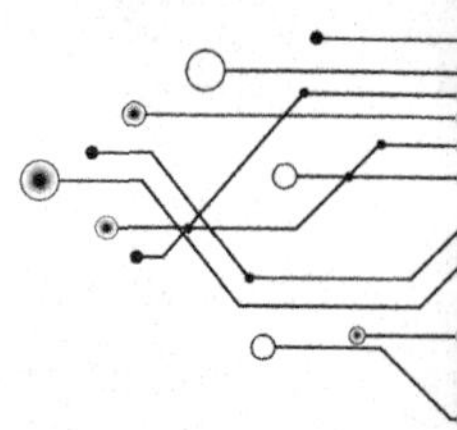

Chapter 16:

WHAT NEXT, SUPERSPY?

—Nik—

For the next hour at least, Nik berated himself back in his stateroom, tossing and turning in his bed. What in the bloody hell was he doing, kissing her again? He'd done so well resisting her, even on the ship in close quarters. Except for almost running into those racing buggers because he wasn't quite on the ball with her next to him. At least no one had been hurt.

He'd thought he could do this, and what was he supposed to do, leave her at the Port Housing Office? Of course not. She had her own bedroom here. He didn't have to hear her tossing and turning, each of them tethered to the wall in their sleep bags while the ship recharged the grav wheel, wondering what nightmares she was having and clueless about how to help her. And now he'd done what for her? Set back any progress she'd made? He shouldn't have pushed her. She'd looked like she was near tears when she'd fled to her room.

Smooth move, dumbarse. Nik shook his head. And she hadn't answered his question. Did she remember now and not want to tell him? Was it really that bad? He rolled over on the cool sheets. Of course it was that bad. There was no best scenario here.

He wanted to find whoever had hurt her and beat them to a bloody pulp nugget. And yet, despite—whatever it was—she was resilient, full of palpable joy at every turn. With her, each new taste was the best thing ever. He'd never known he enjoyed dancing as much as he did when holding her close. He'd never thought himself a teacher until she voraciously wanted to know everything about everything. Simply because she didn't seem to know anything, his first impression was that she wasn't smart. And maybe also because she didn't speak, he winced as he admitted his own stupidity, if only to himself.

He'd quickly found out how wrong he was when she'd soaked up everything he'd shown her as easily as breathing. And if that wasn't enough, she seemed to genuinely love meeting and observing new people. She really gave them her full attention, her full presence in the moment, which was a rare and refreshing quality. She was open and honest, spontaneous and mysterious, and simply… indescribable. She made him feel alive. She made him wish that he, and everyone, could get amnesia so they too could experience life again through new eyes.

He'd have to apologize the next morning for pushing her and help her get into counseling. And, as much as he didn't want to, as much as being with her made him feel like no one ever had, he should remind her that it was best to be just friends, considering everything. Like the fact he was meeting his bride to be the next day. Shite. Thinking about Luminous, he'd almost forgotten the other woman. He didn't know if he could handle a complicated, private romance and a fake, public courtship at the same time.

What was expected of him? What was he even supposed to say to the princess? Princess Paranel. In everything he'd seen of her, she was elegant and stately, and as bloody frigid as the rest of them. He hoped Max had some sort of appropriate present ready for the occasion. He had no idea how their first meeting would go. And he really did have a mission to complete. He smashed his face into his pillow. What next, superspy?

Chapter 17:

THE TRADE TALKS

But the princess had not yet appeared. People said that she was being brought up and educated in a religious house, where she was learning every royal virtue. At last she came. Then the little mermaid, who was very anxious to see whether she was really beautiful, was obliged to acknowledge that she had never seen a more perfect vision of beauty.

Hans Christian Andersen, The Little Mermaid (1836)

—Luminous—

Luminous sat with Astri next to her in the otherwise empty audience chairs, feeling like an unwanted interloper in the next round of peace and trade talks with the Travelers. There were six human delegates at the large conference table, one from each of the five Earth regions, plus Nik. A holographic name card floated in front of each one with their name and the region they represented, rotating between five different Earth languages. There did not seem to be a written Traveler translation that Luminous could tell.

Nik, labeled Prince Nikolas III of New London, and Maximilian, exuding self-importance as the European Union Delegate, were the only two she knew. The others were all handsome, middle-aged people, dressed in well-tailored suits and with perfectly coiffed, thoroughly boring hair.

The only other audience members apart from Luminous and Astri were General Varma and General Martine, who seemed to be observing rather than participating in the talks, and the port sheriff who stood with sharp-eyed suspicion in a back corner of the room.

Nik had had a tough time getting Luminous in, and the other human delegates had only allowed it because she had been the one to find the tiny Traveler recording device. So far, this room wasn't giving her any hints of such a device, but the energies coming from around the room were so intense that she didn't know if she could detect any subtle energy signatures through the tension the humans and Travelers were all giving off. She hadn't been given a seat at the large conference table, but she'd decided it was alright to be in the audience. It wasn't as though she would be talking anyway.

When the Travelers came in, they each were automatically labeled with a floating holographic name card like the humans. As they walked to their seats at the table, all eyes turned to Prince Nik and Princess Paranel's first meeting. He exuded nervousness while she was outwardly calm, as all Travelers were said to be, but her energy was nervous too.

The princess was exotic and beautiful all at once, with her shining brown scales polished to a high gloss all down her arms and legs, sides, back, and the length of her muscular tail. And there was something very elegant about how she held that tail, curved in a gentle corkscrew, swaying behind her and accentuating her well-formed scaly backside as she walked into the room to one of the special seats made to accommodate the Travelers. Her front was the only part of her not covered in scales, and she had clothed it with a long blue silken dress front, tied in place with contrasting red bows, providing splashes of red at the back of her neck and waist. Luminous wondered if she'd worn the patriotic colors of the British flag on purpose to meet her betrothed.

A strange, unpleasant feeling welled up in Luminous as Nik stepped toward the princess with a bouquet of hothouse flowers and greeted her with a gallant kiss on her clawed hand. Princess Paranel immediately handed the flowers to an attendant as if they might bite, and the attendant held them at arm's length while leaving the room. Other than that, Princess Paranel and the five other Traveler delegates, plus three guards, showed no outer signs of emotion, not even unconscious body language. Though Nik seemed surprised at the reaction to his gift, he proceeded, as if working from a script, to ask the princess if she would accompany him to dinner that evening.

Luminous felt a sudden rush of unpleasant feeling and had to stop her examination of the room and turn inward to find that it was jealousy, an ugly, muddy green emotion. She tried to release it, realizing that their betrothal was neither one's choice, and of course he would have to try to get to know her. It was only reasonable. She refocused on the room only to find the princess declining the invitation without apology or explanation.

Seriously? She wouldn't even go to dinner with her betrothed? Luminous felt insulted *for* him, though Nik merely seemed surprised, and relieved. Princess Paranel glanced at Luminous curiously, and then with what she could only decipher as sympathy.

Despite the rejection of Nik's overture at a date, another Traveler, a tall, muscular female standing behind the princess seemed to be glaring at Nik. Her holographic name read, Guard Tynee. Nik studiously looked anywhere but at the definitely *not* tiny guard and Luminous would have laughed if the tension in the room wasn't so high. Astri laughed silently though, garnering them a curious look from the telepath, Cassandra, and then several humans in response. They quickly moved on with the exchange of pleasantries.

They all sat around the large conference table and Cassandra gripped and jangled the bulky black and white crystal stones on bracelets at both wrists while she translated between the species. Her gray eyes went a startling white as she listened to and translated the Travelers mental-speak. It was slow-going. She was keeping most of her emotions well-hidden, but others at the table were not. The human delegates acted visibly surprised and uncomfortable at the Travelers' blunt honesty, or worse, confused and suspicious, like they were trying to understand what the Travelers were really saying. Because, despite Cassandra acting as translator, the words she spoke for them lacked nuance, the emotion and body language that added so much meaning to human speech.

Some of the missing content would have been revealed for all to see in the layers of energy surrounding both humans and Travelers, but humans seemed to be either deliberately or unknowingly blocking. Luminous wasn't sure, but she thought it was deliberate, with how uncomfortable humans seemed to be with some emotions while flagrantly waving others all around themselves. She, in her human body, was bombarded by the emotional layers surrounding every person in the room, so why were the other humans so blind? Though it was exhausting, they were biologically capable. Had they never learned to use that sense? Had they deliberately buried it? The only human who seemed to be able to sense anything was Cassandra, and there was definitely something very odd about her.

Her voice, for instance, didn't quite seem to go with her body, and her energies were indescribably different from all the other humans in the room. Everyone, even the humans, blind as they were to the energies surrounding each of them, seemed to feel uncomfortable with Cassandra. She was, Luminous had learned, the first ever scientifically proven human telepath, but how she'd become that way was still controversial years later. She'd experimented on herself to prove telepathy was real. Perhaps that was the difference. But Luminous felt there was more.

As she sat in the gallery with Astri next to her, she closed the input of her physical eyes and focused, not on what Cassandra was saying, but on her energy. It was dim and pale around her, muddy as it would have been with someone in pain. And it was wrapped in dark, invasive tendrils. Luminous realized with a start that she had felt the darkness of those tentacle-like tendrils somewhere before, with Ix. What did that mean? They clung to Cassandra's energy, sucking at it, at her very essence. The tentacles seemed to reach for Cassandra, coming not from her, but from another source outside the room. And then, as if they sensed Luminous's concentration on them, the tentacles moved. They reached out for Luminous, as if Cassandra was merely a conduit, and Luminous a magnet. She gasped and dropped the connection, her eyes popping open to find Cassandra staring at her with fire in those eerie white eyes, belying her pale, tired energy. One by one, the delegates noticed the exchange and turned to look curiously between Cassandra and Luminous.

Something about it made Luminous wish she could get up and run. But no, this was why she was here. She had to observe the problem if she wanted to fix it. But she raised her own walls protectively, forming a shield around herself.

"Luminous? What is it?" Nik asked quietly, following when she hurried out of the room for a drink of water when the delegates stopped for a break.

"I don't know exactly," she signed. "It's Cassandra. She doesn't…" she paused trying to find a decent sign to contain the amount of ick she felt, "feel right. Like her voice doesn't come from her." She shook her head. "I can't describe it."

"Don't worry. She has always seemed an odd duck, especially when those eyes of hers turn white when she translates," Nik said. But how could she explain it was more than that?

When they went back in the room, the talks resumed. The Travelers, in their straightforward, unemotional manner, expressed their main interest: to trade for a specific material for which humans did not seem to have a word. The Travelers' scans showed a rich vein of this element, deep within the core of Planet IX, which was why they had parked their planet, Traveler One, in IX's orbit in the first place. They admitted this element was vital for refining their fuel source so their planet and ship could use it for long distance travel.

Humans, especially Nik, were on the edges of their seats, thirsty for this kind of knowledge. When the Travelers didn't go into any further specifics, humans tried not to show their disappointment. But Luminous was surprised, and Astri too.

What's Ix going to think about them mining his planet? Luminous radiated to her.

Mmmhmm, Astri replied. *And that the Travelers are asking* humans *permission to do so?* They laughed uneasily for a moment at this new turn of events. Ix was not going to like this, but what could he really do?

The translator, Cassandra, gave a startled look over her shoulder in Luminous's direction, as if she'd heard something she couldn't quite understand. Luminous had to wonder if she could hear them, but if so, she quickly ignored them and got back to work. Now that the Travelers had asked for what they wanted, it was the humans' turn.

Through their chosen spokesperson, the Asian delegate, a balding, paunchy man named Sato, the delegates expressed careful interest in learning about the Travelers and their home planet, and then mild curiosity to learn how the Travelers' planetary travel technology worked. Luminous knew the travel tech was the humans true burning desire, and wondered why they wouldn't just ask for what they wanted.

When Delegate Sato made this deliberately bland statement of mild interest about the Traveler's technology, as one, the pearly black, flower-like sensors on the Travelers' foreheads snapped closed to a pea's size, and they each pulled minutely away. At least the humans noticed something had happened, but they misread the reason why. It took several minutes of niceties, asking about Traveler One's temperature and weather patterns, before those sensors relaxed and began to reopen, though never as fully as before.

Oh, this is not good, Astri radiated to Luminous. *The humans don't even know what they did wrong.*

I know, Luminous thought back to her.

This time, Cassandra turned in her seat to give them both a surprised look before facing forward again, which earned them more curious glances from several delegates and Travelers as well.

Can she hear us? Astri wondered aloud.

Shh, Astri, Luminous replied. Cassandra responded by putting a finger to her ear and jiggling it. Maximilian gave her a look and head shake that clearly said, whatever you're doing, stop it.

A few minutes later, the head Traveler negotiator tried asking again, "What is it the humans would like from a cooperative trading relationship, in exchange for the element we need?"

Delegate Sato conversed briefly with the other delegates before smiling and responding heartily, "We want nothing more than friendship and to learn about the beautiful Traveler people and their fascinating planet."

The Travelers' forehead sensors again snapped shut. They immediately got up and left the room.

"Well, that did not go well. What did I say?" The lead delegate scratched his balding head. Luminous sighed.

They don't even know, Astri moaned, earning an irritated look from Cassandra.

Maximilian turned and blustered at Luminous. "And *why* was everyone turning to look at you and your pet rock? *What* were you doing behind us?"

Pet rock? What's that supposed to mean?

Hush, Astri.

Cassandra was squinting from Luminous to Astri and back, but at least her eyes were back to their normal gray.

"Me?" Luminous signed, pointing to herself. "Do you not know what you did? Is this what's been happening and you haven't figured it out yet?" Her face expressed her disbelief and her arm motions became large and exaggerated with incredulity.

"No, Luminous. Tell us," Nik said quietly.

"He *lied*." She gestured at the Asian delegate and his energy bristled with protective spikes. "First the half-truth of what you wanted, downplaying your desire for their technology, and then the full lie. That all you wanted was friendship and to learn about them."

"What? It wasn't a lie," the lead delegate said. "When they obviously did not want their tech on the table, I downplayed it. And they gave no reaction, except those things on their foreheads opening and closing like they do."

"It's an emotional sensor." Her body language added the "duh" at the end of her sentence. "They could tell you were lying, weren't telling them what you actually wanted in a forthright and open manner. They were offended." She turned and looked at

Nik. "Tell them what you want from them. Only the truth. They may not give it to you, but they'll respect you for it."

"It's a *what?*" the diplomat for the Americas said, her perfectly groomed eyebrows shooting up her forehead into her shiny, helmet-like hair. "Experts don't know what that's for, if anything. It could be decorative for all we know."

Luminous sighed in exasperation. "Of course it's *for* something. Haven't you noticed how open it is when the meeting starts, and whenever you lie, it snaps closed?"

"It closes whenever we say practically anything," the American woman said.

"Yes." Luminous nodded emphatically.

"So, they're angry? How could you tell?" Nik asked.

"How can you not?" She threw up her hands and it felt natural.

"They don't show any emotion. Not since we first met them. I've seen all the vids a hundred times."

"They don't show emotion in the outward ways humans do. That doesn't mean they're emotionless beings, far from it. No wonder you're having trouble understanding them. Everything they say is informed by their emotional energies."

"It's an energy they give off? Why haven't our sensors detected that?" The American woman looked at some strategic pieces of art placed around the room.

"Because you all put off similar energies. You call it an aura."

"An aura?" the American asked, her lip curled in derision. "So, you can read *auras* now, and they tell you all this?"

"Yes."

And *that* was where she hit a brick wall with the humans. Some rolled their eyes while others turned away mentally and physically. And Nik's energy shuttered toward her too, showing he was incredibly uncomfortable with what she'd said.

Cassandra looked mentally exhausted, as if only the creepy dark tentacles in her energy field were holding her up. Luminous stayed far out of her way as she walked to the door.

"I must go rest." Cassandra excused herself and the tentacles led her out of the room.

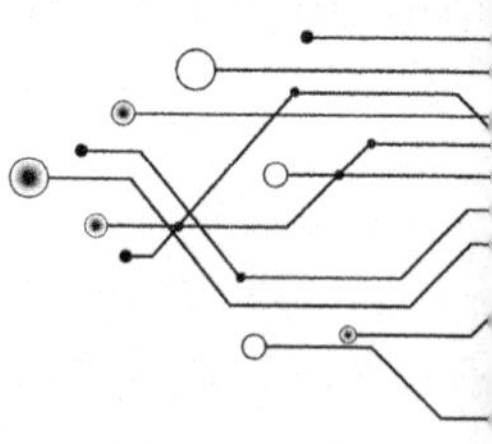

THE TAVERN

—Luminous—

That evening at dinner, Luminous felt alone in a sea of people. While port scientists studied the listening device Luminous had found in the port labs, trying to find a way to scan for more of them, the delegates were afraid to discuss anything of importance in their usual upscale dining hall. Needing to come up with a new strategy for conducting trade talks with the Travelers, the delegates had decided to have dinner in a place they had never frequented before—a noisy port tavern. They'd reserved a special room at the back of the bar, so the dignitaries would still be separated from the public they represented. Luminous sat by herself, off to the side with Astri, after Nik had been called over to another table for next level plotting.

They don't believe me. Luminous moaned into her wineglass at Astri. *I did all of this for them. I became human! And for what? They don't believe me on anything. Every time I tell Nik about something he can't see with his own eyes, he pulls away. Look at him over there, plotting with his advisors. Like he doesn't even want to look at me. Am I imagining it?*

Oh no. They're telling him you're crazy, and he's listening. When you first arrived on his ship and told him you were a nebula, he thought you were having some sort of stress induced episode. But the minute you said 'aura' today, you crossed the line of believability.

But Deb says there have always been humans with the ability to read auras on Earth. More humans would have empathic abilities if they didn't close themselves off.

Yes, Deb heard her name and broke into the conversation. *But they do close themselves, while they're still little children.* She projected some articles onto Luminous's forearm and gave a short digest into her earpiece. *And they've almost always relegated the few who keep themselves open beyond childhood to the realm of the crazies or the charlatans, or both.*

You may as well team up with Cassandra now, Astri said.

Luminous shuddered. *Not a chance. Her energy is… hard to describe, but creepy. And yet, they believe her.*

She had to prove her telepathy in a laboratory. Deb brought up more articles.

And I doubt she ever used the word aura, Astri said.

Luminous hated that revealing her true self had caused Nik to believe his advisors about her, and to pull away. She looked at him again and shook her head. After everything he'd seen, he didn't believe her. What a waste. She may as well throw herself out an airlock and go back to being a nebula. Only then she'd have to go serve Ix. She drained her wine.

And now you look like you're getting drunk and talking to yourself, Astri said.

Well, we can make at least one of those true. She tried to signal a waiter, but got no response, so she walked up to the front bar herself for another glass. Nik appeared not to notice, deep in his strategy conference with his smarmy advisor Maximilian. She was sure as soon as she was out of the room, Maximilian would argue for her removal from the royal suite. She wondered where they would put her. As far away from the prince as possible, probably.

The main tavern was much more interesting than the stodgy, reserved dining room. The bar was noisy with miners off work and Settlers having fun before beginning their long journey. They drank, danced, and played some sort of fascinating-looking game at some knee-high tables up front.

It appeared to have something to do with growing multi-colored crystal trees and yelling, "Durongo!" when the trees fell over. While walking up to the bar, she spotted a mixed-species couple, a human man and a pretty Traveler woman having a drink at a secluded table. Luminous took a seat at the bar near the bartender and looked around. He saw her looking at the couple in the corner and gave a short, derisive laugh.

"You know, when they first started coming in, I thought it was that Traveler princess having a drink with a different man every night, right after it leaked that they wanted her to marry a human prince. Hard to tell 'em apart, you know? But those armbands and clothing aren't as fancy as what she wears. They come in alone, let a man buy them a drink or two, then leave with the poor schmuck. An' I have a theory." He leaned toward Luminous and she found herself momentarily mesmerized by his dancing nose hairs as he breathed heavily, as if for emphasis. "They're her *maids*, see? An' they're doing research on human men for their princess, before she has to marry one. But who knows what they do with the men once they leave here. We get so many Settlers and miners come through, have to wonder if they're ever seen again." He shook his head and grabbed the decanter of wine from below the counter.

"Disgusting if ya ask me, which no one ever does," he grumbled. He finished pouring her a glass and set it before her.

With his blatant prejudice, imagining the worst of the Travelers, and his sour energy, Luminous wasn't thirsty anymore. She was pushing the glass away when an argument broke out at the nearest Durongo table, which caught both their attention.

As far as she'd been able to tell, Durongo was a betting game that required more luck than skill, unless a player cheated, which perhaps *was* the skill involved. Each player, at least two, but sometimes six or more, took turns tossing a color-coded seed, only one, into the dirty, much-used goo on the knee-high table. The goo started out as grey as an asteroid miner's face, but as soon as the first seed hit, out grew a crystal the color of the seed, varying in size from six-inch spikes to three-foot spires, as big around as a person's thigh. With each seed tossed, the crystal grew either at the base or higher up the "tree" until one misplaced seed caused the whole thing to topple and shatter to shouts of "Durongo!" Bets exchanged hands frequently, not only at the end of the game, but per seed as well.

After the game was over, crystal lay shattered on the floor and a stumpy bot swept it up and loaded it all back onto the table with a heavy warning: "For your safety, never touch the Durongo liquid. Thank you." A flick of a switch on the table turned the crystals back into dingy ooze. The same warning was posted on each table and the surrounding walls.

Interestingly though, something about the game made the players' auras invisible to Luminous, as if there was a dampening field around the tables. She felt blindfolded, unable to tell a thing about them. Was this what Nik and "normal" people felt all the time?

Now as she watched from her stool at the bar, a fight broke out between two men, one middle-aged who looked as though he'd come straight from work in the astro-mines, and the other, she'd guess, was a young Settler having some fun before his long voyage.

"You said it was safe to touch!" the Settler shouted while holding his hand up in front of his face and watching transfixed as it crystalized before his eyes. "Do something!" he screamed.

The older man laughed, holding his middle and pointing at the other guy as if this was the funniest thing ever. His victim stopped yelling, his face hardened, and he launched himself at the joker, punching him in the face—with his crystallizing hand—which shattered in seeming slow motion against the miner's cheek. The young Settler screamed again, now holding up a jagged stump, still slowly crystallizing.

The bartender finally came out from behind the bar with what looked like a fire extinguisher and sprayed the arm and stump all over. He turned to the Settler's drunken friends who were watching, looking dumbfounded.

"Take him to Medical, ya lousy layabouts! If you want him to keep his arm that is. Now!" The friends bundled the man and his still slowly crystallizing arm out the door. "And don't forget to come back and pay his tab!" the owner yelled after them, before going over to talk with the other man who was now holding a bleeding cheek and still laughing. "That was a dickhole move, Spetzler. What'd ya do that for?"

"Stupid Settlers think they're so smart. Let's see if they let him get on 'at *Stalwart Mariner* now." The miner sneered drunkenly.

"Just because you have a fake hand," the owner shook his head, gesturing at the man's hand, the fingers of which were tipped in the dingy Durongo ooze. "It ain't funny. This here's a respectable joint."

"What you gonna do, kick an old friend out? Don' forget I saved yer ass more 'n once in the astrofields when we first arrived."

"Sit down, Spetzler. Yer getting outta hand," the bartender grumbled and called for a bot to clean up.

But instead of doing what he'd been told, the miner spotted Luminous watching from her spot at the bar. "Hey, honey. Yer a pretty thing. Wanna see what a fake hand can do?" He swaggered over to her, waving the hand around that still had that ooze dripping from his first two fingers. She saw most of his aura emerge, minus anything nearest his hand, as he got farther from the Durongo table, and closer to her. It was muddied, jagged and malevolent.

Don't let that ooze touch you, Lu, Astri said. *It steals energy.*

Luminous backed away from the man, signing, *No. Stop.* She waved her arms at Nik, trying to signal him across the room. *Nik!* She mentally yelled at him. More than ever, she wished she could speak, wanted to yell, but couldn't produce anything more than a weak, warbling yodel. *Deb, I need you to yell at Nik for me!*

There is a translation program I can download, Deb said calmly. *But the signal in this room is dim.*

Yes, do it! She found Astri in her bag and held her protectively in front of her.

The drunk miner's face hardened. "Ah, the prince's crazy deaf girlfriend," he spat. "I got no love for the royals on Earth, 'at's why I'm out here, an' here he comes inta *my* port, like he's ridin' in to save the day." She looked around him, but Nik was not on his way.

Nik! Look at me! She tried to extend her frantic energy toward him. He finally looked up from what he'd been absorbed in with Maximilian and looked startled, straight at her.

"Luminous!" he yelped and jumped out of his chair. "Get away from her!" Nik yelled and strode toward them, but the miner ignored him and kept coming for her. She kept backing away from the man, and unfortunately away from Nik, toward the entrance.

"Gonna stay with him once he marries that Traveler whore? What does that make you? Let's see him save you now." Without warning, Spetzler flicked his fake hand at her, spraying droplets of crystalizing goo at her. She threw up her hands to protect her face and head, releasing Astri at the same time.

Yaaaa! Astri whistled through the air with a warrior's yell. Time seemed to slow and Luminous watched as Astri first spread to take the droplets on her stony exterior, and then opened wide, and to the astonished man's horror, surrounded and swallowed him whole. In two blinks, she compressed herself back down with a series of horrific crunches to only slightly larger than her usual size. She released a giant, fiery belch that echoed through the now silent tavern, and dropped to the floor.

Luminous picked her up and smoothed her ruffled exterior energies with gentle hands. *Astri, are you alright?* She hugged her rocky sister to her cheek and exhaled a sigh of relief. *Astri, thank you.* She looked up to see everyone in the bar staring at her, dumbstruck. She gave an awkward smile and put Astri back in the velvet bag strung across her chest.

It was a tighter fit now, and she had to work to get the fabric to stretch. Astri burped again and slid inside with a moan. *You owe me, Lu,* Astri groaned, inaudible to everyone but Luminous. *I am so stuffed.*

The people around started to mumble and point. "Where did he go?" someone asked.

"I think her rock *ate* him!" another whispered frantically in reply.

Nik shook off his stupor and crossed the remaining steps to her side. "A new self-defense device I gave her. Looks like a rock, doesn't it? But it did its job and scared him enough to make him run off. I'm sure port authorities will apprehend him quickly enough."

"Oh, he ran off," someone said. Others laughed in relief at having been given a reasonable excuse. "Of course."

"But… did anyone actually see him run off?" someone toward the front mumbled.

"I did, my good man," Nik boomed with a charming smile. "Didn't you? A bit too much of the old starshine, eh?" Nik forced a laugh over his shoulder while ushering Luminous out the door. They got away, leaving Maximilian behind, still performing crowd control and paying the bill.

She heard Maximilian snap at the tavern owner, "Why would you keep such a substance in a bar in the first place? Or any public place?"

The owner's defiant answer drifted in their wake. "Ain't no law says we can't. 'Sides, all the bars have 'em. Folks love their Durongo. A little danger's part o' the fun."

"What the *hell* happened back there?" Nik whispered.

"Astri saved me, that's what." She patted Astri in her pouch, who gave another moan and a burp that made the pouch jump on Luminous's chest. He stared at it in disbelief. "I did tell you she's a nebula, remember?" she said gently.

He shook his head and seemed to try not to think about all that entailed. She sighed. Perhaps he needed time to process. They walked back to the royal suite in silence.

Sign to voice translator download complete, Deb said into her earpiece.

Luminous released an annoyed burst of radiation. *A little late, Deb, don't you think?*

Would you like to begin using it now?

No thanks, Deb. I'll let you know.

Luminous could tell Nik was having a hard time and wished there was some way for her to help him, but she couldn't make him accept what he'd seen with his own eyes.

As soon as they walked through the door, he flopped into a cushy chair and put his head in his hands. She put poor Astri on the dining table next to the floral centerpiece she liked so well. After a few moments he looked up at her.

"OK Luminous. What is that *thing* you carry? And where did it come from?"

She sighed and tried to be patient, but his continued head burying in the face of oncoming destruction was annoying. She patted Astri who groaned and belched again.

"And did that rock just *burp*?"

"I've told you, this is Astri. She is a nebula. She likes this dense, small asteroid shape, maybe because she comes from space and the air pressure in here is a lot higher than what we're used to."

He shook his head and blinked, his energy still closed and disbelieving. "No, I mean, what lab or facility created a device that looks like a rock and can open up and swallow a man whole? And then compress him down to nothing in seconds, all without getting incredibly hot from all that pressure. I mean, the physics of it are mind-blowing!" He grabbed a tablet from a small table hovering nearby and started making furious notes. She looked over his shoulder and saw—math. He was trying to do the math. And he was no longer paying attention to her at all.

She ripped the tablet from his hands and chucked it across the room. *Deb, now.*

Ready for Sign to Voice fine-tuning. Deb said. *Please sign something you would like translated aloud.*

"Why can't you believe me?" she signed with large, angry movements and a female voice came booming out of her ear-piece. Alright, maybe that was a bit much, but at least he was looking at *her* now. He blinked owlishly.

"We came from space, not a lab!" She used somewhat smaller

movements and the voice was a bit lower in volume. "Astri is not a human-made device, but a nebula like I was, until I became human to warn you of impending *doom.* But *you* want to sit there and do the *math*?"

"It's the PTSD talking," he mumbled as if to himself.

"*I do not have PTSD!* If I did, it would be from you not believing me!"

He sighed like he was about to tell a child something for her own good. "Because it's not believable, Luminous. You can't have changed from a nebula to a human. It's not possible."

"How is it not possible? Explain it to me, please, because I'm standing right here." She put her hands on her hips. Yes, that was the right stance for this interaction.

You tell him, Lu! Astri said from the table, and burped again.

"Did the rock, excuse me, nebula in the *form* of a rock, burp–again?" Was that sarcasm? Did he use sarcasm at her? Oooh, he was so not getting on her smooshy side here.

"She's off gassing. As you so brilliantly pointed out, she just ingested a large amount of human! And now she's having to digest all of that at high temperatures in her core to avoid burning through the table! Which is really quite thoughtful of her, so maybe you could say thank you?"

He rubbed his forehead like he had a headache. "I can't believe we're having this argument. Also, that voice does not sound like you."

She chose to ignore the voice critique. *He* might not like it, but *she* was really enjoying having an audible voice at the moment.

"Your ability to believe or not doesn't make a whole lot of difference to reality!"

"OK, Luminous. You want to know why, specifically, I can't believe you are a nebula turned human?" He got up and stomped over to pick up the tablet she'd thrown.

"It's a little thing called $E=mc^2$. Energy equals mass times the speed of light *squared.* It was discovered hundreds of years ago by a guy named Einstein, and despite being ancient, it still holds true for everything we know about the universe."

"Everything you *think* you know."

He continued as if he hadn't heard. "Do you know how big the speed of light squared is?"

"I think I have some concept of the speed of light." Ooh, *now* who was utilizing the sarcasm?

"It's enormous! Multiply by your mass and the amount of energy necessary is even bigger."

"I am going to ignore whatever you implied there."

He closed his eyes and took a breath, before looking at her again. "Luminous, you know you have the perfect mass."

Well, at least she could see he was sincere. She felt her cheeks go warm on her.

"But that's not the point. It's an enormous amount of energy, Luminous! Bigger than a nuclear bomb, until the most recent planet-killers were developed. Only a solar flare has that much in nature. And, even if you could produce that much energy, there is no way to safely store it, because it would *blow up*, not create a living person."

"Yes, there was a lot of energy involved." Until he said it,

you don't trust security drones… or you decided a rock wasn't enough." The general looked directly at Luminous.

Luminous jerked her head up in surprise from inspecting her new whip.

Say something, Astri said. *Say…*

"She's full," Luminous signed and her voice translator spoke for her. Nik might not like the sign translation, might not think it sounded like her, but it sure helped her be heard.

Several Settlers gave a shocked look, gasped and took a step away. But the general paused and gave a full belly laugh. The Settlers followed her lead and laughed tentatively as well.

Nice. Keep the biologicals guessing.

"Well, in that case, after this class you may want to come back for the self-defense martial arts class later today. That goes for all of you. Same time, same place every day because: one, it's important for everyone to be able to defend themselves, and two, it takes practice to master any physical skill. For now, spread out with the heavy bags, keep the power setting on low, and get in some practice releasing the whip and striking immediately. Get your release down nice and fast and give an attacker no warning of what's coming. That's all there is to it."

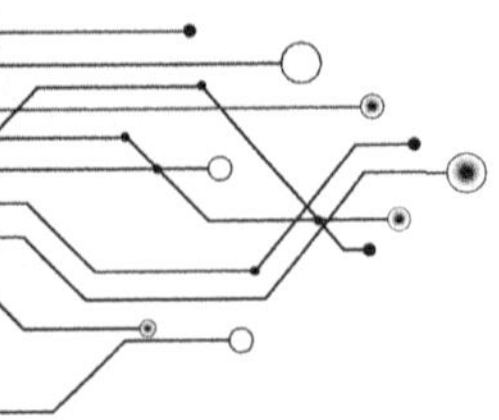

Chapter 20:

NEGOTIATIONS

—Luminous—

Maximilian showed up at the end of class with an employment contract for Luminous to sign. Deb went into full lawyer mode as she read it, keying off Luminous who saw the dishonest, power-hungry gleam in his aura.

"Does Nik know about this?" she asked, her chest giving another ache at the thought. She told it to stop, but it paid her no attention. She straightened, pulling her shoulders back. "Anyway, no." She pushed the tablet away. "I maintain all rights over Astri and myself, and all of our DNA and samples. I have the right to reject any test or procedure for any reason. And of course, the contract should not be with the royal family. I don't work for the prince."

"Miss Luminous, be reasonable. This is only a formality between friends so you can feel more self-sufficient."

Wow, he's some sort of slime, isn't he? Astri said, snug in her shoulder bag. *Space slime. No, port slime.*

"I said no, Max," Luminous signed aloud.

"Maximilian," he sniffed and left in a grumbling huff. General Varma came out of her back office.

"I was listening," she said without preamble. "Your instincts are obviously good, as is your Deb, but you're going to need a real lawyer next round. Fortunately, I have a good one. Would you like me to see if he's available to come by?"

It took all of half a second for Luminous to decide. "Yes, please. I can use all the honest help I can get."

Her eyebrows rose. "Couldn't we all? I'll ask him to stop by. For now, get in there. My sister, Star, will run you through some basics. Looks like you'll be her only student this session. I'll introduce you." She began to walk toward the dojo doors.

"Can I—" Luminous took a deep breath and took her chance. "Can I first tell you something you're going to think is very strange?" The words poured out of Luminous's hands, with more than a hint of desperation. This was one of the generals. One of the people she had to convince to stop a war. Varma turned slowly, and Luminous could see her curiosity, and also a protective wall go up.

Just give her a little bit. Talk to the curiosity, Astri said.

"The Travelers. They're not our enemies."

General Varma cocked her head to the side. "You're sure of that, are you?"

The stars hadn't changed but, "More so all the time." Luminous turned and entered the dojo.

General Varma's sister, Star, was immediately familiar at the first glimpse of her shifting, mysterious energy. She was the only one in the large dojo, practicing some smooth dancing movements that Deb called tai chi when Luminous entered, her cane leaning against the wall.

"Luminous," General Varma said, following her in, "do you have a last name?"

Luminous began to shake her head no; they'd tried to assign Doe as her last name in Medical, which didn't sound right, but now she had a different idea. "Nebula," she signed, and Deb translated it into speech. It sounded just right. "Luminous Nebula."

General Varma raised an eyebrow but didn't comment. "I'd like you to meet my sister, Star Varma. Star is a black belt in several classical forms of martial arts, though by day she's a—"

"Master chocolatier," Luminous signed with a smile that she hoped came through in Deb's vocal translation. She put Astri's bag down on a chair by the wall. "Your chocolate collection was amazing. I ate every one, well those I didn't have to share." She pushed Nik firmly from her mind. She thought about giving Star a hug in greeting, but one thing Deb had warned her was that surprising people with unexpected touching was not always welcome.

"Thank you. I am so glad you enjoyed them," Star replied with a wide smile, reaching for her cane against the wall and immediately finding it with a sure hand.

"And Luminous is—" the general began.

"Our mystery girl," Star broke in, tapping her cane over to Luminous. "The no longer silent enigma on Prince Nikolas's arm, and I hear through the grapevine, a seer of some sort. Welcome." She put out a warm hand, which Luminous gladly shook.

The general sighed. "Star has a special affinity for fortune tellers." Her energy spoke loudly of skepticism. "Now if you'll excuse me, I must go see about preventing this Mafia Don phantom from rigging the Settler placements aboard the colony ships for everyone and their brother," she grumbled, walking out to return to her office with her slightly bouncing gait on her blade prostheses.

"And Moon is quite closed to anything she can't see with her own eyes," Star said quietly when her sister had left.

"Well, that makes sense. And Moon? The general's name is Moon?" Luminous asked.

Better than most human names that have nothing to do with anything, Astri said.

"Mmhmm," Star confirmed. "What do you mean?"

"Uh, what do you mean, what do I mean?" Luminous asked. Was she able to hear Astri?

"You said, that makes sense. What makes sense?"

"Oh, I meant that her energy is protective, her walls are up," Luminous said without thinking, glad Star couldn't hear Astri after all. "Uh, I mean…"

"You see auras," Star said, but her walls didn't go up, at least any more than they already were. "Fascinating. What else do you see in my little sister?"

"Um, well, she is an amazing leader. People follow her without thinking or knowing why. If they could see her aura, they would know why."

"Why?" Star leaned forward, nearly completely open.

"She projects her energies, her will onto others. Because she also projects intelligence and wise decision making, and her intention that what she wants is for the good of everyone, people will follow her anywhere."

"Fascinating," Star said again.

To see what would happen, Luminous asked, "Would you

like to know what your own energies say?" To her surprise, walls didn't go up all around Star, only in one area, the part she was already hiding so well.

"Absolutely."

"You are more than a bit of a mystery. You have shifting layers of qualities around you. Decisiveness, kindness, ability and physical skill, intelligence, and leadership too, different from your sister's but related. I would say you are open, and you are, but for a few definite areas you are hiding. Yes, you hold walls, like everyone does, but I don't see you hiding for reasons of selfish gain, or shame either. You help people, don't you?"

Star took a deep breath when Luminous was through. "Well, that's all positive. You don't really read fortunes, do you? You read people."

"I leave the fortunes to the stars."

"Do you read them too?"

Luminous nodded and Deb said, "Yes."

"And what do they say?" Star whispered.

"War. Nuclear war," she clarified.

Star sucked in a breath. "Here at the port? With the Travelers?"

Luminous shook her head, and Deb said, "No," but that wasn't a good answer. "Near here. The rest isn't specific. My… gut, I guess, says the Travelers don't want war. It's humans we have to watch out for."

"Ah. That's why you were with the prince. To try to intervene."

"Yes, but we've had a fight. He doesn't believe me, and…. I don't know what more I can do." She felt her throat constrict and took a deep breath.

"And so you are here. Learning to fight."

"I have to do something." She snorted. "To prevent a nuclear war. It sounds ridiculous, doesn't it?"

"A bit. But someone has to push the button." Her face changed as something became clear. "And one of those people is my sister."

"Yes."

"Ah, then we should begin. I find tai chi helps me with centering, breathing, and focus. Come stand next to me and copy my movements, please."

They started a sequence of glacially slow, controlled movements. "Rise and breathe in," Star said, raising her hands. "Sink and breathe out." She lowered her arms and her whole body in a gentle, rolling movement. She continued into, 'Withdraw and Push,' and then the same on the other side. 'Stillness with Body' seemed to be merely standing with arms out in front and legs wide, breathing deeply. They continued with moves like these and more for what seemed a very long time. The postures with one leg lifted were a little more difficult to balance, but in all, it was much too slow. This was supposed to help with self-defense? There was a sequence called 'Deflect and Push' that might be useful—to deflect a slow-moving object in zero gravity.

"I hear a lot of sighing over there. Thoughts? You seem to be doing well incorporating new moves," Star said.

"How can you tell?"

"Practice, concentration, and using senses others forget they have."

"Can I ask you something?" she signed after completing 'Grasp the Sparrow's Tail.'

"Go ahead."

"I don't mean to sound ungrateful, but how is this self-defense? Or is it not supposed to be?"

The blind woman walked over to stand right in front of her. "Have you ever been hit?"

She was surely not talking about comets or broken satellites. "No."

"How much martial arts have you taken?"

"None."

"Then we'll take this at half-speed. Ward Off," she commanded, throwing a slow punch at Luminous, who did the move called Ward Off and found herself blocking the punch. "Good. A bit faster, Roll Back." Luminous did the next move and blocked a punch on her other side. "Again. Now you're going to block and then hit me. Ward Off," she called the move, "and Maiden Works the Shuttles. Good! Do you see now?"

"Yes, I think so."

"Now I want you to try to hit me," Star said. She reached out and inspected Luminous's fist with her hands before stepping back. "Now throw a good, solid punch."

As if Star could hear the movement of the air parting around Luminous's fist, she blocked it perfectly with 'Side Guitar', grasped Luminous's wrist and pulled her right around with 'Rolling Side Hands.' Luminous wasn't quite sure how it happened, but she found herself down on one knee with her arm pulled back and her head grazing the floor.

"Ah, tai chi isn't so useless anymore, is it?" Star let her up.

The only response Luminous could think of was, "Show me that again."

A lesson of palm strikes later and they paused for water. This felt good, in a way Luminous hadn't expected. Her muscles did what she asked. Blood pumped hot and alive through her veins. At times she was gangly and untrained, but with every practice, she grew more sure of her movements. This body was graceful and strong. Martial arts was a dance, a give and take, and she'd almost forgotten how much this body was meant to move. She swore she wouldn't forget again.

"Now it's my turn to ask you something."

"Alright," Luminous said.

"Are you always so open with people about what you see? Because that won't help to convince Moon, or the other generals."

"No," she shook her head and gave a little laugh. "Openness hasn't been exactly helpful so far." She thought of Nik and changed the subject. "When Moon, I mean General Varma, yes that still sounds better. When she mentioned stopping this Mafia Don from interfering in Settler placement, your energy practically rolled its eyes at her. Why?"

Star laughed in surprise. "You see even more than I gave you credit for. Very well. I think people should be given a say in their placement, and more than that, a chance to prove themselves. There are people here the military has rejected as potential Settlers because the bureaucrats can only see boxes marked on a checklist. They're not seeing individuals. By their so-called standard requirements, neither she, nor you, nor I would be allowed to volunteer as Settlers. They would see our disabilities rather than our abilities. But Moon won't listen to me."

Luminous nodded her understanding, but didn't comment. When Star put it that way, General Varma's placement process sounded cold and unfair.

Luminous practiced at the Self Defense Emporium through the next three rounds of contract negotiations, which were delivered by drone. General Varma's lawyer arrived and reviewed each one, but they got only slightly better each time. Luminous thought they were not going to come to an agreement at all, until finally on the fourth round, she had a job contract she could live with. She was going to work on improving translations with the Travelers using auric energies, and any other means at her disposal. And the pay was livable, even with the expensiveness of living in the port. She thanked Star and General Varma for their help and promised Star she would return each day to continue her training.

Luminous and Astri were asked to report immediately for testing. They spent the whole afternoon in the labs across from Medical, testing their abilities. It was slow and arduous because the scientists really had no idea how to reliably test for an ability to see auras. When Luminous got impatient and needed to move, she practiced her new tai chi.

"Were you not born in a hospital on Earth?" the doctor asked Luminous. She manipulated some holographic test results in the air. In large letters across the bottom it flashed, *No Match Found.* "You were never chipped. That must have made things difficult for you growing up. Were your parents part of some sort of privacy cult?" The doctor looked at her with apparent sympathy and Luminous shook her head.

The woman's energies were intriguing, a mixture of blues and greens that seemed to express healing and compassion, but there were also the smoky dark strands that Luminous had only rarely seen on other people, winding their way through and around her aura like snakes. She didn't know what they meant on either this woman or Cassandra the telepath, but she felt sure it wasn't anything good.

She wished they were back in the Medical wing. Here in the labs, holographic ads floated across the floor and ceiling in a soup of noise. She didn't know why the signals weren't muffled here. Perhaps some of this equipment needed the connection? In any case, it was annoying. She concentrated on her breathing and the next movement sequence.

The doctors subjected Luminous and Astri to every test they could think of, from mental health and physical exams, to Telepathy, though she told them she was an empath not a telepath. She didn't read minds. She kept her ability to talk with Astri and Deb using nebula radiation to herself for now.

She'd described for each doctor and technician what their energy fields looked like, and what they were feeling, though they all had significant protective walls up, which would have taken no talent to guess. They'd wanted to take Astri away to test her separately, but some instinct made Luminous insist that she not leave her side.

She was currently standing with Astri beside her on the floor, inside an insulated, closet-sized scanner bombarding them with every type of radiation noise the doctors could think of, all shouting gibberish at them. It was loud and maddening, and Astri was angry that Luminous had put them both through such idiocy. The x-rays felt like a violent intrusion to her cells, and with everything else the scientists had tried, she was surprised they didn't try gamma or cosmic rays on her delicate human body.

The infrared scan was next, but quickly got unbearably hot in the little cubicle. She tried to leave, pulling on the door release, but it wouldn't open. Something or someone was holding it closed. She pounded on the door with her fist, making throat noises in her distress.

Throw me, Lu! Astri yelled. Luminous picked Astri up and hurled her at the door with all the force she could muster. There was a *bang* followed by a *pop* and the machine cut off, and Luminous and Astri came tumbling out.

"Hot! Hot!" she signed, waving her arms in emphasis.

"It's only infrared thermal imaging, and we weren't able to finish with your fussing," the doctor said, trying to take Luminous's arm and steer her back in. Luminous thought something was off about her, but she was suddenly having trouble seeing the energies of the people around her, like everything in that emotional spectrum had been white-washed.

"No!" Luminous signed, jerking away from the woman and scooping up Astri, playing hot potato with her too hot exterior. She quickly set her on a nearby countertop. *Thanks Astri.*

That woman was trying to bake us!

"No? Are you refusing the testing the prince ordered?" The

doctor stopped to glare at Luminous with eyes that had at some point had turned a startling white.

"Yes!" Luminous backed away in alarm. Just then, Sarah hustled into the lab, looking at the two of them in concern and the doctor's eyes faded back to normal.

"What is going on here?" Sarah asked, looking confused.

"Uh, doctor," a tech spoke up from inside the scanner compartment, looking strangely from the doctor to Luminous. "There are actual scorch marks in here. And the machine is not coming back online. I think the scanner malfunctioned."

"Well then," the doctor looked around as if she didn't know quite where she was, and her voice changed subtly. "We will have to finish this tomorrow. I will give the results to the prince's attaché when I have them." She nodded dismissively to Luminous. Energies were slowly returning to Luminous's sight and she saw dark tendrils retreating from the doctor's aura, reminiscent of Cassandra's the day before.

Luminous hurried to get dressed behind a curtain, unable to get out of there fast enough. She didn't know why or exactly what had happened, but she was sure the doctor had tried to fry them.

You're quitting this part of the job, right? Astri said. *If I have to go through that again, that doctor is gonna go crunch.*

Yes, definitely, she agreed, though she was distracted by Sarah's anxious energy arriving outside the curtain.

"It's the Travelers," Sarah said through the thin barrier. "Luminous, they say they won't continue without you and your rock."

Luminous stuck her hands outside the curtain. "Astri," she signed. She kept an eye on the rogue doctor through the gap, but she seemed more disoriented now than threatening, and her eyes were definitely back to brown.

"Yes, well." Sarah cleared her throat. "It has been suggested that before continuing the trade talks, we exchange goodwill tours of the ships. We are starting right away, this evening with the Traveler ship, before they change their minds." She was so excited her energy buzzed around her. "Let's go."

When Luminous and Sarah joined the delegates a short time later as they prepared to board the Traveler ship, her gaze zeroed in on Nik like he was sustenance and she hadn't eaten all day. Her chest squeezed painfully and she had to cross her arms and look away to keep from going to him. Sarah maneuvered them into line and Luminous found herself three steps, yet still a virtual galaxy away from Nik. His aura told her he was glad to see her, yet his face held mixed emotions and he didn't take the first step either. The Travelers seemed relieved when she arrived, as if they'd been worried about her. It was confirmation of what she'd told Star and General Varma earlier. It wasn't the Travelers they needed to worry about.

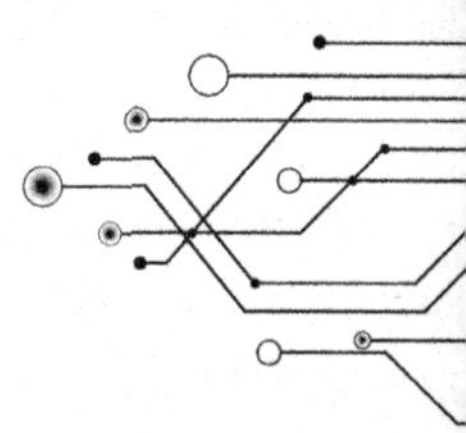

Chapter 21:

THE TRAVELER SHIP

Nik felt himself release a breath he hadn't known he was holding when Luminous walked up with Sarah. He wanted to reach out to her in his relief, but stopped, kicking himself again for their fight the night before. She hadn't returned his messages all day. Why couldn't he have been a little *less* honest with her? He'd screwed everything up.

He'd worried about her all through the previous night, even though Max had shown up late to claim her room, so he knew she had a place to stay. After he'd sent several messages that morning with no response, he'd logged into the new personal security drone he'd bought that was tasked to follow her the night before, when he'd been unable to sleep. The scene of her attack kept replaying over and over in his head and he'd had to do something to protect her. He'd checked the vid feed and assured himself that he wasn't spying on her. He simply wanted to make sure she was okay. The footage had showed her in a dojo, taking what looked like a self-defense class. He'd felt like a jerk for invading her privacy, but had breathed a sigh of relief and set the drone to ping him in case of emergency.

However, he hadn't realized until she walked up with Sarah that he'd been concerned for her safety with the experimental testing too. She looked as fine as ever though, if a little frazzled, and still mad at him.

Despite wishing he'd been more tactful, he hadn't changed his opinion. Insisting that inanimate space objects could turn into people! It was beyond absurd. If that made her angry with him, well that was how it had to be. His responsibility was to make sure she got the treatment she needed. But why did he have this nagging feeling that he was missing something important in regards to Luminous?

Maybe it was simply because he'd missed *her*. He knew she'd needed space that day after their fight, and in his mind he knew that was probably a good idea for both of them. When he'd heard she was insisting on being paid for her services in helping to translate for the Travelers, and proving her theory about auras in a lab setting, he'd thought it was a good idea. He fully supported that. He supported independence and self-sufficiency. Except that it felt like she was attempting to sever all connections with him, and that hurt like hell. Max, of course, thought it was ridiculous what she claimed to be able to do, but Nik had seen her do things he couldn't explain.

She was eerily observant. She'd been able to find that tiny Traveler energy recorder when it was all but invisible. There was the weird thing with her rock eating a man. And, her explanation of how they were offending the Travelers in the talks by not being completely truthful made a strange sort of sense. What if there was another component of Traveler communication most of them couldn't see, including Cassandra? They'd assumed the

Travelers were emotionless and unexpressive, but what if Luminous was right? About that at least.

Nik looked at Luminous. She was standing only a few steps away, and yet it still felt like there was a canyon between them. She looked the same, gorgeous as always, but there was something different about her, something a little wiser, a little wary, a little less trusting. Her joy had dimmed, and he couldn't help but know that it was at least partly his fault.

If there was a scientific explanation, if she could prove she really could read auras, it might make all the difference, for them and for the trade talks. While he'd told himself to stay out of her employment negotiations, when he'd heard she and Max still hadn't reached an agreement after three rounds, he'd told Max to agree to whatever she was asking. They only had so much time and they needed to find out if she was right about the Travelers. He'd keep her story about being a nebula to himself for now.

His intuition had been whispering nagging doubts all day about his assertion that it was impossible. *Before Cassandra, no one believed in telepaths either,* it had reminded him during the long, sleepless night. *There was a time people believed the Earth was bloody flat too,* it whispered at breakfast without her. *Just because something hasn't been proven, doesn't make it impossible,* it told him while he was supposed to be meeting with Max. And, *do you really think you know everything about space, you dumbarse?* it berated him as he'd mooned out the window at lunch.

And now, *you don't have time for this. Get your head in the mission.* As if to remind him, Max budged his way into the icy canyon between him and Luminous.

They had gotten word that morning that the Travelers had suggested a break in negotiations, and as a sign of good faith, to exchange tours of the Traveler ship and one of the three colony ships. After much debate over potential dangers, the delegates had agreed, and had spent half the day arranging security for the *Stalwart Mariner.* Nik had tried to get mentally prepared to see inside the Traveler ship for the first time, and to stealthily record holo-vid scans of everything, especially the technology.

They were about to board and he felt his heart rate pick up. This would be their first glimpse into Traveler culture and habitat, the first look at how they chose to live. And, the first glimpse of their capabilities, including possible weaponry. He had to be ready for any opportunity. He could not be focusing on Luminous.

He looked out the port window at the gleaming white ship. A stumpy appendage stretched and grew out of the side of the ship, into a long tunnel. They'd seen it before, when Travelers came to port or returned to their ship, as if the ship's hull was made of some gelatinous liquid. He wondered what else it could do. The tunnel suctioned itself onto the side of the port and the light over the port door turned green. The door slid open into a glowing astrobridge. They stepped into the solid, stable tunnel and Nik couldn't help but notice Luminous stiffen on the other side of Max and look back worriedly at the group remaining behind.

"It'll be fine," he found himself reassuring her, and himself. She took another step away from him and Max, difficult in the tunnel considering she was already as far from him as she could get. Bollocks. He needed to talk with her, but this wasn't the time to get into it now.

For security purposes, only half the delegates and two of the generals would go aboard at a time, though the full reason remained unspoken. At least three generals were necessary to order a military strike and access the port's nuclear reserves. He really hoped they would never have to test that system.

Luminous squinted over at him and he had to wonder if she could see his nerves. He worked what he hoped was a subtle calming exercise. Could she really see his aura? He had a sudden rogue thought about how useful that could be in the bedroom and had to again rein himself back in as they crossed the threshold into the Traveler ship. And he also reminded himself that he didn't believe in auras.

Two burly guards suddenly came into view on either side of the door. They stared straight forward, as unthreatening as two large alien guards could be, but he couldn't help but notice that they each gripped a long, poled weapon behind them with their tails. The tips of the dark gray poles glowed with a flare of yellow that stood out like a warning beacon. Princess Paranel chose that moment to take her place as their tour guide next to Cassandra, Paranel's muscular guard Tynee close by her other side.

It felt humid inside, and dim, and smelled of a rainforest. The walkway beneath his feet was slightly springy, reminding him of a carpet of leaves or pine needles underfoot. The edges of the walkway glowed, and the walls seemed to be covered in some sort of green plant-based substance, with a subtle glow all its own. The humans had not been allowed to bring a reporter or any recording devices aboard, but he'd already instructed his Deb to record everything through his earpiece and a special contact lens

Max had given him earlier. He felt like a thief in a jewelry store and he hoped the Travelers weren't as perceptive as Luminous had made them out to be.

They followed as Princess Paranel glided through the ship, giving the tour with her devoted guard on one side, glaring at anyone that got too close. Cassandra walked awkwardly on Paranel's other side, backward and translating. The tour group walked through a galley, where they were offered traditional Traveler refreshments, which all seemed to be moving. Everyone politely declined.

Travelers were seated at tables enjoying plates, raised on pedestals, of what looked like live ants. They would turn the plates and lick the edges with their long tongues, like humans licked ice cream cones before they could melt. Another favorite dish seemed to be a soup with one lobster-sized insect swimming in broth and surrounded by pea-sized vegetables. Nik tried not to stare as a Traveler delicately turned the insect over, removed the carapace and used a tiny immersion blender on its insides, before tipping the whole mess into the broth and slurping it all up with his long tongue.

Nik tried not to let his disgust show. Humans had been eating lab-grown meat for nearly two centuries now. Raising and killing animals for food was considered wasteful and barbaric. A few Travelers looked up from their meals to see the humans and watched with apparently equal curiosity as the tour group exited the galley and continued down a glowing hall.

The humans were allowed to file briefly through a shuttle bay which held what they were told were compressed emergency pods, and then into the room Nik was most interested in, the engine room. He saw huge, quietly thrumming engines that seemed to be made simply of glass and light, pulsing with a glowing dark energy that he did not recognize and did not understand. He made sure to slowly rotate and take everything in from floor to ceiling. It was exciting and frustrating at the same time, knowing that *this was it*, the tech that would make all the difference in human colonization. Humans even had a name for it: dark energy, and yet they had no idea what it *was,* how to get it, or how it worked.

Along the walls, there were also pulsating, shifting… boxes, for lack of a better word. A few were as big as a small apartment back on Earth, and others as small as a jewelry box.

Paranel said the large ones held the refined dark energy powering their engines, while the small ones were empty. "As you can see," Cassandra translated for her, "we need to refill those small tesseracts, or we won't have enough fuel to get Traveler One home."

Nik had so many questions, but tried to hold back. *Let the others ask the questions,* he reminded himself of the game plan. *Your task is to blend in to the back and try to be invisible. Act casual.*

Sure enough, the delegates asked a flood of questions about this energy source, what it was, how it worked, what kind of engines those were, where exactly Traveler One called home. Nik had other questions, but he tried to merely look around from the back of the group. Paranel and the other Travelers predictably declined to answer anything of importance, saying that humans would have to make these discoveries for themselves in their own time. Through Cassandra, one of them even used a phrase that humans already knew well: "There is no shortcut to scientific discovery."

Nik saw Luminous react but couldn't tell what she was thinking. The rest of the human delegates were left with sour expressions but no real argument, and Nik was left with a nagging question. How did they know a famous human saying, or did Cassandra merely translate the meaning of what they said into that specific sentence?

Max gave him a look that seemed to remind him. *No questions. Just blend.*

Paranel tried to regroup and get back on the right foot. She gave a sweeping, grand gesture toward the door and forward down the hall. "Now, if you'll follow me, we're coming up to the part you've all been waiting for. The control room."

The group perked up and followed her out, but as much as Nik wanted to see the controls, this, the engine room, was where the magic happened. He dallied behind the others, and ducked back to hide around a corner while the others left. This was his chance. He took a signal blocking bag out of his inner pocket and reached for one of the small, shifting energy boxes. He hoped it held the remnants, even a mere drop, of Traveler fuel technology.

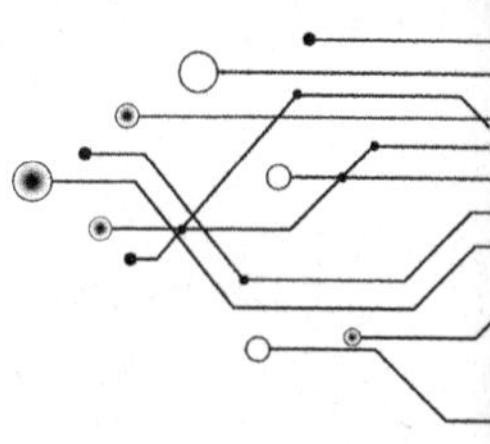

Chapter 22:

THIEF

—Luminous—

Luminous hadn't realized how attuned she was to Nik's energy until she didn't have it all day. Now that she had it back, she was quickly aware when it faded behind the group. She quietly fell back as the tour moved forward and retraced her steps, looking for where they had lost him. She reentered the engine room and turned the corner to find him using some kind of sparkling cloth bag to cautiously pick up one of the small tesseract boxes from the stack of empty fuel cells. She squinted at him. What *was* he doing?

It twisted and rotated in his hands as she approached with quiet steps, like it was a living thing, excited to be held. The cloth bag seemed to calm it, and dampen its energy field somewhat. And then he tried to hide it under his shirt.

She felt her jaw drop in very human surprise and quickened her steps. He was stealing? How *dare* he jeopardize the peace talks this way?

"What are you doing?" she signed angrily, instructing Deb not to translate audibly for her now. She felt like a housecat must when it arches, hissing its displeasure with an idiot dog. "Put that back." She tried to grab it from him.

"No!" he whispered, turning away from her reach. "Luminous,

we need to be able to study their technology. Don't you see? Earth is overcrowded. People are dying from drought, and flooding, and famine. We need to be able to travel like they do, to get people off the planet quickly, to new worlds that can sustain us for a new start. Or the loss of human life will only grow. This famine season is predicted to be one of the worst on record."

"And how bad will it be when you start a war with your dishonesty?" she signed, her movements sharp and agitated. "The Travelers are negotiating in good faith while you try to steal from them? This is what I was trying to warn you about. But I never imagined *you* would be the one to provoke a war!" They heard heavy footsteps in the hall.

"Quick, help me hide this." He tried to put it in her bag with Astri. Under his shirt the movement was not subtle.

"No!" Now it was her turn to move away. She would not be a part of this, this *theft*. And she also couldn't let the talks be derailed by letting the Travelers find them in here stealing. She yanked the box from him and thrust it back on the pile, but that wouldn't be enough. Any Traveler, guard or not, would be able to tell she and Nik were hiding something. The footsteps entered the room and she threw her arms around Nik's neck and smashed her lips to his.

He froze in surprise, then seemed to get on board with her hasty plan. He wrapped his arms around her and pulled her closer, kissing her back, and she forgot for a moment where they were. What she was doing, again? How could he be a thief when he tasted like chocolate and sunshine? She melted into his embrace.

She realized she'd gotten carried away when she heard a raspy sound that had to be a Traveler clearing their throat. Luminous and Nik sprang apart, and they didn't have to feign guilty embarrassment for the guard who had found them. They apologized profusely and allowed themselves to be ushered back to the tour group. When they rejoined the humans, Luminous stayed on the other side of the group from Nik, both of them standing with arms crossed. Anyone looking at them could see they'd been having a fight. Maximilian smirked with happiness.

∞

The next morning Luminous again joined Nik and the human delegates and two generals as they toured the *Stalwart Mariner* with the Traveler delegation. They were led by the ship's captain, a bright eyed, energetic woman with close-cropped brown curls. In her mid-thirties, she seemed young to captain such an important mission, but then, everyone aboard the colony ships would be young. The huge, 5000-occupancy ship was tethered to the port on the protected inner ring, flanked by its two sister ships. The guards flanking the doors when the tour group entered were much more visible, and more heavily armed, than the Traveler guards had been the evening before.

No Settlers were aboard yet, while final preparations were being made, so the Travelers could tour the approved spaces without crowds. From the start, Princess Paranel and the other Travelers seemed nervous, excited, and worried all at once. They were looking for something, but Luminous wasn't sure what.

The tour started with the crew quarters, as yet empty, pristine and utilitarian in their small, double occupancy rooms and communal bathing rooms. Next were the equipment bays, already loaded with the newest in mining equipment and heavy machinery for building a settlement. There were rows of escape pods lining the walls, though what good the short-range vehicles could do in deep space was dubious. There were storage bays filled with vacuum-sealed space suits and crates of clothing, tools, and supplies of every kind.

But Princess Paranel seemed to grow impatient with every new storage bay. She stopped the captain mid-explanation about upgraded medical and security drones to ask a question.

"Where do the animals live aboard this ship?" Cassandra translated for Paranel.

"Uh, animals?" The captain cocked her head at her in surprise. "Well, Princess, we don't have animals aboard. They would require additional food, care, and resources that we must save for our Settlers."

"But," Paranel paused and exchanged a look with her guard Tynee before continuing, "the pangolins from Earth, who we have heard that we so resemble. Are they not going with you to the new world? Are they still aboard the port?"

"Erm..." The captain was thrown so far off her expected speech it took her several long moments to recover. "No, Princess. I am sorry if someone told you that. There are no animals aboard this ship, or the port either, for that matter. However, the port holo-suites would have access to some lovely nature holograms from Earth if you wish to view them." She took a breath and smiled. "Now, if you have no more questions, I'll continue the tour. The most interesting parts are still to come."

The tour moved on, but Luminous could see in Paranel and Tynees usually calm blue-green energies that they were surprised and disappointed, as were the other Travelers, and now their auras held anxious orange prickles. She wondered who had told them there were pangolins aboard the *Stalwart Mariner*, and why.

The group next turned their attention to the largest storage bays yet, and most of the Traveler delegation moved forward to view huge stainless steel potable water vessels, stacked layers of photobioreactors growing algae, and crates upon crates of rations. The Settlers would have to mine for water along the way, both for drinking and bathing, and also for electrolysis to make air, but their ability to grow fresh food aboard the ship would be extremely limited. How much water they had to mine from comets and asteroids depended in large part on the algae. It required only light and water mixed with nutrient solution to grow, and it would filter carbon dioxide and make oxygen, as well as being the only source of fresh food aboard, growing already popular seaweed varieties.

In addition to the algae, and in case the photobioreactors failed, they had to take enough preserved rations for 40-50 years, and the sheer amount took up half a large bay by itself, floor to ceiling. That was a lot of foobars. And the large crates they were stored in were made of an organic compound that, when soaked in water, made the nutrient solution for the algae. Everything on the ship was useful and nothing would go to waste. The *Stalwart Mariner's* Captain seemed proud of her state-of-the-art ship's many efficiencies.

But Princess Paranel's energy was troubled, not impressed.

She asked the captain through Cassandra if she was sure they had enough rations. The captain assured her they did, yet Luminous saw that Paranel's energy remained concerned and unconvinced as she looked at that half-full storage room. Her guard Tynee put a hand on her arm and seemed to be cautioning her about something. Luminous wished she could understand what they were saying, but if Cassandra knew, she wasn't saying.

The tour group was moving on when Luminous, lagging at the back of the group to avoid Nik, noticed they had left Paranel and her ever-present guard behind. She felt a strange, expansive thrumming energy behind her and backtracked to find out what it was, while the rest of the group rounded the corner and proceeded on. She peered back around the corner to see Paranel aiming a device at the room of foobar crates and firing a wide energy beam. Her guard's energy looked tense and unsure, as if they were doing something against the rules.

Unfortunately, Nik chose that moment to come back to talk with Luminous about what had happened between them the past few days. He snuck up beside her and peered around the corner too.

"Hey! What are you—" he yelled in surprise, running back to Paranel only to stop with his hands up at the end of Tynee's orange glowing weapon. The rest of the group ran back to see what the yelling was about. Many of them, not only the human guards, pulled blasters and aimed them at the two Travelers. The rest of the Traveler delegation stepped quickly in front of their princess, extending compact pole weapons that glowed orange, and taking defensive stances.

The delegates and ship security were all yelling at once for the Travelers to stand down, but Cassandra had her hands over her ears as if it were all too much. Her energies were pale and laced with those sickly dark tendrils. The Travelers had no one to speak for them.

Luminous jumped in between the Travelers and human security, her hands up, then signing.

"Wait!" Luminous had Deb turn up her volume. "They're trying to help!" The humans looked at her.

Nik, with his arms still raised at the end of Tynee's weapon, moaned. "Lu, get out of there!" he said, his energy frantic and worried for her. But she had no time to consider that. She focused her words on him.

"They're helping. This isn't what you think it looks like."

The group paused and seemed to collectively take a breath.

"Lu, what do you mean? Can you understand them?" Nik asked.

She had to shake her head. "But I saw Princess Paranel's energy. It was only helpful. Now it's alarmed. Put your weapons down so we can sort this out."

"Tell them to put *their* weapons down."

"I can't," she signed, frustration making her motions jerky. But she gave them all a lowering gesture and miraculously, weapons began to cautiously lower on both sides.

Luminous took a breath. Paranel seemed to try to say something, gesturing at the storage room.

"Cassandra, we could really use your help here," Nik called out to her, but she stayed curled into the wall, hands over her ears.

"Let's simply… look," Luminous signed and raised her hands to cautiously step by the Traveler guard, Tynee, who Paranel was trying to calm and pull back by the arm.

Luminous looked into the room and her jaw dropped in surprise.

"Luminous, what is it?" Nik asked. "What do you see?"

She looked back at him. "The crates of foobars," she signed, "they've—"

"What? Disappeared? Caught fire? Exploded?" The ship's head security officer growled, taking a threatening step forward.

"No." She gave calming gestures again. "Calm, please. They've multiplied."

They all slowly came forward to gasp and stare in amazement at the room full of crates, floor to ceiling, all the way to the door.

In fact, when counted, the crates had more than doubled and they appeared to be exact duplicates of the originals, including the contents. Nik looked stunned as Princess Paranel relinquished her ray gun device to allow them to inspect it. The delegates sent it and a selection of the bars off to be tested before cautiously calling for a break for the rest of the day. The Travelers returned to their ship and flew off to Traveler One, promising to return the next day. The lead security officer grumbled that they would probably never see them again. The next morning, the results came back. The bars were perfect. And the Travelers returned to the trade talks like they said they would.

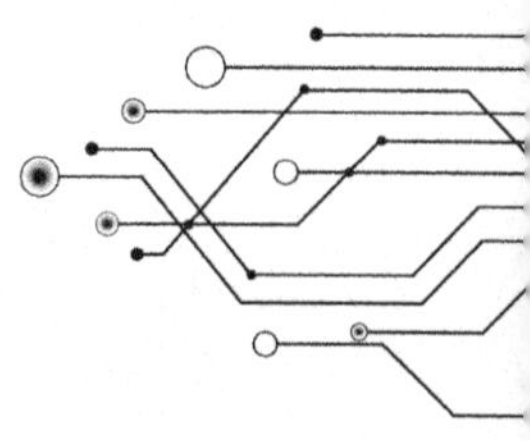

Chapter 23:

GIFTS

—Nik—

Nik's jaw was still on the floor the morning after the Stalwart Mariner tour. He had to admit it, though he didn't understand the science, that he'd been wrong. An energy beam of some sort had *become* or *created* matter aboard the *Stalwart Mariner*. He had no idea how, but there it was. And if that was possible, what else was possible? Was Luminous possible?

They had tested Princess Paranel's "weapon", and the foobars she'd used it on, all through the day and half the night until the device had run out of juice. Nik and the port's best scientists and engineers could not find a way to charge it with any form of power they had. Nik had stayed in the lab with the scientists and though he didn't understand how it worked, it was clear the device was a hand-held food replicator, not a weapon. As far as they could tell, it didn't work on anything besides food. Not living creatures, not weapons, not metal or bio-synth, and only worked on inedibles if it was wrapped around the food like the biodegradable foobar wraps, and the algae nutrient storage crates. The extra bars would be split between the three ships and offer a much needed cushion in their travel time.

The device was like magic, a miracle he'd witnessed with his own eyes, and now he needed to convince the Travelers to let them keep it and teach them how to charge it—somehow.

The meeting started with pleasantries as usual. Luminous was again in the audience with two of the generals, though this time she was greeted by the Travelers by name. When it came his turn to speak, Nik put the hand-held food replicator in front of him on the table with an almost reverent caress, then pushed it toward the Travelers. The human scientists had taken recordings, tried to take it apart, and failed. Despite the abuse it had taken, it was still white and gleaming like new, and completely useless. How was he going to convince the Travelers that they *needed* this? He looked over at Luminous and decided to be honest.

"Nine million people die every year of hunger and malnutrition on Earth." He let Cassandra translate and saw understanding enter the princess's eyes. Her expression didn't change, but she seemed somehow sad. He continued. "Despite all our advances in technology, the death toll from that one cause remains the same as it was 250 years ago, due to the damage we've done to our planet. For perspective, there are about 30,000 people here at this port, with 15,000 set to launch for the unsure hope of a new world. We have limited our population growth on Earth with some success, but understandably, people don't take well to the government telling them how many children they can have.

"Over the centuries, we have poisoned our food chain, starting with our oceans. We are making great strides in reducing the trash and pollutants, but we've lost much of our sea life and what remains is too toxic to eat. The land we grow food in is constantly ravaged by mega storms that destroy crops and take lives.

The storms are a direct result of global warming which melted most of the ice caps, altering ocean currents permanently. This altered the airflow from the oceans that used to keep the continents temperate, but now creates a constant stream of hurricanes and tornadoes. It will take thousands of years for the Earth to realign itself, but of course, we don't have that long. That's why we've begun the long journey to colonizing a new world. Thank you for the compassion you've shown in replicating additional food for those ships.

"What I'm asking you now is to allow us to keep the device, and teach us how to recharge it, to save lives on Earth. I am asking for your friendship. I'm asking for your help." Throughout this speech, he saw the black pearl on Princess Paranel's forehead relax and open, flower-like. He hoped that was a good sign. When he looked back over at Luminous, she was beaming at him in a way he'd wondered if he'd ever see again. He tried to tell her with his eyes that he was sorry for their fight. He would tell her as soon as he got the chance.

The human delegates had sucked in a collective breath when he'd begun talking and they seemed tense, laying Earth's problems out on the table like that. It was a gamble, but Luminous had said that stark honesty was the only way forward, and after everything he'd seen, he had to go with her instincts. He held his breath while Paranel turned to her fellow Travelers and their forehead scales fluttered like petals in the wind. After what seemed an eternity, they turned to Cassandra. Her eyes as usual when she was translating mental speak, shifted to white.

"We have an offer for you," she translated for them. As was

often the case, it was difficult to tell which Traveler had spoken, but one of them walked to the door, took something the size of a loaf of bread wrapped in fabric from a guard outside and placed it on the table next to the defunct food replicator. He motioned calmly for Nik to unwrap it. As soon as he did, it began to shift and move in the light. Nik gasped. It was one of the tesseract boxes he had tried to steal, and this one was partially full of the dark swirling energy he desperately wanted the chance to study. He wanted to grab it, before they changed their minds, but forced himself to stay still.

The Traveler who had brought it in reached over and lifted a small, palm-sized cube from the top, and Nik was instantly riveted. It was covered in what looked to him like mathematical equations, though the symbols were different from Earth's number systems. Mathematics was supposed to be the universal language. If he could decipher theirs, what secrets could it hold? The key to everything?

"Whoa! Hold up." The port sheriff stepped in, hand on his holstered blaster. "How do we know that thing doesn't contain something that's harmless to you, but would kill us? How did you get it into the port without a thorough vetting and inspection by my team?" He squinted around at the Travelers while Cassandra translated.

The Traveler slowly put the small cube down on the table, as if trying not to alarm anyone. "Of course. I had forgotten that aspect of human history. You are used to attacking others to get what you want, and you expect that we would do the same." At this, the other Travelers gave him looks with sharp forehead flutters that seemed to say, hush! But the humans barely noticed, trying to hush up their own port sheriff.

"Human history?" the sheriff said. "We are talking about that thing you have on the table right now."

Princess Paranel stepped forward with her hands raised in front of her. "We assure you that we mean you no harm," Cassandra translated.

Delegate Sato bowed respectfully to her and asked for a few minutes for humans to conference. Then he quickly joined the delegates huddling together around the port sheriff as they shuffled him toward the door.

"Sheriff," the delegate from Oceania hissed at him. "It is a gift of technology we have never seen. We need to test it."

"Well then, get it out of my port! You want to test an alien device with completely unknown capabilities, you do it out in space, not in a port of 30,000 people, like you did last night!"

Nik could see his point. "We used the high security labs in the military base last night," he said. "They are more than sufficient." But it was clear the sheriff did not understand their capabilities.

"Those labs are still connected to the rest of the port!" the sheriff protested, but by this time, he was at the door.

"Besides," Nik said, lowering his voice to a whisper. "If they were here to pillage and destroy, they would have done it already." He watched as the conference room doors closed in the sheriff's incensed face.

Nik tried not to think about Luminous's warnings about a coming nuclear war. Could she be right? In being so desperate for this tech to save lives on Earth, could he be making a fatal mistake? He glanced over at her, but she was not paying attention to them, or the Travelers at all. She was watching Cassandra.

When the delegates came back to the table, the Traveler slowly picked up the food replicator, showing his every movement, and placed it where the small cube had been, atop the tesseract. Like a thick liquid, the tesseract enveloped the replicator and the swirling energy inside shifted up to surround the device.

"We cannot give you our travel technology. That you must discover for yourselves," Cassandra translated in the voice that ever since Luminous had mentioned it, really did sound off somehow, like it didn't belong to the telepath. Not that it couldn't be made by her vocal chords, it obviously was. The feeling was hard to pin down.

"However, we anticipated that you would want technology in exchange for some of the element in your Planet Nine's core, and this is the first part of what we are prepared to offer you." He gestured toward the tesseract. The Travelers didn't so much as glance at Nik, but it couldn't be a coincidence that this was a bigger version of the box he'd tried to steal. The other humans eyed it with a mixture of hope, interest, and fear as it continually shifted shape on the table, apparently, hopefully, charging the food replicator.

"The tesseract holds the dark energy inert. With your permission, we propose that we use non-invasive mining to remove the element we need from the core of Planet Nine. If you would like, you may send a team to observe this advanced mining technique." Luminous seemed to tense.

"What?" he signed to her silently.

"The mining," she signed. "Don't send humans."

"What?" he signed back. Of course, they wanted to observe and record this new type of mining. She merely shook her head, still tense. He'd have to ask her more later.

Meanwhile, the American delegate wasn't happy with the offer. "A fancy box and a mining technique we likely won't be able to duplicate?" The others jabbed her in her side.

"The easiest way of course, would be to destroy the planet." The humans' faces and energies showed shock and fear at this before the Traveler continued. "But you'll be happy to know we are long past mining that way." A nervous twitter of relief ran through the humans at this statement.

"In good faith, we will allow you to observe how we collect and store the element." The Traveler waved at the shifting box on the table. "A second tesseract like this one will be provided to hold a measure of it and prevent decay while your scientists study it." The darkly shifting energy inside the tesseract moved down and the hand-held food replicator seemed to float up to lie on top. "And yes, you may keep the food replicator device. It is most efficient when used on large stores of food at once."

The humans side-eyed each other and Nik could tell this last piece would be the bone of contention. The delegates huddled together.

They all tried to speak at once, but Nik chopped his hand through the center of the group, grabbing their attention. "We will come up with a fair and civilized way to share this equally for our peoples. Otherwise, we don't deserve it. Agreed?" A small amount of grumbling, and everyone nodded. He motioned to the lead delegate, who turned to the Travelers and bowed in traditional Japanese style.

"We, the delegates of Earth, accept your proposal." Delegate Sato motioned a robot forward, shaped like a small, hovering table, and two traditionally attired attendants followed. He took the first of a stack of beautiful silk kimonos from the hovering table. He turned and presented it with another bow to the nearest Traveler. The delegates had wanted to give the Travelers goodwill gifts when they first arrived, but Cassandra had strongly advised that for the Travelers it was customary to wait until a deal had been agreed upon.

"In honor of our guests," Sato continued, "and in celebration of an honorable treaty, we present gifts from each of the five regions of Earth. From my homeland, traditional Japanese kimonos, with a few small changes."

The two attendants came forward to assist the male and female Travelers into the beautiful robes. Each had a long slit up the back for tail mobility and the Travelers seemed quite pleased, running their finger pads gently over the silk. Meanwhile, another delegate quietly instructed the robotic table to load the shifting tesseract and the food replicator and take them to a high security lab at once for testing. A contingent of armed guards accompanied the robot and its prize. Nik wished he could sneak out to follow and resume testing immediately. But that would be rude and he should stay. He envied the team of mathematicians who would get first crack at deciphering that control cube.

Nik sighed and waited as the other delegates each presented traditional forms of art from their home regions, each one priceless in its own right. Softly gleaming black and tan pottery from the Americas, a sculpture of mother and child from Africa, an ancient tattoo kit from Oceania, the carved handles stained black from years of use. Max pretentiously presented a Stradivarius violin from the European Union as if it was the pièce de résistance. But Nik saw Paranel reach toward the ancient statue of mother and child from the cradle of civilization and knew that was the piece she most admired.

Despite the Travelers' lack of outward emotions, Nik thought this was going well. He looked at Luminous for confirmation, but she seemed completely absorbed watching Cassandra talk earnestly with Delegate Sato. He wasn't certain what all Luminous saw, but when he watched Cassandra touch Sato's arm, all the color in his eyes momentarily faded to white.

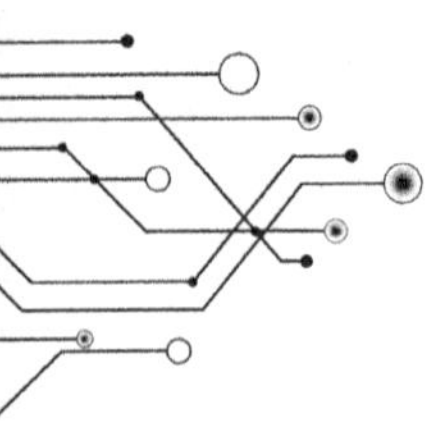

Chapter 24:

THE SATELLITE

—Luminous—

Luminous watched as Cassandra stood talking with her hand on the delegate's arm, something Luminous had never seen the telepath do before. Up until that moment, she had seemed to deliberately go out of her way not to touch another person. Luminous could see her from where she stood at the side of the room, but no one else seemed to notice her eyes. Like when she mentally translated for the Travelers, Cassandra's eyes turned opaquely white, but the Travelers were all paying attention to the gifts, and their energies were open and non-deceptive. At the same time, Cassandra's energy swirled with dark tendrils, even more than usual, so much that they seemed to overtake her. What was going on?

Delegate Sato wasn't moving, seemingly listening intently at first glance, but then Luminous realized his energy, the man himself, was… paused. Frozen. At first, nothing happened. But then, the dark tendrils from Cassandra reached out and twined themselves up and around Delegate Sato's arm, and into his auric field. And his eyes turned white before fading back to normal. His energy restarted, but remained… invaded. That was the best word she could think of.

Cassandra pulled away, but the darkness stayed, woven

through both of their energy signatures. Since everyone knew that her telepathy, and simply being around others, wore her down, no one paid her any attention when she excused herself as soon as the Travelers departed with their gifts. Cassandra left the conference room and Luminous felt she had to follow. What was *that?* Was she infecting auras all over the port?

Lu, what are you doing? Astri said in her bag at Luminous's side. *You saw what she did to that man. What if she does it to you?*

I have to talk to her Astri. I have to find out what that was.

Astri heaved a silent, beleaguered sigh. *Do not let her touch you. Do you have your flashy belt weapon on? I do not want to have to eat that energy of hers.* Luminous could feel Astri shudder and silently agreed.

She kept Cassandra in sight, giving her as much distance as possible, but soon Cassandra pulled a single person hover out of her bag, hopped on, and sped off into general port traffic. Luminous ran to keep her in sight, but was quickly losing her.

Deb, where does she live? Can you tell me how to get there? Deb helpfully pulled up a port map marked with Cassandra's residence, and Luminous chased after Cassandra, Astri banging against her side. She thought about hailing a mini-cab, but how far could it be? The answer to that turned out to be as far as possible.

Luminous finally arrived, panting in the crowded, not so great side of the port. Hawkers and cat callers yelled at her from all sides. Why would Cassandra choose to live here? But Luminous soon saw the reason. Cassandra's small satellite was tethered on the unprotected, least occupied side of the space port. Though inside the port was busy and loud, outside, she had unoccupied space on all sides of her satellite. A dingy, accordion-style tunnel was shared with two distant neighboring ships to connect them to the port.

Luminous hoped Cassandra was already aboard when she directed the tunnel to the correct residence. And, when Cassandra didn't answer her call, she walked nervously down the dim, flimsy-feeling tunnel to knock on the hatch door. Astri meanwhile promised to keep her feelers out for incoming space debris. Luminous felt vulnerable in her human skin in this flimsy tunnel. Though she'd seen the impressive meteor defense lasers in action ever since she and Nik had arrived, this felt anything but safe. Now the port's cannon lasers seemed even more vital as she nervously watched through small, porthole windows in the tunnel as they targeted and eviscerated incoming debris. She wished Cassandra would hurry up and open the door.

She was starting to think Cassandra was going to ignore her out there. She almost gave up when the door slowly opened, Cassandra's jangly bracelets with their black and white stones knocking against the doorframe as she ushered Luminous inside. The satellite was dim and quiet after the noise of the port. The only sound was a softly burbling fountain in one corner. The small space smelled of something herbal and burnt and Luminous could see that the windows were covered with black, sooty cloth. Light from amethyst, quartz, and blue lace agate lamps cast shadows on thick cushioned wicker furniture, and made the walls sparkle. They seemed to be encrusted with multi-colored crystals.

"Here, hold these." Cassandra thrust one black and one white crystal into either of Luminous's hands, but didn't continue touching her. "You have his energy all over you," she said in an accusing tone. "You're here to spy on me for him, aren't you?" she said without preamble.

Who, Nik? No, of course not. She thought the answer at Cassandra, unable to use her hands with the crystals in them, and unsure Cassandra would understand.

Cassandra squinted at her suspiciously and grasped two of the stones at her own wrists.

"Don't pretend. I know you're one of them. An energy being like Planet Nine. You use the same radiation speak."

Ix? How do you know about Ix? she asked in shock.

"You're somehow hiding your true purpose from me," she shook her head. "It's exactly what he does when he…" She suddenly looked about to cry.

Hey, it's alright. I'm here to— Though she'd previously thought the woman horribly creepy, now Luminous couldn't help but feel sorry for the telepath. She awkwardly reached out to comfort her.

Luminous, don't touch her! Astri said. Luminous pulled her hands back uncertainly.

"Wait." Cassandra commanded and picked up a black, feather shaped stone and began sweeping it up and down, close to Luminous's body but not touching. Luminous didn't know what to think, so she just stood there until Cassandra was done.

"His negative energy is tenacious. And you've obviously not been cleansing yourself," Cassandra said.

Uh… sorry? But she could see dark energy tendrils drawing into the black fan stone. She wondered if that would work on the others with tendrils in their auras. She started to speak, but Cassandra put her hand up.

She lit a small bundle of sage and swept the stone repeatedly through the smoke, before repeating the stone sweeping down her own body, drawing away murky, sticky tendrils. Again, she swept the stone through the smoke before extinguishing it and turning on a small filtered fan to clear the air.

"There," Cassandra nodded. "Now you may speak, energy being."

Luminous put the stones in her pockets so she could sign. "I—how did you know?"

"Your energy is related to his. He is the one who changed you into a human?"

Luminous nodded.

"For what purpose?"

"The stars predict war, Earth-ending war. I am trying to prevent that."

Cassandra nodded, seeming resigned but not surprised.

"How do you know Ix? And can he hear us now?"

Cassandra shuddered. "He comes to me often. He attached his energy to me when I was studying his planet. I wish I'd never gone there. And then the Travelers showed up and parked their planet in his orbit and contacted me to ask for a trade deal with Earth."

"Hold on. They contacted you, not Ix, not Earth?"

"Yes, and was he ever steamed that they didn't even know he was there, but he took me over and talked to them through me, as me, while they asked for an audience with Earth. I had contacted Earth as soon as they arrived of course, and they sent their delegates, and all the while Ix plotted. And now that Earth needs me to translate for them, he interferes. He's tried to derail the talks. He is where that silly idea comes from for the prince to marry the Traveler princess. He told both sides, through me, that to refuse would be unforgivably offensive."

"Why? Why would he care who gets married?"

"He doesn't. He wants war, because Earth has their planet ending bomb stored here, in the military base. You know, the kind of bomb we tried to jumpstart Callisto's core with, but ended up blowing it up instead?"

"Is that what happened?" Luminous had only known that humans had blown up the poor moon, but had never known why. "Ix wants humans and Travelers to blow each other up?"

"No. But he desperately wants them to try. He plans to somehow absorb the thermonuclear energy, to become a star again."

"He was a star? When?"

"You're an energy being. I thought you would know more than I do."

Luminous shook her head. Cassandra sighed and continued. "Long ago, when the solar system formed, he became attached to what we call a brown dwarf star. He was kicked out from his original binary orbit with our Sun, into his current hugely elliptical orbit in the outer reaches of the solar system. Over time, the brown dwarf lost all its radiation, and became dark Planet Nine, but Ix was still stuck there. I don't think he can leave."

"You mean he's imprisoned? By who?" Even though she asked the question, her brain whispered the answer, *Sagita.*

"Sagita?" Cassandra read her mind and seemed to digest the

thought. "Yes, I think so. What is certain is that he's power hungry. He made you give him your radiance, didn't he?"

Luminous nodded.

"And yours isn't the only one. But it's not enough. It'll never be enough until he can become a star again."

"And to heck with Earth and Traveler One that get caught in the crossfire." Luminous realized. Traveler One would be too close and burn up in the thermonuclear reaction. And Earth, if not targeted by Traveler One's weapons, would get pulled out of its normal orbit. Even a little shift in Earth's orbit would be enough to produce catastrophic climate shift.

"Why don't you tell the humans?" Luminous asked. "They listen to you. Get the delegation to back away from the talks before they get conned into starting a war." The delegate. Luminous had to tell Cassandra about the Asian delegate, unless… She wasn't talking with Ix now, was she?

"I can't." She shook her head. "Here in my satellite, I've done everything I know of to block him. Yes, you're talking with *me* now, but in that meeting room, he takes me over. I can hardly think for myself, let alone speak." Her shoulders slumped and her energy showed her feelings of defeat. "Besides, the delegates are so determined to get the Traveler technology, they wouldn't leave the talks for anything."

"Then we have to get them to listen."

"But how? They already think I'm halfway to bat-guano crazy, and now you too."

Luminous was about to admit that she had no clue when a laser blast hit right outside. *It's alright Luminous,* she told herself.

This is probably normal out here. Finish what you came to say so you can get back to the port.

"Do you know what he did to that delegate you were talking with—and touching—at the end of today's meeting? Why did his aura change like that?"

"Like what? What did I do?" she shook her head, looking horrified. "I don't remember," she whispered. She closed her eyes and wrapped her arms around herself. "His mental grip on me tightened at the end of the meeting. I was struggling to see, to hear anything, but he pushed me down, deep into my own subconscious. Do you know what that's like?" She held a hand to her throat, remembering. "I had to struggle to make it back up to the surface of my own mind. To regain any bit of control until he let me come back here."

Luminous felt incredibly sorry for her. She wasn't a threat, she was a victim. Well, she was a threat too.

"What did he do?" Cassandra whispered, even as the satellite shook again.

"The dark tendrils in your energy, that's him, right?" Luminous asked. Cassandra nodded. "Some of them transferred to Delegate Sato."

"Oh god," Cassandra looked sick.

"And, what's more. I think I've seen a couple others," she realized, thinking back. "Have you had physical contact with a doctor, and a nurse, in Medical?"

"Yes," she whispered, "of course. They ran tests on me, like they have on you. You're not, you're not losing time, are you? He's not speaking to you, is he?"

Luminous shook her head no. He wasn't speaking to her, or taking her over, yet. But she wasn't sure he couldn't. She looked down at her aura.

"His touch on you is less than it was. Less than it is on me still, and always," Cassandra whispered. Luminous could see her panic rising. "Oh god help us, it's spreading. Ix is spreading and he's using me! I'm the carrier." Another blast rocked the satellite.

"Spreading? Ix is spreading? What?"

"Don't you get it? Once he gets his tentacles into you, he can control you. Well, maybe not *you* because you're an energy being like him, I don't know. But people. Humans. In here, I've managed to muffle him, and he's let me, to rest I thought. But now you tell me he's spreading. Is he controlling other people?"

"I don't know. I'm not sure," Luminous had to admit. Two more blasts, then three more, one after another. "What is going on out there?" She ran to the nearest window, lifting the black curtain. She squeaked in fear and dropped it, wishing she hadn't looked.

Deep breaths, deep breaths Luminous, she told herself. If this was what fear felt like, turning her warm body to ice, she didn't like it one bit.

Cassandra went to look, and Luminous knew what she saw, like the image was burned into her retinas. Hundreds of meteors, comets, and asteroids were coming straight for them, bombarding their side of the port. Outside the window, space was lit up with red and blue laser blasts, coming uncomfortably close to their hull. And emergency beacons on the port hull flashed, warning people to take shelter in the port. The satellite rocked and the two women swore together.

"You blocked *all* incoming signals? Even emergency messages from the port?" Luminous gasped.

"Yes," Cassandra's voice was small. She seemed frozen. "Do you know what this means?"

"That Ix's orbit has crossed into the Kuiper Belt? Soon he will be the closest he's been to Neptune in thousands of orbits."

Cassandra nodded. "He'll try something then."

"I think he's trying something *now*." A hit rocked the small satellite, worse than before. "Shite." Well apparently she'd picked up something from Nik. "We've got to get back to the port!" Luminous ran and hit the call button for the tunnel. She watched through the window at its glacial speed. The laser jockeys seemed to notice the movement and realized someone was still aboard Cassandra's satellite. They concentrated their blasts on protecting the tunnel. As a result, a nearby ship at dock was pummeled with debris and the two women watched in dazed horror while a large asteroid sped directly toward it. The ship exploded in an enormous fireball and Luminous recoiled, protecting her eyes with her arm.

"I can't go back there," Cassandra panted. Deb told Luminous she was hyperventilating and offered the advice of giving her a paper bag. Luminous mentally swore at her to shut up. Where was she going to get a paper bag?

"You have to. You can't stay here!"

"No, *you* have to." Cassandra dashed over to where the cleansing rocks had fallen and scooped them up. She ran back with an armful of rocks and half-burned sage and shoved it all into Luminous's arms. "You have to cleanse them. Like I did with you. Maybe you can save them." She started shoving dry, crumbly sage bundles into Astri's bag.

Get a grip, woman! Astri snapped.

Some small debris hit them, and the shield integrity alarm started pealing a warning.

"Well at least you didn't turn that off, huh?" Luminous signed and clapped her hands over her ears. The tunnel was almost there. Almost attached. They were rocking and rolling, holding onto whatever they could.

"Ix is doing this," Cassandra squeezed her eyes shut and grasped her crystals to her. "I know he is."

"Why?"

"He doesn't want us talking. Ever since I layered this place with Durongo crystals he can't control me here, or fully see what I'm doing. But maybe he could still hear us, some of what we were saying."

"So he's trying to kill us?"

"It appears so!" She grabbed more crystals, shoving as many as she could hold into a bag and slinging it over Luminous's shoulder. The hull took another hit, the biggest yet, and the inner walls shattered, spraying them with crystal shards.

Luminous threw her arms up over her head and face. "You can't be serious, Cassandra! You can't stay here. It's suicide!"

Cassandra looked at her as the light above the door finally turned green, indicating the tunnel was finally pressurized. "Maybe it's for the best."

She threw open the door and pushed Luminous out into the tunnel, just as a small meteor made it through the laser defense system—and the rickety, accordion tunnel exploded. Luminous was thrown back into the satellite, and suddenly they were adrift. The whole satellite was blown away from the port.

They tumbled violently inside the satellite, while it tumbled out into unprotected space. Their precious air was almost instantly sucked out into the vacuum. Emergency sirens blared and everything that wasn't attached, crystal lamps, cushions, and wicker furniture flew toward the door that had gotten jammed open. Luminous and Cassandra hung on to anything they could while being pelted with debris as they struggled to push the door closed without being pulled out themselves. A wooden side table crushed into Luminous's side, nearly throwing her out, but Cassandra caught her and pulled her back, right before Cassandra was hit herself, above her ear by a large, pink salt lamp. Luminous watched her go limp and fumbled painfully at her body as it slid by, finally grasping Cassandra's collar, pulling her back. The door slammed shut.

The satellite still tumbled through space, debris now flying about the cabin. Luminous curled tightly around Cassandra's body, trying to hold herself together in the near vacuum with no air to breathe. She was freezing, and her eyes felt like they were being pulled out of their sockets, but the emergency atmosphere stabilizers kicked in. She felt heat and air wash over her skin in relief.

She opened her eyes, and looked around frantically. The satellite looked like a tornado had torn through it, Cassandra was floating limp, but breathing, and Astri's bag was nowhere to be seen. She looked out the window again to see their tumbling was slowing and a hazy, shimmery mist surrounded the satellite—Astri!

Luminous saw Nik come up alongside on a mining speeder that he must have commandeered, looking frantic. She waved to him awkwardly, the pain in her side making her gasp. She was sure she'd broken a rib or two, but all in all her body was intact. A look of relief washed over Nik's face, though he was busy dodging incoming meteors. Astri stretched herself to encompass Nik and his speeder, and she drifted with them back to the port. Only a few minutes had passed, but the double ring port was small in the distance, remarkably far away.

Parking attendants and dignitaries alike gaped in amazement as Nik's ship and the satellite floated into the nearest docking bay surrounded by a protective nebula shield.

Astri, thank you, Luminous said, looking out a window at her sister, and holding her side as every breath was a jabbing pain. *But you have to leave, quickly. You know they'll want to study you now. No matter what contract was signed, I don't know if I'll be able to protect you.* It pained her to admit it, but she made herself radiate the last words. *You have to go.*

Reluctantly, Astri agreed. *I won't be far if you need me. I don't know how, but we'll find a way.* As soon as she had them all safely inside the repair bay, Astri withdrew into space and shrunk herself down to her usual asteroid density. She flashed a goodbye at Luminous and sped away.

Nik rushed out of his borrowed speeder to pull pieces of shredded tunnel out of the way. Luminous climbed over debris to the door and tried to work its air pressure mechanism, finally getting it to unlock. She stumbled out into his arms and was hit by the waves of desperation coming off him.

"Luminous!" he cried, pulling her to him.

"Ah!" She wheezed, pulling her injured side away.

"You're hurt!" The medics were pushing past them to get to Cassandra inside the satellite and Nik scooped Luminous up, cradling her good side against his chest as he carried her out of the way. He sat down against a side wall, still holding her. A medic came over to check her for injuries.

"Lu, how did you survive?" Nik looked bewildered. "What *was* that?"

She gave him a look of exasperation. "How's Cassandra?" she asked the medic rather than answering.

"Unconscious, but alive. The medics will take good care of her."

"Lu?" Nik began again hesitantly. She closed her eyes and simply enjoyed being in his arms for a while, not ready to look at him and see his deliberate disbelief again. But his energy field surrounded her anyway, bombarding her with… warmth, awe, and what's more, openness. She looked up into his face and saw the wonder there.

"It's—it was Astri, wasn't it?" he whispered. "I mean, I saw it—her, unfurl." He shook his head, blinking. "It's what you said all along, isn't it?"

"Yes." She looked at him, not daring to believe he had finally opened his eyes to the obvious.

"Wow." He kept blinking, as if that was somehow helping his

brain to process what he'd seen. But he didn't let go. He sucked in a breath. "Wow." He put a hand on her cheek, to the annoyance of the medic trying to scan Luminous. But they only had eyes for each other, and Nik placed his forehead to Luminous's and hugged her gently.

"I'm sorry. I was an arrogant know-it-all who turned out to know nothing, wasn't I?"

She nodded, and tears blurred her vision. But he was here and open to her. She didn't need to see what she could feel in his warmth surrounding her.

"I'm keeping you with me. I'm not letting you go again. If I still have to marry the Traveler princess, well, we'll deal with that. But they can't make me love her, and they can't make me stop loving you. Oh, bollocks, I'm really messing this up, aren't I?"

She laughed a little laugh and looked at him side-eyed. "Love?" she signed.

"I love you, Lu. I know this is all crazy, and I tried not to, but I can't help it." He paused. "Shite, shite, shite. I'm sorry, I didn't mean it that way. I—"

She put a finger to his lips. "It *is* crazy. And I can't help it either." They kissed, and they didn't let go for a long time. Even when the medics insisted they needed to put Luminous on a hover stretcher to go to Medical, and Maximilian showed up hissing that this was hugely unwise, Nik held her hand and walked at her side.

Chapter 25:

THE HOSPITAL, THE DAGGER, AND RAINBOW HATS

She saw her siblings rising out of the flood… "We have given our hair to the witch," said they, "to obtain help for you, that you may not die to-night. She has given us a knife: here it is, see it is very sharp. Before the sun rises you must plunge it into the heart of the prince; when the warm blood falls upon your feet they will grow together again, and form into a fish's tail…"

Hans Christian Andersen, The Little Mermaid (1836)

—Luminous—

That night, Luminous was still in Medical in the recovery ward. It was weirdly quiet at first, with no holo-ads floating all around having to be batted away every ten seconds. But now it was so late, it was early. She'd done so much resting in bed that she was wide awake, and she'd had enough of the port holo-news. She'd seen the report about her and Cassandra's close call with the meteor shower and the strange shield that had saved them at least ten times now. They were big news, along with the head-smacking warnings to *not* to silence the port alarm system in personal conveyances. Maybe the port-wide mocking was the reason Cassandra was still in a coma across the room. Luminous kept the noise and lights low so as not to disturb her, thinking her brain probably deserved some down-time, even though she was desperate to talk with her again.

Earlier, she'd told Nik everything, as he gently cuddled her bruised body in the recovery ward in front of a cozy holo-fire. She was so relieved to have him back, to simply be with him. All the horrible feelings she'd had when they were apart faded away, and she appreciated how he was trying to accept what she said even though he was still struggling to understand. He'd seen proof with his own eyes that Astri was a nebula, and that she was telling the truth. The new pieces he had to grapple with were that a malevolent energy being named Ix inhabited Planet IX and was trying to cause war between humans and Travelers in order to become a star. And, that Ix was capable of controlling humans through infection with his dark energy. Some of it was quite difficult to explain, particularly since she'd only just learned it herself from Cassandra, but she did her best.

However, the one thing she needed his help with immediately turned out to be the hardest. The Travelers had wasted no time in beginning their "non-invasive" mining of Planet IX, and Nik had no way of stopping it, or at least of stopping human observers from being infected by Ix. There was no evidence that Travelers were susceptible to Ix's mind control, but Luminous and Nik also had no way of knowing how Ix would react to his planet being mined. Even "non-invasive" mining would take this element from his core without his permission. What would, what *could* he do? They didn't know.

Without being able to explain to the delegates why, Nik's plea to not allow close human observation of the mining fell on deaf ears. Neodurium—what scientists were calling the substance they knew almost nothing about—was alternately touted as either the greatest discovery of their lifetimes, or a trick to enslave them all. Luminous worried that the pessimists were on the right track, though it wasn't the Travelers they had to worry about.

Nik left for the night, telling her to get some sleep, but she stayed up, watching Tersa Tellus holo-news. She kept waiting to hear of some sort of accident, some crazy event, miners going insane with white eyes. But so far, that hadn't happened.

The ward's bio sensors showed an uptick in her anxiety levels and automatically turned the station to the holo-weather and port events calendar. Despite Planet IX getting closer and the laser jockeys working overtime targeting incoming asteroids, port administration was still going ahead with the Intrepid Settler Festival. Almost everyone at port was busy either planning or joining in the festivities, which included a Farewell to Fresh Food Banquet, another Proxima b Fashion Show, a Shipmates Meet and Greet, followed by a Zero Grav Collision Dance, and of course, a Durongo Tournament—which ironically would probably be the safest place from Ix's mind control.

The festival also, to Luminous's head shaking disbelief, still included the ever-popular Mining Tractor Races, outside the port, now with the added excitement of incoming asteroids! It seemed a ridiculous risk, but she was here to try to save the whole human race and the solar system. She didn't have time to worry about a few adrenaline junkies.

With that, the holo-tainment system shut off all together.

There were no windows in the recovery ward, so Luminous couldn't even watch the lasers zap meteors outside. If she couldn't do something productive, she was going to go bonkers. Nik had said he'd be back in the morning, and he'd promised to bring her a change of clothes, but she had things to do. Now. She instructed Deb to disengage her from the monitors and made her escape in her hospital gown, flimsy robe, and slippers.

With Ix getting closer, she had to figure out a way to keep from being controlled, and to protect Nik, Cassandra, and the generals too. The generals most of all. And the events calendar had given her an idea.

Her first stop was the site of the ProxB Fashion Show, which had ended hours before. Thankfully, the place was empty and the ridiculous looking helmets shown in the ads were still there, ready for warehousing in the morning. Unfortunately, the clothiers hadn't left any clothes, but they apparently weren't concerned about the unpopular helmets.

They were silver, with horns on the forehead, which, after taking a few self-defense classes, Luminous felt must be for head-butting. But she merely needed their solid form. Assuring herself she was justified in succumbing to theft, she grabbed a large bag and helped herself to a whole stack of them.

Her next stop was the Durongo tournament, set to begin the next day. The closest venue happened to be her *favorite* twenty-four hour tavern. She paused outside the door as a pang filled her, missing Astri. Could she really do this? She imagined what Astri would have whispered to her. *Walk in like you own the place.*

Luminous lifted her chin and walked into the nearly empty

tavern at 4am, dressed in her medical gown, her body covered in bruises and with a large fashion week tote bag on her arm. She went straight over to an unoccupied Durongo table with a sign floating above that indicated it was reserved for the tournament. She took the first helmet out and carefully dipped it in thick, gray Durongo liquid, letting the excess drip off.

"Hey, you!" the tavern owner yelled and started running over to her. She looked up and stared him down. He stuttered to a quick stop on recognizing her and retreated back behind the bar.

She then plunged the helmet into a nearby bin of multi-colored seeds, yanking her hand away as crystals sprouted over the horns. But she saw her instinct had been right, and the crystal growth quickly stopped. She pulled out the crystallized helmet and admired her handiwork. A thin coating of liquid, plus a plethora of seeds had resulted in many small crystals, coating the surface of the helmet, and now safe to the touch. She jammed it on her head and all types of radiation noise around her went silent. Excellent. Cassandra had said something about Ix not being able to reach her in her satellite due to coating the wall panels with Durongo crystals. Luminous now just needed that effect to be portable.

A while later she left behind a few bewildered tavern patrons and its owner. Despite the fact they never saw Astri, because hey, she wasn't there, they were so scared from last time that they hadn't said a word against Luminous crystallizing a whole stack of helmets. Unfortunately, as she'd found out when she'd dropped one, they were now brittle as glass, and useless as actual helmets. But that wasn't their intended function anyway.

Now she needed to get one to Nik. Thankfully she had a good idea where he was. She was walking along the marketplace, which was much calmer than during the day or evening. Now, in the very early pre-simulated-dawn, the market held vendors arriving and setting up, the smell of food grills warming, and the optimistic sounds of a new day. And something caught her eye out the window. Astri was knocking gently, like pebbles in space against the clear polymer. Their nebulae siblings were surrounding her on either side, twinkling, though not as brightly as usual, to get Luminous's attention.

Her siblings rolled something long and solid through their gaseous forms. Luminous leaned in but could not quite make it out. It looked like a jagged shard of some kind of dark, pitted metal.

The nebulae started down the outer curve of the port hull, radiating at Luminous to follow. Not far in that direction was the hanger bay where Astri had brought Luminous and Cassandra in the satellite. She headed that way to meet her siblings, hoping they had some good news for her.

The hangar bay was mostly used for repairing ships. It had a force field on the bay door which allowed ships through, while keeping air pressure in, which was very helpful for Luminous to sneak in and hide behind the damaged satellite, its hull crushed and misshapen, already being cannibalized for parts and scrap.

Despite the early hour, the bay was busy. Several mining vessels were under repair inside while another pulled up outside with one landing strut hanging awkwardly from its underbelly. Watching from her hiding spot, Luminous saw her siblings slip the object into its undercarriage before the damaged mining tractor carefully backed into the repair bay.

The ice jockey pilot climbed down from the cab, a blaster holstered on either hip, and strutted around back to hook up ice warmers to her cargo. Repair bots bustled up and she pointed them to the landing strut, leaving the vehicle resting precariously on the remaining three. She started the pump that would offload her water cargo and walked around her rig, checking off items on a holographic inspection chart hovering in front of her.

Luminous could see the object, whatever it was, glinting darkly from under the back of the chassis, above one intact landing skid and below a bank of lights. But she couldn't simply run over there and take it. This woman looked like she took no shit from anyone messing with her rig. All Luminous could do was wait, and watch. She saw the moment when the woman spotted the object too. She reached under her rig to pull it out and Luminous reached out a hand from her hiding place as if to stop her. Noooo! But she pulled back and stayed quiet.

The ice jockey turned the item over in her hands, and Luminous could now see what looked like a thin shard of iron, dark and pitted. The woman ran a finger over one edge and jerked back, quickly sticking her bleeding finger in her mouth. Luminous held her breath, as she saw the woman stiffen and her eyes go milky-white. She turned toward Luminous's hiding spot and smoothly put the jagged shard down on the floor and slid it over to her, regarding her with those creepy eyes.

Cautiously, Luminous stopped it with her foot and stared down at what she could now see was a dagger, made of some dark, pitted metal. Though crudely formed, the point and wavy edges on either side looked sharp as obsidian blades. The woman's eyes could only mean one thing: it was a gift from Ix.

But why? And why would her nebulae siblings have delivered it?

"Luminous," the woman intoned in that now-familiar voice that didn't sound quite like a human voice. Ix's voice. "Nice hat," her lips curved in a smirk. "You have found a way to keep me out of your weak human mind, temporarily. But no matter. I have a new deal for you."

"What have you done to my siblings? Taken part of their radiance and forced them to do your bidding?" She felt her anger bloom, and took a step forward, but then stopped. It wasn't this woman's fault.

"Tch, tch. They each gave it willingly, for the chance to have you back with them. Take the dagger."

She shook her head. "I remember our deal. When this body dies, I have to go to you and serve you forever." She wished now that she hadn't been such an optimistic idiot.

"Yes, you made your bet to save the humans and you are losing on all counts, aren't you? But now, I'm giving you a chance to double down." He cackled though the poor woman's mouth. "Look at the stars. The humans' mini supernovas are inevitable now and with them I will take my place in the pantheon of stars. My new gravity will shift this solar system ever so slightly, enough to shift the Earth into an ice-age and make humanity nothing more than another failed experiment. But for you, one of my own, I am in a generous mood. Use the dagger. Kill your prince with it, and prove your allegiance to me, to our kind, before I become a star again. Your debt to me will be cancelled, your radiance returned. I will even return the radiance of your siblings so that we can all celebrate my coming glory together, as a family."

She gasped. "You're insane. I can't kill Nik!"

"Then you can experience human death with your newfound brethren before coming to serve me. It is your choice."

The white faded out of the woman's eyes and the black tentacles in her aura faded into background noise. She shook her head. "Hey, what are you doing here?" she asked, in a voice that made sense this time.

"I was just leaving," Luminous signed and the ice jockey's eyes widened. Luminous quickly stooped down to pick up the dagger with the hem of her hospital gown, not really wanting to touch it.

"Hey, aren't you— What's that in your hand? Didn't I..." she looked confused.

"It's nothing." Luminous turned quickly to leave. Her next stop would have to be the Self Defense Emporium's twenty-four hour supply shop for a knife sheath while she figured out how to get rid of the dagger. And she hoped she could find something else to wear too.

By breakfast, Luminous was back in the recovery ward, contemplating her new form-fitting, move-any-direction exercise suit. It covered everything, but felt like she was wearing nothing, except the light energy whip on her waist and the now-sheathed dagger in its new cross-body bag, just like the one she'd lost with Astri. General Varma hadn't been in so early in the morning, but

Luminous had left her a stack of crystalized helmets with instructions to get them to the other generals, and that when they saw people with eyes turning white around them, it was time to put them on. And also, for all of them to come see her in Medical.

She knew the note was cryptic. She knew Varma wouldn't believe her. But, without being able to get into the military compound, it was the only avenue Luminous had open to her.

She was still plotting when the Traveler princess, Paranel walked in with all her shiny scales and exotic beauty. And here Luminous was, bruised all over, completely unglamorous. Paranel acknowledged her and paused, seeming to want to say something, but not knowing how. She released a breath and continued over to Cassandra's bedside. She pulled up a chair, and sitting beside her, took her hand.

Paranel's energies were sad, and caring. She took deep breaths and, from Luminous's perspective, her aura swelled to encompass Cassandra's murky, stuttering energy field.

Luminous must have made a noise because Paranel turned and gave her a calming signal. The energies she touched Cassandra with were healing, regenerative, kind. Luminous nodded, and Paranel went back to focusing on surrounding Cassandra in her green-blue healing field.

They had understood each other, at least that much, Luminous realized, without a shared language or cultural background. She watched what Paranel was doing closely, and when she finished, Cassandra's energy had improved. It wasn't entirely better, but it was steady now and no longer felt so lost.

Paranel turned to Luminous and pointed at her, but her

energy was as non-threatening as ever. She gestured at her eyes, and then around herself, tracing her aura.

Luminous nodded in surprise. "I see auras," she signed. Paranel turned her seat to sit next to Luminous. She held out her hands and they began to try to sign together. Without a Deb that would work for Paranel, there was no sign language dictionary the princess could use or holo-vid examples. Her clawed hands were clumsy and jerky at first as she copied Luminous's signs for things in the room that one or the other pointed at.

A day and a half later, they were still working at it, but had made outstanding progress. They'd stopped for meals and to sleep, and Paranel had returned first thing in the morning to continue.

"You are not like the other humans," Paranel signed. She picked up signs remarkably fast for someone with no Deb, though sometimes she hit a block and had to take a break. Sometimes a sign from Luminous was taken completely wrong by Paranel and vice versa. The middle finger, for example, meant something to Travelers that was completely different from what it meant to humans.

It wasn't perfect by any means, but Luminous thought, hoped they were speaking the same language now. The trade talks had been postponed until Cassandra woke up and recovered enough to come back to work. Luminous thought that was why she wasn't awake yet. The mining of Planet IX was quick and almost done, and she wondered, with everything, how long the Travelers would stay afterward. Paranel seemed to have a sense of urgency about her. They had things to talk about. But first they had to be able to talk.

"No, I'm not," Luminous agreed. Their communication was slow, stilted, and at times frustrating, but they both seemed to know this was vital.

"Why?" Paranel wanted to know. With the princess's limited vocabulary, it was hard to explain, but Luminous tried.

She gestured at the lights on the ceiling and walls in the room. "I am light-energy, in this body."

Paranel cocked her head to one side in a very human-like gesture. Luminous got up and walked Paranel around the room to all the things that expressed energy: the electric drawing pad they were using to call up pictures, the lights, the holographic scenery panels that showed Earth landscapes and the starscape outside. She pointed at each of them and then back to herself. She mimed the laser blasts outside and signed, "Me."

Paranel looked thoughtful. She took off the jeweled armband she always wore on her upper arm and turned it over in her hand. Her guard, the same one who was always first by her side, dashed into the room, but she put up a hand to stay her and gave the guard a warm smile. Paranel's aura lit up at the sight of the guard, and Tynee's for her, but Paranel turned back to Luminous with the device in one hand. Using one sharp, manicured claw, she popped open the back of the armband and showed the inside to Luminous, a tiny, glowing, shifting orb. A power source. She pointed at it, then at Luminous.

"Yes," Luminous signed enthusiastically, "I am," she made a sign mimicking the tiny moving ball of energy there, "energy."

"I understand," Paranel signed, closing and putting her arm band back on. The guard relaxed a bit, and said something quietly into her own device at her shoulder. Paranel held up a finger. "But… aren't we all energy," she used the new sign, "inside?"

"Yes!" Luminous was bouncing, practically jumping up and down now on her toes.

"Humans are not?" Paranel asked.

"Yes, humans are, but they don't *know* it." Her body movements emphasized the not knowing. She asked Deb to call up a holo-vid of a human newborn beside another of an energetic nebula and pointed to each in turn. "I was not a human baby. I was a nebula. Now I am human." She didn't know if this would come across, the past vs present. It was hard to teach everything in only a few days with Paranel unable to look up signs on her own.

Paranel held up her finger again, then a full hand. "Wait. Stop." Out of her arm device, she drew a holo-vid of her own. It surrounded them in a holographic room, a completely submersive experience. Sound, sight, smell, even a hint of the taste of forest air through open walls. The only thing missing was touch as Luminous's hand went right through everything. Wow. She looked around at the scene, her breath stuck in her throat for several moments. Paranel, still next to her, got her attention and pointed to the scene unfolding in front of them. A Traveler woman had just given birth.

Paranel pointed at the baby, then herself. "Me." The scene then dissolved and they were back in the recovery ward. Paranel pointed at the nebula picture on the tablet, then at Luminous. “You?”

Luminous nodded.

“How?” Paranel shook her head in wonder.

And Luminous did her best to explain about Ix.

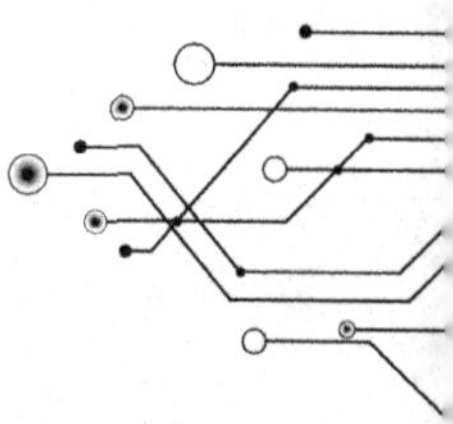

Chapter 26:

STRANGENESS MULTIPLIES

—Nik—

“What are they doing in there?” Max asked as he and Nik peeked into the recovery ward through the small window in the door. Nik had taken a break from the lab and trying to work out that wanker of a control cube with its bloody unsolvable mathematics only to find this.

“It looks like Luminous is teaching the Traveler princess to sign.” The impossible girl he loved and his alien future wife were getting chummy. Aces. Also, Lu was wearing the sexiest catsuit he’d ever seen in his life.

“Maybe she can convince them to give us more technology,” Max murmured. Nik rolled his eyes. The man had a one-track mind. “At least Luminous is not wearing that ridiculous hat at the moment. I see you’re not wearing yours either.”

Nik grunted, and knew he probably should be. Ever since Luminous had told him the newest in unbelievable stories, he’d been seeing people all over the port do strange things. He couldn’t see whatever it was that Luminous saw around people, but he had definitely seen a port geologist, still in her sleek spacesuit having just come from observing the Travelers’ non-invasive mining of Planet IX walk headfirst into the bio-scanner security door to the military compound. Over and over. She had been taken away to Medical, strapped to a stretcher, and mumbling incoherently.

Later, he'd requested the security vid of all the doors into the military compound. He'd watched ten people in total—medics, miners, Settlers, even one of the delegates—test those doors. None were able to get through. And then he'd seen Delegate Sato walk up, touch a soldier on the arm while talking to him… and the soldier had turned and walked right through, into the central military base. The eyes on that soldier had been white. He'd watched it multiple times to be sure. All their eyes had been white.

The ridiculous helmet that Luminous had given him was in a bag currently slung over his shoulder. Hers was on a chair inside the room. He thought he recognized them from the fashion show advertisements, only different. They were crystallized, from the bulbous helmet part to the small spike-like horns on the forehead, with multi-colored, rainbow crystals. She'd said it would keep Ix out of his head, but had warned it would be as durable as brittle tinfoil. He was determined to never wear it, and yet, he kept it with him.

He glanced back to the two incredibly different women in the room. They were communicating, without it appeared, any help from Cassandra's telepathy as she lay still asleep in her hospital bed. Luminous had said she would help them communicate with the Travelers and here she was, teaching the Traveler princess sign language. This was fantastic! A breakthrough. Why had no one else thought of it, and were they all a bunch of buggering vocal gits?

Even Max, not at all a fan of Luminous, was excited. He

walked a short distance away to ping the news to the other human delegates. They might be able to continue talks without Cassandra.

But then both women were both looking very serious, not only Luminous who expressed it in her face and body language, but the princess too, who was usually near impossible to read. She stiffened, which was a lot for a Traveler, and seemed to ask clarifying questions as they talked. Uh-oh. He had a pretty good guess what Luminous was telling the princess—about Ix. Should he interrupt? There was still no proof of this crazy story. But Luminous had shown him enough proof of everything else, she had earned some faith on this.

The princess looked at her guard every few seconds as if relaying the information to her. The guard then placed the back of her hand to her forehead sensor and he thought he must be witnessing a telepathic communication with other Travelers, or their ship.

"Uh, what's she telling her in there?" Max asked.

"Um, well…" How was Nik supposed to tell him this? But he didn't get much of a chance. Paranel got up quickly, she and her guard hustling out of the room, straight past him and Max without so much as a glance, and out of Medical.

"What happened?" Max demanded, striding in to confront Luminous. "What did you say to her?"

Nik followed, feeling protective. "Max, calm down."

Max spun around. "Calm down?" he repeated, looking incensed. "We need to know what was said! You know, don't you? You were watching. She has completely brainwashed you, Your Highness!"

"No, she hasn't, Max. It's us who've been brainwashed by our own bloody egos, thinking we know everything, when we obviously don't. And yes, I do know what she said. Max, you're going to need to sit down for this."

While they were telling an incoherently sputtering Max that a being he didn't believe in inhabited Planet IX and had been trying to cause a nuclear war between humans and their new, much more powerful ally, Nik's Deb buzzed. He and Max pressed their earpieces at the same time. Nik turned to Luminous while Max crumpled in his chair, whether in relief or disappointment, he couldn't tell.

"It's the Travelers." He shook his head in amazement. "They've bloody well left. Every single one aboard the port just—dissolved—into tiny bubbles where they stood. And then their ship, zoom, vanished. And now," he put his fingers to his ear as if to hear better. "Uh, repeat that please?" He waited a moment, looking stunned. "And blimey, the planet, also. Our sensors indicate… Traveler One is bloody-well gone."

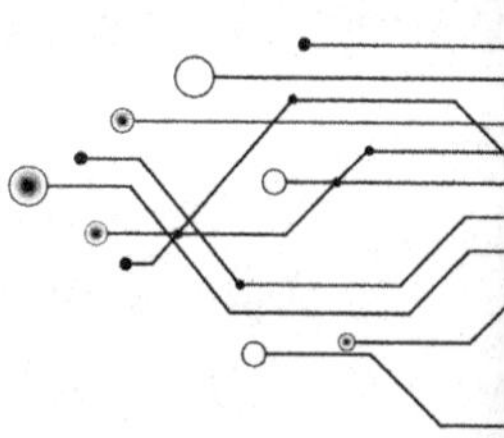

Chapter 27:

THE GENERALS

—Luminous—

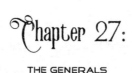

The Intrepid Settler Festival was now in full swing, a celebration of success on multiple fronts. The Travelers had gotten what they needed from Planet IX, and had left in all haste and without incident, leaving behind the food replicator and its charger. The Settler ships were ready to launch as soon as the asteroid storm passed. And Nik hadn't had to marry the princess after all. Luminous should have been stoked. Too bad the stars hadn't changed their predictions of multiple mini supernovas.

Cassandra had awakened convinced that Ix would try something else soon, and Luminous had to agree. Considering that two of the five generals, Martine and Garcia, were in the military base and unable to be contacted, they highly suspected that Ix already had control over them. Nik was the only other person who believed them. He was on board with their plan, and for that Luminous was grateful.

They'd had to act fast to keep Ix from gaining control over any of the other three generals. But, when Luminous, Cassandra, and Nik had tried explaining the situation to Generals Varma, Okafor, and Ngata, they didn't believe them, and they didn't agree to remain in Medical so they couldn't be infected and forced to fire thermonuclear weapons at Planet IX.

Now, Varma's calculating stare across the recovery ward was cold and disheartening. Of course, Luminous, Cassandra, and Nik *were* technically holding the three generals hostage. The energies from that side of the room were not exactly positive.

They had gotten the generals to come to Medical by telling them part of the story: that a rogue agent would try to get them to fire nuclear weapons at Planet IX, and Cassandra, still in recovery, had important information to share with them. Nik had backed them up, saying that while he didn't have proof of this, they could trust what Luminous said. His support felt great, but as time passed and nothing happened, Luminous began to wonder how long they could keep the generals there before their support troops broke down the door. Especially after they'd scoffed at Luminous's helmets and tried to leave. Cassandra had hacked the ward's safety protocol to place the three of them behind a padded force field and prevent them from calling anyone. It wasn't going over well.

Luminous sighed and went back to watching the Mining Tractor Races with Nik on the holographic newscast. Miners in souped-up mining tractors raced around the port like comets orbiting a binary star system with their tails on fire. Their wheels, usually used for navigating the surface of moons and asteroids, were tucked into the vehicles' bellies as impromptu bumpers, not to protect themselves and other tractors, but to protect the expensive saws, drills, and laser grinders housed underneath. The idea had been floated to require removing the cutting tools for safety, but that had quickly been shot down. It was already against the rules to use any type of laser against an opponent or their rig, but that didn't mean it didn't happen from time to time. The racers adamantly refused to give up what they saw as protection from unscrupulous drivers who weren't going to follow the rules anyway.

Spectators lined the viewing deck all around the port. The track was laid out in an enormous figure eight that wound around and through the port ring, crossing at the center and marked with color changing buoys lining the track. Single operator mining vehicles lined up at the starting line, rear hydrogen ion engines ready to flare to life. Their snub noses were lit with banks of headlights, their pilots in full view through large bubble dome driver compartments that gave more than one hundred and eighty degrees of visibility to the pilots. Short blasts from small ionic thrusters on their sides slowly propelled and kept each tractor in position until the lights turned green and they blasted forward with fiery tails of white, blue, and orange. Bigger units with more powerful engines took the lead first, but the smaller tractors were able to fire longer and caught up at the first turn where they jockeyed for position.

And all the while, Luminous, Nik, and Cassandra watched on a holo-screen while holding three of the generals hostage. They'd done all the explaining they could, that Medical was the only place in the port where there was enough signal dampening that Ix's brainwashing could not reach them. They'd shown the generals Nik's holo-vid proof of the brainwashed folks with white eyes trying to get into the military base, which only made the generals want to leave more. Nik and Luminous had explained that they believed Ix already had two of the generals, and they couldn't let him get his tentacles around any one of the others. But the generals didn't believe them and were losing patience.

"When are we going to see any real proof of what you say?" General Okafor of the African Alliance asked from behind the glimmering medical force field. "A rogue entity on Planet Nine wanted to cause nuclear war with the Pangaloids, erm, Travelers, and force us to fire first, for no reason. Moreover, now that the Travelers are gone, this entity still wants us to fire at Planet Nine, and if we leave this room, we risk being somehow brainwashed and forced to fire our planet killers. You have no way of proving any of this and we're supposed to stay here indefinitely on your word and nothing more?" She shook her head. "My patience is wearing thin."

General Ngata made noises of agreement, but Varma was absorbed with her Deb projection on her forearm. Cassandra had disconnected those from the military base, but whatever the general was doing could not be good news for Luminous, Nik, and Cassandra. Luminous hoped something happened soon to prove their theory or they were going to end up in the brig.

"Generals, I understand your frustration," Nik said, trying to keep them calm, "but we won't know if you can be manipulated until you go out there, and by then it'll be too late. The helmets might protect you. Then again, they haven't actually been tested."

Luminous tried not to feel guilty that she hadn't told Nik that the helmets had been tested by Ix himself. But she hadn't wanted to tell him about the knife and Ix's demand that she kill him.

Just then, on the wall hologram, they saw one of the racers outside miss a turn. They all turned to look as the tractor veered off course, straight for the side of the port. *Wham!* The outside wall of the hospital medical bay shook with the collision.

"What the—" General Ngata from the Oceania Federation exclaimed. They all stared at the hologram showing the race outside and saw and heard the mining vehicle scraping to attach to the port's smooth surface. Then *Wham!* and *Wham!* Two more hit the port hull and began attaching themselves as if to an asteroid they were going to mine.

The holo-broadcast announcer was beside himself. "A terrible accident, folks! Several mining tractors have collided with the port. Have you ever seen anything like this, Jim?" But Jim didn't answer and the same announcer continued. "Now the crowds are starting to disperse, but in the most organized way I've ever seen. It's almost… precision. Jim, do you have any idea—Jim? Jim, your eyes! No, don't—!" and the incessant announcer's voice went silent.

"What is going *on* out there?" General Okafor asked.

At the same time, General Varma had been working furiously at her Deb on her forearm. Suddenly, she stopped and looked up in triumph as the medical force field fell.

"Hand over the blasters now. You're under arrest for conspiracy," General Varma said, striding toward them. With the medical field down, her words carried weight again. Three small security drones detached themselves from the ceiling and hovered down in front of them, blaster barrels glowing and whirring in warning.

"Uh, ladies," Nik began. "I'm not willing to have a bloody shoot-out with the people we're trying to protect." And Nik placed his blasters on the floor, and put his hands up. "Plus, I really think we should all get out of here."

Wham, wham! There were five, now six, mining vessels that had abandoned the race. A terrible grinding sound started on the port hull, signaling that some of them had completed the attachment phase.

"They're cutting their way in!" General Ngata got on his Deb. "Stop those miners! They're going to breach the port hull!"

Cassandra put her hands up as well, looking frantic. "It's Ix, I know it! This is proof of what we've been trying to tell you all along," she yelled at the generals. "He's trying to get to *you!*"

Luminous's mind was racing as she too, slowly raised her hands. If the generals left without putting on helmets, Ix would control them. If the port hull was breached, they would all get sucked into space and probably die, although Ix might have worked out a way to save at least one of the generals, since he needed three of them. They had to get the generals to put on the helmets, and then get the hell out of Medical. She'd work out where to go later. But General Varma had another idea.

"Drones, arrest them!" Varma ordered.

One drone descended for each of them, two attached, glowing loops held in front, the right size for handcuffs. But Luminous had an idea.

Deb, if I can talk to you with nebula radiation speak, can I talk to the drones too? She didn't wait for Deb to answer. *Drones! Power down,* she ordered. The drones paused, inches from their hands with the glowing cuffs, and then hovered back up to their ceiling docks.

General Varma looked confused. "Drones! Put these three

under arrest," she repeated. They hovered back down and formed cuffs in front again.

"Put your hands together in front of you, please," the drones intoned together, coming closer. Luminous cringed and tried again.

Drones, cancel that last order! Protection mode, for me and my companions, she ordered.

The three drones hovered up to fly in interweaving circles above her head.

"How are you doing that?" General Varma demanded, incensed. "Drones—"

"We have bigger problems than that," General Okafor said. "I can't get in touch with Generals Garcia and Martine." Varma stopped, her head whipping toward him at this news.

"We already told you that!" Cassandra said.

Nik scooped up his blasters again. "Cassandra, is there any way that the medical force field could be used to keep port atmosphere in, in case of a hull breach?"

"On it!" she answered, lowering her hands and going to work on her Deb.

Across the room on the holo-cast, a small projectile streaked across the view outside, catching all of their attention. The race had been abandoned by the holo-crew and the camera remained focused on the mining vehicles now cutting at the side of the port hull with neon bright lasers. Then, a small asteroid shaped like a football pelted at the nearest mining vehicle.

"Astri!" Luminous signed and cheered. She was followed by five other small, dense asteroids and they all watched as one of them was shot by port defense lasers and exploded into bits. A bright, pure golden energy was visible for a moment before Luminous's sibling gathered the bits and dust together and wobbled off.

Astri, be careful! Luminous radiated at her, hoping their sister would be alright. Astri and the others dodged the laser blasts, targeting and colliding with one of the mining tractors attached to the port, knocking it off the hull before turning on the next one.

"Finally," General Ngata grumbled as they saw a swarm of android troops fly out of a nearby repair bay like human-shaped silver missiles. They turned toward the mining vehicles and fired, ignoring the nebulae-asteroids.

"Now do you believe?" Luminous asked Varma, the security drones circling her head and pointing their built-in blasters at the generals.

Varma shook her head muttering, "That's impossible."

They were at a stalemate. Varma's energy showed she was not as sure of her path as usual. In fact, all three generals seemed downright unsure of what was going on and who to believe.

Outside, the grinding noises stopped but then started up again in different spots. As quickly as Astri and the android troops could disable and arrest the miners, Ix recruited more. But Luminous couldn't see the port sheriff or his deputies coming to help, and she had a suspicion that they were already compromised. The androids went untouched by Ix and one by one they blasted the mining tractors off the port hull until the grinding stopped.

It was during this impasse that the recovery ward doors slid open and in poured dozens of rainbow-crystal-helmeted folks, led by none other than Star Varma, her hand on Sarah's shoulder like she was her seeing-eye person.

"Alright, we're in," Sarah said.

Star spoke something into her wrist that sounded an awful lot like, "Close and seal the recovery ward, authorization Infinite Dawn."

The doors slid closed and a red light above indicated they were locked. Star extended her white cane to the floor and Luminous remembered that Mafia Don had been involved in the construction and completion of the port itself. Meanwhile Star seemed to be listening now, locating everything and everyone around the room.

Medical was not a small space, but now it was so full of people in rainbow helmets that they had to perch on every bed, chair, and counter. Star had at least fifty of her own "troops" with her, shop-keepers and business owners, prostitutes and hawkers, and ordinary port folk of every stripe. Luminous would be willing to bet that every one of them Star had helped in one way or another.

"Star?" General Varma gasped. "*You're* Mafia...Dawn?" She looked gobsmacked. "How is that possible? You— you make chocolate."

"She is everyone and no one." Star walked over to stand beside her sister, her energies a calming balm. "You said it yourself, Moon. Mafia Dawn is a phantom."

"You were *spying* on me? My own *sister*?"

"We all do what we must. Can we discuss this later?"

Meanwhile, Nik was gasping in surprise as well. "Sarah?"

"Sorry, Your Highness. Living out here is a lot different from life at the palace." She shrugged and turned to Luminous. "We saw your note for the general and the helmets you left. We made more when we saw people with their eyes turning white like you said, all over the port. We outran them, but we think they're coming here."

Before anyone could get too comfortable, a new sound began—a pounding on the recovery ward door. It quickly got louder and louder and they all backed slowly away. The *pound, pound, pound,* became like a rhythmic battering ram, but the door held strong. Luminous had all but forgotten Cassandra was there, but now the telepath hesitantly walked over to the wall next to the door.

"One-way window," she commanded the wall. It turned clear and all they could see out in the wide corridor were people, hundreds of unnaturally calm people, not talking, yelling, or pushing, but pounding and pressing on the wall and door, in unison. They turned their heads as one, and it seemed like a thousand wide, blank eyes stared at them through the supposed one-way view wall.

"Cassandra!" their mouths said as one, and though no sound penetrated the insulated wall, Cassandra fell to the floor with a cry, curling into a ball.

Luminous grabbed her under the arms and dragged her back and out of view. She pointed emphatically at Nik and then at the wall with the blank-eyed people staring in, chanting and pounding rhythmically as one. He understood her urging and told the wall to become opaque again. But that didn't seem to help Cassandra.

"No, no. He's here," she mumbled.

"Where?" Luminous signed and had to shake the telepath by the shoulders to get her to respond. "Where?" But Cassandra simply moaned and squeezed her eyes tightly shut.

"Everywhere. Everywhere," she said. Sarah handed Luminous a crystal helmet and they slapped it onto Cassandra's head.

The generals' expressions still held disbelief. Star's and Sarah's held a need to understand.

"*What* is going on?" Okafor said.

"What is wrong with those people out there?" Varma asked. Luminous gave them an incredulous look.

"What do you know, Luminous?" Star asked. With Nik's help she did her best to explain for the newcomers what they already had for the generals. She'd barely finished when they heard the noises of the crowd outside change.

"What is *that*?" one of the generals asked. No one moved. But there was only one way to find out.

"Sorry Cassandra." Luminous put on her own horned, rainbow-encrusted helmet and walked to the wall by the door. With a look of resignation, Nik put his on as well. "One-way wall," she said.

The sight that met their eyes was breathtaking, and not in a new-kitten, lovely-sunset kind of way. The wall was opaque in spots, for some not immediately apparent reason. Ix's brainwashed masses, the Ixies Luminous decided to call them, were stepping aside with robotic precision. Several others stepped forward with buckets and beer mugs of something grey and thick, and splashed it on the wall and door, covering most of the window-like view into the hall.

Luminous peered closely through the wall at the substance. It looked like....

"Paint?" General Okafor asked weakly, seeming out of her depth.

"No," Luminous shook her head as they watched. "Paint wouldn't do that." She gestured at the last clear spot, where they saw two of the brainwashed Ixies get splashed with the thick ooze. They just stood there, not reacting at all as crystals grew up to envelop them. At the last second, their eyes went back to normal, they looked down at their crystallizing forms and screamed out their last breaths before becoming crystalline statues.

"Get back!" Luminous signed and Deb's voice yelled her instruction. "Helmets on! Protect the generals!" She dove away from the wall, pushing people back.

"What?" someone started. But their words were swallowed when the wall shattered, an explosion of shards spraying in every direction.

The wall, previously battered but unbreakable, was gone, and the Ixies climbed in. Their white eyes focused on Generals Okafor, Ngata, and Varma.

"Come with me, Generals. I need your assistance in the military base," the Ixies said together in a creepy monotone that stood Luminous's hair on end. They held out their hands as if they were one being and advanced.

Star's mishmash of an army stepped in front of the generals, but there was no space, and nowhere to retreat. As if blind to everything but their goal, the Ixies walked straight through the disturbing crystal statues, each with a person's agonized face in faceted relief. Amid gasps and cries, the statues toppled, shattering noisily on the floor. Luminous made herself look away from the red interior crystals.

"I order you to stop, or we will be forced to fire. This is your only warning." Varma threw her will outward with the order, but even the strength of her aura had no effect on the Ixies. Everyone with blasters took aim. So many innocent people were going to die. Was there no hope for shocking the Ixies out of Ix's mental grasp?

Luminous shoved her way quickly through the people in front of her and whipped her energy whip off her waist. She had to try. She aimed and tazed the front three Ixies in quick succession with its glowing tip. At the same time, she radiated at them, *Snap out of it!* trying to push her aura out at them like a wave.

They fell back, into their comrades, and shook their heads as if confused. The dark tendrils in their auras appeared to slip and everyone who wasn't brainwashed held their breath. But, all three Ixies got back up, merely slowed. They were still under Ix's control, and continued forward.

"Fek," Nik said, having pushed his way up next to Luminous. The sentiment was echoed by everyone still in control of their mouths.

"Ready. Aim—" General Varma began.

"Wait Moon!" Star yelled at her sister. "Luminous, turn it up to max and try again!"

Without taking the time to wonder how much Star could sense, she turned her whip up to maximum power and cracked the nearest Ixie again, a young Settler woman she recognized from her self-defense class, this time screaming her radiation at her like an invisible fire hose, forcefully spraying Ix's dark tentacles out of her paused aura. The young woman fell back, her body jerking against the nearby wall before falling to the floor—and so did the Ixies on either side of her, also hit by Luminous's radiation. But the tentacles clung tenaciously to the auras of the people not tazed. They got back up, leaving the young woman who'd gotten the brunt of both attacks on the floor, apparently unconscious.

"Ready—" General Varma began, but was again cut off by her sister.

"It works! Set your weapons to max stun until we know the full effects!" Star barked over her sister's order. Star's civilian troops did as she said and soon were firing and whipping tazer strikes at the Ixies, and Luminous sent blast after blast of her radiation at the stunned people, like tsunami waves breaking over them. The generals hung back, as if they didn't know what had happened to their authority. The next wave of Ixies, roaring Ix's displeasure, climbed over their fallen comrades.

Luminous cracked lightning at them with her whip and Nik fired his blasters beside her, while the three security drones orbited over their heads firing stun blasters. A barrier of fallen, unconscious bodies grew in front of them. Star's army fought with whatever weapons they had, and they all worked to push the Ixies back into the wide corridor.

Luminous's whip buzzed at her through her hands with every hit, and she saw a diminishing bar of red lights on the handle. The light of the tazer tip faded down to a dim glow before it stopped tazing altogether. She ran to the side where the first young Settler woman she'd hit was, against the wall, and reached for the whip at her waist. She looked at the woman's face only to see her eyes open, wide with fear and confusion, and *brown* in color. Her aura held no sign of Ix's dark tentacles. Luminous pulled her up to sitting, and motioned to a few troops behind her who'd paused with their blasters to let her through.

"It worked! She's clean!" she signed exuberantly and checked the others. So far, their auras were clean too, and some were waking up. "Pull them out of the way," she signed.

"Luminous?" Nik yelled. "We need you back here doing, whatever it is you were doing!" She grabbed a second whip and ran back to the front line.

"Nik, it's working!" she signed to him, before blasting another giant wave over the Ixies who'd been stunned in her absence.

"That's great, but I'm running out of juice. I need to reload soon."

"Here." She handed him the second whip she'd grabbed. He looked at it and shrugged, holstering his blasters, and extending its length.

Minutes, or what seemed like hours later, Luminous turned to see if Cassandra was alright and saw that she had gotten a door open at the back corner of Medical. The door had blended in so seamlessly that Luminous hadn't even known it was there. It was a glimmer of hope, a path out from the waves of never-ending Ixies. For each one they saved, there seemed to be ten more.

"Generals, fall back! Through here!" she signed and Deb yelled over the crowd for her. She ran to the door to usher them through. Okafor was in first, and the other two were on their way.

Luminous turned back to yell over her shoulder, "Nik! Everyone who's not brain dead, come on! We've gotta get out of here!"

But when she turned back to the door, Cassandra was blocking it, with her hand on General Okafor's arm, her helmet shattered on the floor and her eyes turning white. Tears streamed down Cassandra's cheeks, but her mouth was curved up in a mad grin. She cackled. That was when Luminous saw that her helmet had a big crack, right down the middle. As she watched, it fell off her head and shattered.

"I win," was all she said, in that voice that was not her own. And, she closed the door. The mass of Ixies began to laugh, together, in a sound wholly eerie and unnatural.

Luminous pounded on the door with her fist, but it didn't open. Now they were trapped with a seemingly never-ending wave of white-eyed miners, Settlers, and civilians of all kinds coming toward them. She turned and blasted the room with her nebula radiation, trying to make up for the time she'd lost in her attempt to get everyone to the door.

Between radiation blasts, Luminous put her fingers on either side of the crack at the edge of the door and tried to pry it open. Nothing.

"Agh! She's sealed it!" Luminous signed and Deb yelled for her.

Deb? She asked. *Cassandra opened this door somehow. I need to know how to open it, or another one.*

Security access for authorized personnel only, Deb replied.

Well then, how did Cassandra open it?

Unclear. It appears Cassandra may have been able to hack the security database.

Well, let's do that then!

I am not authorized to facilitate the hacking of security protocols.

Agh!

Meanwhile, the two remaining generals had returned to the fight against the Ixies. Ngata was good, but General Varma was a whirling, blasting storm unto her own making. She'd seen the way their fortunes had turned, and had given up trying to save people. Her blade prosthetics glowed orange along the edges like a warning. As she kicked and spun at the closest Ixies, her blades sliced and crackled, and at the same time she blasted away at more distant targets. Her energy blades seared effortlessly through dull-eyed, brainwashed Ixies.

"No!" Luminous yelled. It wasn't their fault! But, as much as Luminous and her friends tried, there were too many to save. Recovery was quickly filling with bodies. And yet, the Ixies kept coming.

"Luminous, how's that door coming?" Nik growled having taken up a position in front of her.

"I'm working on it!" She wondered how Deb could know her mental inflections so well, and yet not be able to open one stinking door.

Deb, tell security it's an emergency! We are under attack and have to get out of this room. Tell them there's a fire or something!

Sensors do not detect a fire.

Well then, the sensors are faulty! Get us out of here!

Immediately, sprinklers burst open from the ceiling, soaking everyone in fire retardant. But the hidden back door remained closed.

Agh! That's not helping, Deb!

"Luminous, I'm coming," she heard Star yell. "Sarah, get me to that door so we can get it open."

As ordered, Sarah led Star over the bodies and crystal rubble that was rapidly piling up. They had just made it and started work on the door, when something caught Luminous's eye in time to see an Ixie slip through the far side of their front line while Nik and the others were distracted. It was an Ixie woman, carrying a glass beer mug dripping with crystallizing Durongo ooze. She locked on Luminous, Star and Sarah, trying to get that back escape door open, and her mouth stretched up into a creepy clown-like grin. She swung the mug back to throw and Luminous cracked her energy whip, right across the woman's arms. The mug spilled down her front to the floor, and the electric charge only increased the crystallization speed. In a blink, the woman became a crystal tree atop a rapidly crystallizing base, but only until it was all shattered by Ixies coming from behind.

The floor was now covered in shattered red crystal, and bodies scorched by blaster fire, or Varma's energy blades. And yet, Ix had no shortage of soldiers in this battle. Luminous and Nik, Varma and Ngata, Star and her civilians, were losing. A shattered helmet, an unexpected hand on an arm, and a person who used to be on their side, turned, eyes white, and joined the Ixies. Suddenly the ally Luminous had just been fighting next to became her enemy. And the same was happening all over.

It was in this chaos that an Ixie got through to Ngata. It

seemed that Ix wanted all three generals for his own. The big man's helmet shattered and in the blink of an eye, General Ngata belonged to Ix. He turned his blaster fire on General Varma.

Star abandoned the door to dive in front of her sister, knowing what was happening in the way that only Star could. She took the blast, a direct hit to her chest and spasmed to the floor. Varma and Sarah ran to Star's aid, and Ixies rushed them from all sides. A lucky swipe shattered Varma's crystalline helmet and Luminous watched the general's Sun-like energy pale, and her eyes turn white.

Ixies surrounded both remaining generals and within moments, Varma and Ngata were marching out, shoulder to shoulder as if of their own accord. Star was down. And, the remaining Ixies turned back toward Luminous and Nik.

"Uh, Luminous? My whip is dead, and my blasters are about out of power. This is not looking good." Nik kept firing as the Ixies climbed over the mound of bodies to get to them. His voice sounded final. "They're coming, Lu. I don't think they're looking to take us with them, either."

Luminous saw Sarah join the Ixies as they came close and surrounded herself and Nik against the wall. Their normal human auras were dim and murky gray under the writhing black tentacles. They stopped in front of Luminous and Nik who huddled against the wall, and laughed as one, a low-pitched cackle.

"You've lost, Luminous," the Ixies said together. "You and your human prince. You should have taken my offer to kill him for your freedom. But now, the generals are readying the thermonuclear bombs to feed me the energy I need and there is no one left to stop me. I will be a star again. And now, I have no use for either of you any longer."

The Ixies stepped forward and raised their arms together to strike. Luminous and Nik crowded together and took one last look into each other's eyes. She could see his were filled with regret.

"Luminous, I—" he began, but he could not continue.

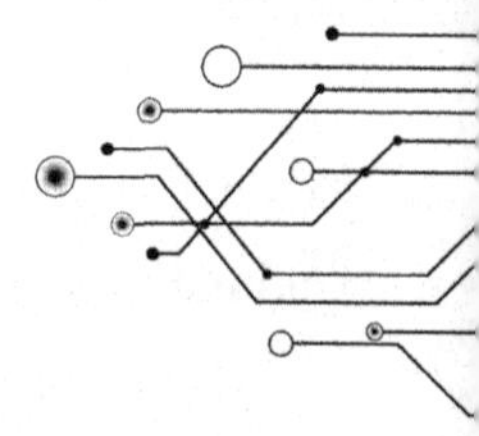

Chapter 28:

DISSOLVING

—Luminous—

Luminous felt the Ixies move forward and saw from the corner of her eye their fists come down, but she did not feel the blows. Instead, she felt something strange. Her body seemed to dissolve where she stood, into a fine mist. Her vision went fuzzy, into tiny bubbles and then nothingness, and a strange dysphoria took over.

She began to feel and smell… humidity. And as her body was coming back together, the ground turned squishy beneath her feet. She was still holding onto Nik but she could not move for another few seconds. His beautiful face resolved before her eyes. His mouth began to move again.

"Love you," were the first words she heard him say and they both collapsed to the squishy floor, gasping to take air into their resolidified lungs.

I love you too, she tried to tell him with her eyes, refusing to let go. After a few moments they looked around. They were in a place with the smell and feel of a rainforest, and the clean, utilitarian look of a spaceship. The Traveler ship, but how they had come to be there, she could only guess. Two Traveler figures stood watching them and Luminous immediately recognized

Paranel, with her guard Tynee at the controls. Paranel was making calming motions with her hands.

"It's all right," she signed.

"What? How?" Nik demanded shakily, pointing one hand at them as if he still held his blaster, which he did not. His other arm let Luminous go, to her dismay, as he checked that his other blaster was gone too. Luminous's energy whip was no longer in her hand either.

"Where are our weapons?" Nik demanded.

Paranel made the calming motions again, then looked to Luminous to translate for her. But Luminous asked her own, more urgent question.

"Can you get the generals out the same way?"

Paranel shook her scaly head. "We have no way of knowing which human is which inside the port. We only knew who you were because you were under attack."

Though Nik could obviously read sign language, Cassandra's voice rang out, translating anyway. She stood at the back of the control room, arms wrapped around her middle, looking apprehensive.

How dare she? Luminous stalked over to her and grabbed the telepath by the throat, never wanting to kill someone more.

You betrayed us! she mentally screamed. Cassandra winced. Nik pulled Luminous back and Cassandra rubbed her throat.

"She took the only escape and locked us out!" Luminous signed furiously. "We lost the generals because of her!"

"I know, Lu, but killing her won't help anything."

"He took me over again. I had no choice. I'm sorry." Cassandra seemed sincere, her voice choking up.

"Ix started taking me over when I lived in his orbit," Cassandra explained verbally and mentally to Paranel and Tynee, who seemed to be the only Travelers aboard, left to catch up with Traveler One later. "At first, I had no idea there was an entity there, but then he began talking to me. Ever since humans blew Callisto trying to jump start its core, Ix was obsessed with human thermonuclear weapons, and getting humans to fire them at him. He had a plan. He would open his gaseous body to absorb the bombs, jumpstart his own core and thermonuclear reaction. He wanted to become a star again.

"I'm sorry, but he was using me in the trade talks, trying to get the generals to fire on your planet, which of course was in Ix's orbit. He used my mouth, my voice, to tell the human delegation that your people would not keep their word, would take all the resources from Planet Nine and leave us with nothing for the future."

Tynee drew herself up, and to Luminous's surprise, began to sign. Luminous hadn't been aware the guard had been learning along with her princess. "We are not a people who lies about our motives. But we do not have time for that discussion. If the humans fire their weapons at Planet Nine and this Ix is able to absorb the energy to change the planet into star, that would change the orbits of the other planets in this system, pulling Earth into an immediate ice age." The two Travelers looked at each other, communicating before turning back to Luminous.

"What can we do?" Paranel signed. "We have to stop him."

Finally, people who believed what was going on! "We have to stop him from firing, but how? He has all the generals now. They'll be firing any minute," Luminous signed.

"We'll have to stop the weapons from reaching Planet Nine." Paranel's energy looked determined.

"Or, we could increase their explosive power by a factor of one hundred," Tynee signed.

They all stopped and looked at the guard.

"Would that be enough?" Paranel asked.

"You're right, better make it a thousand."

"Uh—" Nik looked dumbfounded. "You can do that?"

Tynee nodded.

"Enough to do what, exactly?" Cassandra spoke up quietly.

"But," Luminous ignored her, "wouldn't that just increase his power and mass as a star?"

"Not if we cause an overload."

"You mean—?"

"Make him explode." Cassandra's voice was hard. "Yes. Let's do that."

"Get the ship in position," Paranel said to Tynee. "Everyone hold tight. This is going to get rough. I don't think we'll have too long to wait."

Tynee sped the ship toward Planet IX, a mere speck in the distance that grew larger by the second. She didn't bother dodging or shooting meteors that were still coming from the planet's passage through the Kuiper Belt. Even direct hits by large debris merely rolled off the malleable skin of the ship.

They got in position between the port and Planet IX. Tynee

was right. They didn't have long to wait. Though, was that what she called rough?

All they could see of the port in the distance were bright flashing lights. The emergency beacons.

"The bombs are on their way," Nik muttered tensely and Luminous held out her hand to him. He squeezed it tightly and turned to Paranel and Tynee. "How exactly did you say we could increase the power of the bombs?" Luminous had to let go of his hand to sign for him.

"We didn't," Tynee signed. "But the skin of this ship is designed to absorb and redirect large amounts of energy."

"We're going to absorb the *bombs?* That's your plan?"

"Incoming," Cassandra murmured. She was practically vibrating with excitement.

Nik swallowed hard and pulled Luminous to his side as they both stared at the giant bomb hurtling toward them on the view screen. Two more followed on slightly different trajectories, probably having been fired from different points on Tersa Tellus.

Tynee worked the controls and the ship danced from the first, to the second, to the third bomb, rolling and absorbing each into its gelatinous skin.

"Brace," she warned. They were thrown to the floor as three powerful explosions rocked the ship, one after another. The humans held their hands over sensitive ears, though the explosions were felt body deep. The lights went out and the ship floated, momentarily aimless through space.

"Wait for it," Cassandra said in the dark. Unable to see, Luminous didn't know if she was speaking for herself or translating for Paranel or Tynee. "The explosions knocked out the ship's organic circuitry. They'll heal momentarily."

The lights flickered slowly back on and Luminous could see Paranel signing. "Here it comes."

The pointy rear end of the ship targeted Planet IX and lit up brighter than anything Luminous had ever seen as a human. Too bright to look at even through the viewscreen, but she couldn't look away either. Pure, white light blasted like a giant laser at Planet IX for what seemed an eternity while the entire planet's atmosphere seemed to boil, escaping in columns of steam into space. They could see the remaining planet's icy crust heat from the inside, turn red, and crack. Rivers of fire spewed out all over the surface, which got brighter and brighter, and Ix got what he wanted. He became a star. And still, the thick white laser continued.

The star brightened through the whole dwarf star spectrum until the long ago brown dwarf could burn no hotter. Planet IX went nova mere seconds after becoming a star. A bright white shockwave blossomed outward and huge chunks of debris pelted out in all directions.

While Luminous was hoping the port's best laser jockeys were still alive and back to their old selves, she noticed something left behind, at the center of where Planet IX had been—a malevolent, ugly energy. It was expanding and contracting like the flexing of a long unused muscle, and then it opened, like a single yellow eye. Cassandra began to cackle behind her.

With a deep sense of foreboding, Luminous turned to look at the telepath, who was levitating off the floor, arms wide, head thrown back, laughing. Her entire aura was constricted by thick ropes of black.

"Freedom!" she crowed, and the malevolent yellow energy took off in a streak toward the center of the solar system. Cassandra collapsed to the floor and curled into a moaning ball of misery. Her nose dripped dark red, and she rocked back and forth, the black fading from her aura.

"Cassandra!" Despite her earlier anger, Luminous crouched next to the terrified woman. "Is he gone?"

Cassandra nodded, continuing to rock. "He's gone. To take over the Sun."

Chapter 29:

THE CHASE

. . . [S]he glanced at the sharp knife, and again fixed her eyes on the prince, who whispered the name of his bride in his dreams. She was in his thoughts, and the knife trembled in the hand of the little mermaid: then she flung it far away from her into the waves.... She cast one more lingering, half-fainting glance at the prince, and then threw herself from the ship into the sea....

Hans Christian Andersen, The Little Mermaid (1836)

—Luminous—

The Traveler ship chased Ix across the solar system, Tynee's hands racing over the control panel. They hadn't destroyed Ix, Cassandra had moaned before seeming to go catatonic. They'd *released* him. And now he was going to inhabit the Sun, and enslave every human on Earth.

Luminous watched as Paranel turned and quickly walked from the room without explanation. As always, the Travelers seemed outwardly calm, but now their energies were frustrated and frantic. Though she wasn't sure exactly why, this mattered to them deeply.

Paranel quickly returned with a small, shifting tesseract box and set it on a shelf that grew out of the wall. "We'll need to capture Ix in something that can hold his energy," she signed in explanation. She removed the control cube from the top of the tesseract and placed it nearby.

For a while, the ship seemed to gain on the fiery yellow energy that was Ix. But then he began pulling away.

"Faster!" Luminous signed. "We're losing him!"

"This is as fast as we can go," Paranel signed.

Nik scoffed. "Really? You travel the galaxy, maybe farther, at less than light-speed. We're bloody well supposed to believe that?"

"We travel long distances using a jump gate system that hasn't been invented in this time yet." Paranel's tail twitched irritably as she signed, displaying more emotion than Luminous had ever seen from a Traveler. "It was developed to avoid miscalculations and drunken idiots jumping their ships into planets. The asteroid you think killed off the dinosaurs? That was no asteroid. By law we can't jump anywhere near an inhibited planet, or star for that matter. We could end all of us."

"Ix is going to end life for humans as we know it! Break the bloody law!"

"We *can't*. The ship's speed is automatically limited inside solar systems. Tynee is working to disable the system now, but it will take time. Time that we don't have. Ix will already be to the Sun."

Luminous saw Nik grind his teeth. She squeezed her eyes shut, wishing she were still a nebula. *She* could catch Ix. Nik seemed to be thinking along the same lines and turned to her.

"Luminous, how fast is Astri? Can she do it?"

She shook her head. Neither Astri nor their nebula siblings

had ever wanted to work on their speed with her. She unconsciously reached for Astri in the replacement bag still slung across her chest, momentarily forgetting she wasn't there, but feeling something else instead. She pulled it out. The dagger.

She pulled the dark, pitted metal shard out of its protective sheathe and stared at its razor edges, gleaming and obsidian-sharp, remembering Ix's words in her head:

"Use the dagger. Kill your prince with it, and prove your allegiance to me, to our kind, before I become a star again. Your debt to me will be cancelled, your radiance returned. I will even return the radiance of your siblings so that we can celebrate my coming glory together, as a family."

She was so absorbed in her thoughts, Nik had to repeat his question to get her attention.

"Luminous, answer me! What *is* that? Where did you get it?"

She shook her head and dropped it in horror, kicking it away from herself so its tip imbedded harmlessly in a squishy, living wall of greenery. Nik walked over to it.

"No, don't!" she signed, but he picked it up anyway, turning it over in his hands.

"Luminous?" He looked to her for an explanation, but it was Cassandra who spoke. They all looked over to see the telepath awake now from her previous catatonic stupor, though she still sat clutching her knees to her chest.

"Ix gave it to her. Its purpose is to allow her to return to being a nebula, and cancel her obligation to serve him when her human life is over."

Nik seemed to realize part of the significance immediately. "It's you, isn't it Luminous?" he whispered. "You're the one who can catch Ix, in your nebula form. But you have to…" horror dawned in his eyes as he looked from her to the crude dagger in his hands. But she shook her head, unable to make herself sign the words.

It was again Cassandra who spoke. "The dagger isn't meant for her. It's more of a test of her loyalty. To Ix."

Full realization dawned in Nik's eyes. He stared down at the dagger and gulped, slowly turning the point of its blade to his own chest.

"No!" Luminous signed, Deb yelling the word for her. She ran over to Nik and tried to knock the dagger away, but he caught her hand instead, wrapping it around the handle of the crude iron dagger and holding it there, looking into her eyes.

"No," she whispered, staring back at him. Cassandra and the two Travelers didn't move, but only watched. They showed nothing on their faces, and sadness in their auras.

"Yes," he said. "You have to. Luminous, listen to me. You can catch him as your energy self. You can," he insisted while she continued shaking her head, trying to pull away. Her own heart beat too fast in her human chest and her throat felt tight. Tears threatened.

"You have to, Luminous. We're losing Ix and you're the only one who can catch him. The box will hold him. It's our best shot. But you have to get it out in front of him." He put his free hand on the side of her face. "I have faith in you, Luminous. If this is what it takes to save my people, to save Earth, I give it gladly. I know you can do it. I love you," he whispered. He placed his lips softly against hers. And he plunged their hands forward together, until the dagger was up to its hilt in his chest.

"No!" she tried to cry, her voice coming out in a wordless moan as he gasped and fell back away from her, onto the floor, pulling her with him. He looked at her, coughed and struggled for breath, blood quickly appearing on his mouth.

"Nik," she mouthed, and found his image wavering on her. With the last of his strength, he pulled the dagger out of his chest and his arms dropped to his sides. His last breath shuddered out of his body, leaving her with nothing but a bloody dagger in her hands. She wanted to ignore it and collapse over him. But Cassandra interrupted her misery.

Honor his sacrifice.

Numbly Luminous got up, ignoring the wetness gathered in her eyes, lifted the shape-shifting tesseract box from the shelf where Paranel had left it, and walked to the airlock. Tynee wordlessly let her through the door and closed it behind her. Warning lights flashed as she opened the outer door and allowed herself to be sucked violently out into space. She tumbled into the icy darkness and felt the pain immediately in her human body as it started to freeze and fail. Astri appeared unfurling from an asteroid, calling their nearby nebula siblings who flashed to Luminous's side. She blew the last of her warm air out of her lungs in a frozen cloud. The nebulae soberly gathered around her, but not to save her human body this time. To witness her death.

Painful minutes later, Luminous emerged, tiny and brilliant, a pure light. Her siblings wrapped her in a new body of gas and dust and she immediately felt—nothing. Nothing but cold and empty. But she would have time to think about all that she had lost later. For now, she wrapped her new nebula around the tesseract and tumbled it with her as she stretched herself into her undulating two-dimensional wave toward Earth and the Sun.

She spotted Ix as he was almost to Earth. He was a dark comet, a ball of icy, dark fire with a large, inefficient, showy tail. No doubt he wanted humans on Earth to witness the splendor of his arrival, but it had allowed her to catch up. Now he veered toward Earth and she worried that she'd been wrong. What if he decided to take over and inhabit Earth from the inside instead? He was heading right for it, and she wasn't going to make it in time.

He swerved at the last minute, streaking a giant, cresting aurora across the northern hemisphere as he soared on past. She felt numb relief when he continued on to the destination she had suspected, the Sun. He would be the star he'd always dreamed of being and a controlling god to the humans on Earth at the same time. She felt the Earth shift the tiniest bit as if every human turned to watch Ix flame by.

She pushed herself to her limits, passing Earth as Ix approached Venus, passing Mercury as he approached the Sun. The solar winds increased in intensity and began stripping away her new gas and dust. The box started to slip. She was having a hard time holding it with her gaseous appendages. She had to hold everything in close and tight and yet stretch herself to top speed. A solar flare tore through her and she barely managed to hold on. She fumbled, trying to open the tesseract. She had to get it out in front of him.

She stretched out as far as she dared, surfing solar flares that tried to sweep her back. She inched past Ix and spread herself like a disk, a shield in his way, with the Sun burning directly behind her.

He merely laughed and powered right through her center, as if showing her she was nothing, that even the densest part of her shield could not hold him for a second.

"You think you can hold me with your cloud of gas and dust? You can't even slow me down."

And that densest spot, that's where she held and opened the tesseract box as he burst through her. Its energy vacuum was even darker than Ix. So dark, no energy could escape, not even light, and she had to strain with all her might to get behind it, to not allow her own energy to be sucked in as well. His scream of rage cut off as the tesseract snapped closed. Its surface shifted and stretched in all directions as he tried to get out. She eyed it warily, afraid to touch it, but it held.

Seconds later, Astri caught up, and pulled her back, shielding her from the Sun's burning winds.

Thanks, she whispered, in the language of radiance. She was more tired than she'd thought a being made of energy could be. What now?

They towed Ix into Mercury's shadow and stopped to rest. After some time, Luminous wasn't sure exactly how long, the Traveler ship caught up too. It drifted, silent in front of the two nebulae for several moments, and then, hands appeared on the outside of its white hull. Paranel was projecting herself onto the hull somehow, mostly her hands, but also a ghostly outline of her arms and upper body, the colors of her aura appearing around the projection. And she began to sign.

Luminous, you did it! Thank you! Paranel paused and her aura projection held uncertainty. *However, we do not know how long this solution will last. Our scans indicate the tesseract is already beginning to destabilize. It was designed to hold refined dark matter, not such a being.*

Luminous eyed the stretching, shifting tesseract and silently swore. He was breaking out already?

And, there is another issue: the control cube for that tesseract.

The ship expelled something small out its side to float in space. The cube. Although it now floated on the opposite side of the ship from Ix's tesseract, Ix immediately tried to undulate toward it, though with little success.

Ix has been trying to communicate with us through it, to convince us to release him ever since you caught him. Even for us, it was too tempting, and we had to induce sleep in Cassandra. So, we have two problems. Do you have any ideas?

Luminous thought for a moment, and formed her gaseous cloud into the shape of hands as best she could. *For the control cube, yes.* Luminous paused and called out for her nebulae siblings. *For Ix himself, I have one possible idea. It's risky,* she signed slowly. *But first, I have to know. Is Nik…dead?* She held herself tight and still, awaiting Paranel's answer.

We have the prince in stasis and are working to save his life. The damage to his heart was extensive. We believe our technology may be able to fix it, if we can modify it for his physiology. And even then, nothing with a human heart is certain. Luminous had to silently agree. She acutely felt the loss of her own.

However, when that tesseract breaches, it will not matter. If Ix escapes, inhabits the Sun and enslaves humans on Earth, the future of the human race is, at best, highly uncertain. The projected hands paused. *And, our future with it.*

Luminous digested that and pieces began to fall into place. *You are descendants of humans?*

Yes, from a branch genetically altered for survival on our planet, and far in the future. We came merely to observe the launch of the first colony ships from Earth, the beginning of what we call the Alliance. But we made our fair share of mistakes, including misjudging our own ancestors. And we had never met your kind. We did not know you inhabited our ancestral solar system at all, and could become human! Paranel's aura was filled with amazement. *What's more, we had no idea about Ix. Despite all our advances, this trip has been humbling in many ways. Perhaps we are not as advanced as some of us would like to think.*

You don't know how to imprison Ix again. Luminous watched the tesseract box as it stretched and rotated chaotically, trying to move toward the control cube, the power inside desperately seeking escape.

We do not. We must ask, again, for your help.

I have only one idea, Luminous admitted. *But I need your word first, Paranel, because I know how you value honesty above all else.*

What would you have me say, Luminous?

First, that you'll do everything in your power to save Nik and return him to his people.

We will, you have our word.

And second, that you'll keep your promises to the humans, and then leave, and never return. Allow them to evolve on their own, without your interference—or your tourism.

The feel from the ship was distinctly ashamed as Luminous waited for Paranel's answer.

I agree and you have my word that I will do my utmost to convince my people. The ship glowed with the promise and Luminous touched its energy briefly with hers to seal the deal. That was as good as she could expect.

Luminous and Astri's nebulae siblings arrived and Luminous was glad to see their sibling who had been hit by the port laser cannon had recovered. They communicated the controller problem and their five siblings swept the small cube into their gaseous appendages and immediately left with it. Ix's rage burned even hotter inside the tesseract.

So Princess, how do you feel about black holes?

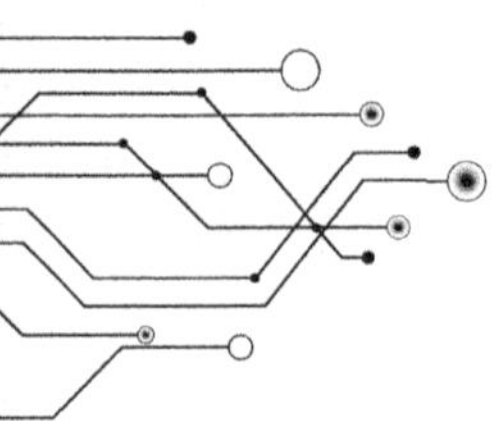

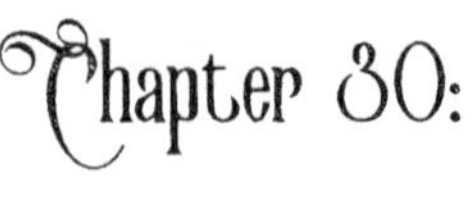

Chapter 30:

THE MATRIARCH

—Luminous—

Sagita, The Matriarch, was doing exactly what she had been when Luminous and Astri had last seen her, enthralling and devouring entire solar systems with world crunching inevitability. Paranel and Tynee had offered to catch up in their ship, but they would have had to travel from the Sun, the solar system's center, to its outer edge before they could create their jump gate. However, with the tesseract beginning to break down as they spoke, they weren't sure there was time.

As it was, Luminous and Astri were not at top speed themselves, but did their best, having to tumble the chaotic energy contained within the tesseract along with them, ingesting supplemental gas and dust along the way to replace what Luminous had lost. Instead of following, Paranel and Tynee took off for Traveler One, as that would be their best chance to ensure Nik's survival.

Matriarch! Luminous radiated as brightly as she could into Sagita's whirl, hoping the all-powerful force could hear her, while simultaneously trying to will the tesseract to stay intact. She could already see bright, hairline cracks starting to form on its shifting surface and had no idea how much longer it would hold.

What are you waiting for? Throw him in! Astri whispered.

Do you really want to be on the bad side of The Matriarch?

You again? Sagita noticed them finally. *Here with more questions, or here to join me? And you brought, who is that? Ix? Ugh. I recognize the energy.*

They brought him forward in his tesseract to the event horizon. He was desperately trying to break free now, as if he could sense where he was. As she watched, a tiny fissure in the tesseract's skin pulsed and grew bigger, exposing a sliver of Ix's dark yellowish light from within.

Ah, I see. The biologicals freed Ix from the imprisonment I gave him, and now you seek my help to reimprison him.

You imprisoned him? If Luminous could have been sweating with the exertion, she would have.

How else do you think this power-hungry being became entrapped in a brown dwarf star? Yes, he came to me when I was forming your solar system and tried to force his way into a star. So I gave him what he wanted, a star, but as you can see, he was not satisfied with my generosity.

He would enslave humans and make himself a god, Sagita. He is already close to breaking free. Luminous watched as the fissure seemed to stretch and widen. *Matriarch, we were hoping you could help.*

You see me as destruction. You think a trip through me would end him. But you do not know is that I perform my own small role in creation as well. Everything that eats must at some point disgorge. And I don't want his negative energy inside me forever either. Sagita seemed in no hurry.

Please, Matriarch. He is close to breaking free already. What do you ask of us?

Very well. Yes, you may send him in.

With a great feeling of relief, Luminous and Astri shoved the tesseract across Sagita's event horizon as hard as they could.

I will encase him in something a little less grand than a star this time, I think. He will look a mere asteroid, but not just any. I will surround him in the most solid and dense elements in the galaxy. And then I will excrete him to drift forever through the cosmos.

Excrete? Luminous blurted, trying not to laugh.

You have only seen me from this side. Did you think I kept everything I consumed inside forever? Sagita, something about her, laughed. *For now, I will have a little fun.*

And Luminous saw Ix begin to swirl down, on the fast track toward Sagita's gullet. The crack widened and she saw Ix's glowing yellow eye stare out at her in desperation. But it was too late. With one last scream, he was sucked in.

And now I have something to ask of you in return, Small One.

Luminous felt trepidation rise within her. What could The Matriarch want of a little nebula like her?

Go back to your home and fill it with love. For that is the most powerful agent of positive change in my galaxy.

*But I—*Luminous began. *I don't know how,* she was going to say.

Look through the eyes of love and you will figure it out. I have faith in your energy. You can do great things if only you believe in yourself. Now go.

Luminous went, Astri trailing along with her, lost in thought. Luminous felt determination rise within her. And, as she stretched herself back toward Nik, she thought she heard Sagita say, *And I do so love a happy ending.*

Now, Luminous only had to figure out how to become human again.

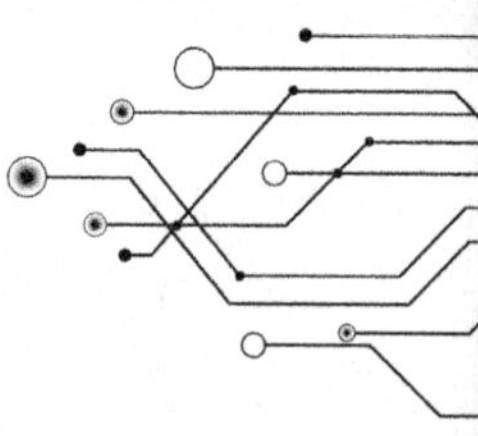

Chapter 31:

A HEART IN THE MIST

—Nik—

Nik looked out the port window from the hospital bed in his private suite, as the entire recovery ward in Medical was closed for investigation and repair. The port was still picking up the pieces from Ix's attack, but things were starting to return to normal, for everyone except Nik.

He didn't want to believe Luminous was gone, turned back into a nebula to save the solar system, but that was reality and now he had to adjust to life without her. Paranel and Tynee had stayed, though the rest of the Travelers had not returned to port. Paranel had signed stoically to Nik that they must marry after all. It was, she said, Luminous's last wish. Hearing this he'd felt, again, stabbed through the heart.

Luminous, Paranel had explained, had gone to Sagittarius A, the black hole at the center of the galaxy, to destroy Ix once and for all, but she hadn't known if she could survive the deadly pull of the black hole. If she had, she'd be back by now, wouldn't she? But would he even know if she was here?

He got up, surprised that he wasn't more sore after receiving a new lab-grown heart. Traveler One had been a lush forest paradise, but he hadn't been allowed to stay. As soon as he was stable, they had brought him back here to the port to recover. He walked slowly to the window and looked out into the darkness of space, placing his hand to the thick polycarbonate.

Why had no one come up with a better plan? The delegates, the generals, the royals back on Earth, they were all going along with it—again—insisting that he not offend the Travelers, and marry their princess. But the one and only girl he could imagine saying his vows with, and meaning them, had stabbed him in the heart and thrown herself out an airlock to save the solar system. And the crazy thing was, it seemed to have worked. All the people who had been controlled by Ix and survived the battle had returned to their senses, many of them not wanting or able to believe what had happened, even though they were still recovering from injuries.

The generals had all survived, however they only had memories of what had happened before they were overtaken by Ix. Star hadn't made it. She'd died of heart failure after being hit by Ngata's blaster on max power. Sarah was recovering from broken ribs and a broken wrist. Max claimed he had been searching for Nik throughout the entire ordeal, but Nik suspected he'd hid in the suite until it was over.

As for Nik, Paranel and Tynee had given him a new heart, like it was easy, like they grew on Traveler trees, but he thought there was a mistake because it still felt broken. He felt incapable of doing the simplest tasks, like preparing for his upcoming nuptials. He left it to Max to come up with a suitable gift for him to give his fake bride. He pressed his forehead to the window. He closed his eyes and breathed in and out, trying to feel her presence, but he wasn't sure he could feel anything. He opened his eyes and saw a cloud, and for a moment, his new heart leapt.

"Luminous!" he shouted. For a moment he thought she was with him and then he realized it was only his breath, clouding the glass. He hung his head, letting it *thunk* forward against the cool window. When he looked up again, he wrote L+N in the fog and surrounded it with a heart. Just in case she was out there, he wanted her to know.

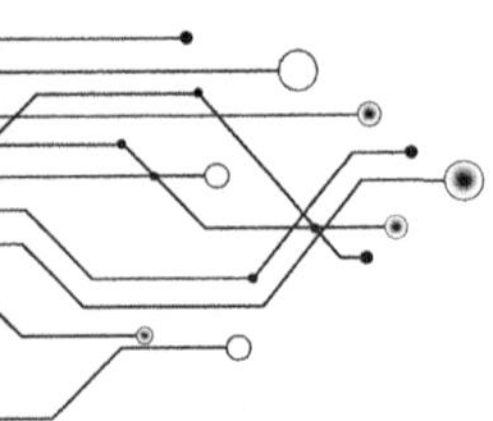

Chapter 32:

$E=MC^2$

—Luminous—

By the time they were getting close to their small home solar system, if Luminous had had any hair, she would have pulled it all out. How? How had Ix done it? He'd changed her energy into living human flesh. But *how?*

She should be happy. They'd won! She'd completed her mission. Ix was becoming black hole excrement, never to terrorize anyone ever again. And the stars spoke of peace, a new joining of old foes.

And yet, her soul mourned for all she had lost.

Astri and Luminous were passing through the Proxima Centauri star system, the unassuming nearest neighbor to their own. Why had she never visited before? It had a small red-dwarf star, uninhabited thank The Matriarch, and several planets, including a beautiful blue-green one with an atmosphere that looked perfect for surfing. But she felt no interest in that now. She and Astri were about to pass on through when several of their nebulae siblings approached.

What's happened, what's wrong? She radiated at them. But she could see their energy was positive as soon as they were within range. Still, why had they ventured so far out of the solar system to meet them?

Nothing is wrong. Ask us what's right, their radiation seemed to sing giddily.

Please, I don't have time for another riddle.

Ah, but you will want to hear this. First, yes, we smashed the controller cube to bits and spread the pieces to the solar winds to drift forever in all directions.

Good, thank you. At least that was one thing.

And we bring news of your human. They twinkled with excitement.

Luminous went very still, afraid to move. *Yes?*

He is alive!

And thinking of you!

Isn't that romantic?

How do you know this? Astri asked when Luminous couldn't respond.

He was at the port window.

He saw us and thought we were you!

He drew this in the fog of his breath. And three nebulae made themselves into a giant heart while the other two made the letters inside: *L + N*

Luminous knew she no longer had a physical heart, but she felt it leap inside her all the same. And then, if Luminous could have wept, she would have.

But there is a problem. Her siblings' twinkling dimmed.

What?

He seems sad. And the humans seem to be preparing for a large gathering.

Well, a lot of people died. They are probably having a funeral service for Ix's victims.

No, they have already done that. This gathering is a happy one, and it seems to be for your human and the Traveler princess.

What? Luminous's radiance fairly shrieked. *They're back to getting married? Why? Why would they do that?*

Uh, Lu, Astri began, *remember you did tell Paranel that she had to keep her word on everything they told the humans. The first agreement they made was that she would marry Nik, remember?*

Agh, no! That's not what I meant! Dang it, now I really need to get back there, and back to being human. She felt herself wilt. *But how?*

She felt Astri and their siblings surround her with support. Despite their not understanding her wanting to be human, with the short life-span that entailed, they supported her, and she was grateful. Through their circle, she heard the voice of Sagita, brought to them on the galactic current.

Oh my child, remember what I have told you, and all that you have learned. Love can make the impossible possible. Search, find the love within yourself. Then you will know what to do. And with that, The Matriarch's words faded into the galactic background.

With nothing to lose, Luminous did as she was told. She went inward, and found her love. Not just for Nik, but for *being* human. For the growth, and change, and the promise of each new day. She remembered becoming human the first time. The power of it. The speed. The energy. She remembered Nik telling her how much it would take. More than a nuclear bomb blast.

Ix gathered radiance from all his victims, she began slowly, an idea taking shape. *Why? Besides greed, he needed to power the next change, but he was imprisoned at the far edge of the solar system. But we—we can travel, and I know where we can collect plenty of energy. Will you help me?*

Luminous, of course we will. Their energy was warm, and excited to be part of the adventure.

Then come on! And hold on to me. I'm gonna teach you all to speed. And she started off again, undulating determinedly toward the nearby red dwarf of the Proxima Centauri system.

Where are we going? Astri asked.

Spread yourselves thin everyone, thin but strong. We're going to catch ourselves a solar flare.

∞

It had not been easy, and Astri kept insisting on stopping for snacks of replenishing stardust, but they made it back to the port, with a small-to-medium solar flare churning inside their nebula-made tesseract. Luminous had gotten the idea from the Travelers and it was working! Now she "only" had to jump.

I can do this. I can do this. Luminous said to herself.

We *can do this.* Astri said to her. *Alright, everyone ready? You all know what to focus on?* The other nebulae flashed their assent. *Go, Lu. Faster than lightning. You've got this.*

And Luminous disengaged from the nebula tesseract and backed away. Her siblings groaned with the strain, but their tesseract held. Luminous zoomed around them, around and around she spun the tesseract, faster and faster into a tornado-like whirl until it began throwing sparks and lightning strikes, and right when it was about to fly apart, she hit it, with one last burst of all her speed into the heart of the storm. Astri would later say it imploded, nearly sucking them all in, but all Luminous felt was the energy and speed and she held the image close of the amazing person she wanted to be in this life. Exactly as she had been before.

It wasn't that Ix had gotten anything right or wrong the first time. It was that she had grown to love her body the way it was. And her vocal chords, well the doctors had said there wasn't anything physically wrong with them. Maybe she would learn to use them, and maybe she wouldn't. Either way, she wanted to experience a lifetime with the physical expression of her self. And with Nik, if she could have that chance. There was only one way to find out.

She awoke, in the warm womb of her siblings as they drifted near the spaceport. She looked down at herself and her warm brown skin, and realized, this time she could breathe. And a glittering golden swirl of a gown made of stardust was forming itself around her body.

Astri, thank you, she said to her sister and truly her best friend, realizing she had not been stopping for snacks along the way as Luminous had assumed.

Yeah, well, you learn a few things the second time around, Astri replied. *Now, let's get you inside, huh?*

They floated Luminous into the nearest mining repair bay and set her down, gravity once again taking over. Luminous waved as her siblings backed out through the force field, and then turned to run on bare feet toward the door into the port proper, but skidded to a stop at the sight of a wide-eyed, gape-mouthed technician.

"Which way to the wedding?" she signed determinedly, but

he merely shook his head, not understanding. Oh, she wished she had her Deb back. Luminous strode to the nearest wall and slapped her hand on it, signing for it to bring up a map of current events. It popped up, Royal Wedding flashing prominently, directly on other side of the port from where she was. She groaned and picked up her skirts, ready to run, when the technician spoke.

"You—you're her, aren't you? The prince's nebula girl."

She nodded, rolling her eyes. Obviously. And turned again to run.

"Wait. Here." He ran over to something in the corner of the room and returned—with a souped-up hover-cycle. "I was brainwashed and you saved me. Take this."

She grinned at him in gratitude, gathered up her long skirts, tying them at her waist, and threw her leg over. She shoved the helmet he handed her over her corona of riotous curls and revved the solar-engine.

"You do know how to ride, don't you?" he called after her when she bucked a little at the start.

She gave a quick shake of her head but didn't wait for whatever else he had to say, gunning it and accidentally popping a wheelie out the door and into the promenade at full speed. Pedestrians jumped out of the way and Luminous overturned an orange cart with her thrusters as she went sideways. Oranges scattered in every direction, and she had to marvel that it was the same cart as on her first day at port. This time, she ignored the seller's obscenities, righted herself and kept going. It was the story of her human life: she got the basics. The rest she would figure out along the way.

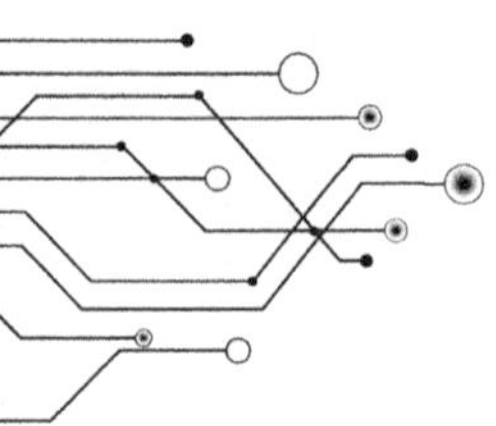

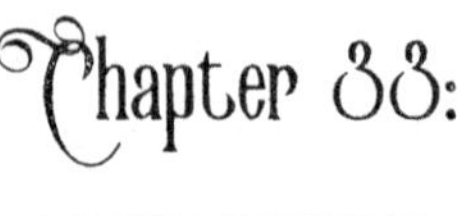

Chapter 33:

A ROYAL WEDDING

—Luminous—

Luminous blew through the doors of the chapel before skidding to a stop. She handed the cycle over to a surprised attendant and strode toward the front of the beautifully decorated chapel, hundreds of shocked eyes on her, her sparkling gown swirling as if weightless around her legs, but she only had eyes for Nik. He had been standing there in his traditional tux, in the process of lifting his bride's veil, looking handsome and determined—and now stunned like everyone else at her dramatic entrance.

Luminous realized she was still wearing her helmet. She pulled it off, shaking out her glorious cloud of hair—just as guards tackled her from all sides.

"Luminous!" Nik yelled as she struggled on the carpeted aisle. Ow. That had not gone as she'd envisioned.

From her vantage point on the floor, the wedding decorations were gorgeous, all white and deep starry blue, with swaths of exotic tropical flowers that had to come from the Traveler home world. Paranel looked beautiful and serene, as always, even amid the chaos and her guards surrounding her. Scales glowing to a high polish, she was dressed in a gorgeous white silk gown in deference to her groom's cultural traditions.

From Luminous's spot in the aisle she could see the full back of Paranel's dress, complete with a long train hiding her lovely, powerful tail. Suddenly, that was the saddest thing ever. Paranel was hiding who she really was, to marry a man she didn't truly care for. This, what should have been a couple's happiest day, had been turned into the biggest lie. All in the name of politics.

The only thing that betrayed her calm was the tightly closed bud of her forehead sensor. Luminous looked around at the Travelers in attendance on the bride's side. All their sensors were closed as well.

"Let her go!" Nik yelled through the commotion. All she could see of him as he ran up were his shiny dress shoes. The guards hauled her to her feet with her hands pinned behind her back.

"Luminous? You're alive? But you died in space! How is this possible?"

She shook her head, and tugged at her hands.

"Let her go! You will not silence her!" Nik took an enraged step toward the guards. The crowd gasped and the guards dropped her arms.

"It's not the same body, no," she signed. "I had to make a new one, with a lot of help. It wasn't easy, and yes, light speed and solar flares were involved." He looked flabbergasted, but his aura remained open to her.

"Your Highness!" Maximilian budged his way through the guards with several of the other delegates. They were quiet but stern. "You are supposed to be getting married now, Your Highness."

"This spectacle is offending our honored guests, who came back specifically to see you and their princess married," Delegate Sato said.

"One minute, please!" Nik snapped. He turned back to Luminous. "Luminous, you know I…" and for a minute, his face expressed everything he couldn't say.

"Nik." She smiled and put a hand on his face before pulling back to sign, "Don't you see?" She tapped her fingers to her forehead and then encompassed the whole wedding with her hands. "A lie about love is the biggest lie of all."

"Luminous," his whisper was strained. He looked around at all the human and Traveler guests in attendance, the priests waiting on the pulpit, one for the bride and one for the groom. But most of all, he seemed to focus on his bride's face, and he must have seen something there because his aura cleared of any indecision. He straightened. He strode back to the pulpit to take his bride's hands and kissed each in turn before looking into her face.

"Princess Paranel," he said. An interpreter standing nearby used the signs Luminous herself had taught the princess. "Any man would be lucky to have you for his wife. But I am not the person you love." He walked her over to Paranel's bewildered guard and placed her hand in Tynee's. Their faces were at first reluctant to believe, but they were quick to grasp each other's hands.

"Prince Nikolas!" Maximilian exclaimed.

"Quiet Max. You're fired," Nik said before turning and speaking to the crowd, but mostly to Luminous. With faulty tear ducts fogging her vision, she saw his words being signed to the Travelers.

"I was reminded just now, no matter our good intentions, our desires to not offend our new allies, a lie about love is the biggest lie of all. We want trade with the Travelers, yes. We also want to be able to travel the way you do, but most of all, we want lasting peace and friendship." Luminous blinked and saw that slowly, all around the room, the Traveler flower-like third eye sensors were opening, their energies softening.

"Princess Paranel deserves to be with the person she loves and who I believe has given her heart in return. As much as I admire the princess, that person is not me. For my heart has been silently and thoroughly stolen by another." And Nik, staring at Luminous, left his bride with her love. Paranel, with joy in her eyes, reached back to tear the back and train clean off her gown, freeing her glorious tail and her true self.

But Luminous's eyes were only for Nik, who came to kneel before her, and take her hands in his. Her breath caught in her throat.

"Luminous, I've been blind. I thought you were somehow lost, that I was saving you. But now I see what you've been trying to tell me all along. *You* were saving *us*, despite my fumbling efforts to muck it up. Can you forgive me?" She nodded, hardly daring to believe, and he smiled. "Will you, Luminous Nebula, do me the honor of marrying me? Of staying with me?" he asked. His smile faltered, "Please?"

Luminous felt every human emotion bombard her at once, and her tear ducts failed her again—she was going to have to get those looked at—and through the overload, all she could do was nod, but that seemed to be enough. He stood up and took her in his arms, and kissed her lips like a prayer.

"Please don't ever cut my heart out and leave me again," he whispered, his cheek to her hair. She laughed, hugged him tighter, and promised. And it was several moments before they walked to the alter together.

They stood next to the happy Traveler couple, Princess Paranel and her Royal Guard, Tynee. They were holding each other as if they would never let go, their sensors wide open. Luminous looked around and saw that happiness glowed from Traveler and human auras alike, and hands were offered and clasped in acceptance across the aisle. The two ministers bowed to each other and separated a few feet apart, seeming relieved, each to officiate their own cultural bonding ceremony.

After the wedding, during the reception and the many, many toasts to the happy couples, Nik seemed nervous as he summoned the gift Maximilian had ordered from Earth for him to give his Traveler bride. Sarah was even more nervous and muttered to Luminous that Maximilian had delegated the task to her. At a loss, and still recovering from her injuries, she had used a computer algorithm to scan all the holo-vids of the princess to come up with a gift and order it from Earth while Nik was recovering from surgery. Nik still didn't know what it was. Luminous patted her arm.

"It will be alright," she signed.

A short while later, into the ballroom walked two snappily dressed, zookeeper looking people, each carrying a scaly anteater wrapped around and up one of their arms. A mated pair of endangered pangolins from Earth.

Nik gulped next to Luminous. "I am going to kill Max," he muttered, standing up and pasting a fake smile on his face to walk toward the zoologists and bring them and the gift animals they held to Princess Paranel and her new wife. Luminous walked with him and tugged on his hand. He looked at her, and seemed to understand. He nodded and dropped the fake smile, taking a deep breath.

"Princess, Tynee, I apologize," he began as they stood up, staring at the pangolins and not signing a word. "I was not in my right mind when I delegated the task of choosing a gift to someone else. This gift is obviously inappropriate—"

Paranel stopped him with one hand, holding the other to her mouth in a rare display of emotion. Her forehead sensor was wide open and fluttering.

"She's happy," Luminous signed to Nik. "They both are." And they watched and waited to see what Paranel and Tynee would do next.

Paranel looked at her new wife, and they both stepped forward to take one of the pangolins in their arms, cradling them, Paranel rubbing her snout against her pangolin's as if it were beyond precious. Finally, after several minutes in which only breath fell in the entire ballroom, she and Tynee handed their pangolins off to others of the Traveler delegation, who seemed equally as taken with them.

"Prince Nik, Luminous," Paranel signed, taking one of Nik's and one of Luminous's hands in her soft scaly ones and squeezing for a moment before continuing signing. "This is the most welcome, wonderful gift you could have given us. We are honored beyond words. And, as much as we would love to take them with us to Traveler One, we know that they belong with humans, with this time. We must ask a favor of you."

Nik nodded and she continued.

"We would be most honored if these pangolins could be treated with the utmost in care and travel with humans on their next adventure, on the *Stalwart Mariner* to bring pangolins to the new world." Everyone in the Traveler delegation seemed to hold their breath.

Nik seemed stunned, but quickly recovered. "Yes, if that is what you wish, I will make the arrangements. You have my word." An expression spread across Paranel's scaly face that could be called nothing short of a smile.

That night, Humans and Travelers together ate delicacies from both worlds, danced to "The Blue Danube Waltz", and drank champagne until dawn, celebrating, because in the end, both the prince and the princess married their true loves side by side, sealing their cultures' bond of friendship. The celebration echoed all across the port, all through the night. The next day it would spread to both planets as the news reached Earth and beyond.

"So," Nik said, his arm around Luminous as they finally retired to their suite, holding her as if he'd never let her go. She tilted her head up to see his glowing face, radiating happiness at her, a mirror of what she herself was feeling. "Do the stars still predict disaster now, or can we relax into happily ever after?"

She signaled to the room sensors to draw the curtains before smiling up at her prince. "I'm done trying to decipher the stars. You and I, we'll make our own future."

Dear Reader

Word-of-mouth is crucial for any author to succeed. If you enjoyed the book, please leave a review on your favorite book sales or review site. Even if it's just a sentence or two. It would make all the difference and would be very much appreciated. Search for: *Karen Harris Tully* on any book review site such as Goodreads, BookBub, Amazon and more.

Thank you!

Learn more

and follow the ripple effect of Ix's actions in **The Giltter of Gold** from J.M. Phillippe

Take a sneak peak at Chapter One on the next page...

PART 1: A Poor Man's Daughter

Once there was a miller who was poor, but who had a beautiful daughter. Now it happened that he had to go and speak to the king, and in order to make himself appear important he said to him, "I have a daughter who can spin straw into gold."

The king said to the miller, "That is an art which pleases me well, if your daughter is as clever as you say, bring her to-morrow to my palace, and I will put her to the test."

And when the girl was brought to him he took her into a room which was quite full of straw, gave her a spinning-wheel and a reel, and said, "Now set to work, and if by to-morrow morning early you have not spun this straw into gold during the night, you must die."

Jacob and Wilhelm Grimm, Rumpelstiltskin

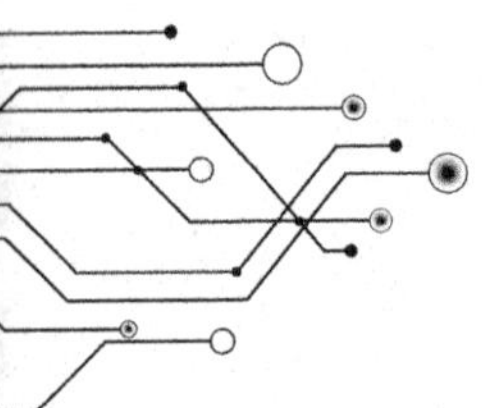

Chapter 1

THE PROMISE OF GOLD

Gwynn Flaxenhart pressed in the final code and held her breath. For one glorious moment, she watched as the pale green crystal in the chamber withstood the pressure and energy flowed into the converter, causing a series of lights to glow brightly. She tried to keep one eye on the clock and the other on the lights. Five seconds. Ten seconds. Fifteen.

Maybe, maybe. She was afraid to hope after so many disappointments. But…twenty seconds. Twenty-five.

The light began to flicker, and her eyes flew back to the crystal. Was that a crack?

"No no no no," she muttered, leaning over the console to look at the readings her computer was taking. "It's not a crack, it's not…."

But the readouts were confirming what her eyes were seeing—the energy level generated by the crystal was dropping. Thirty-two seconds. Thirty-four, and the lights were very dim.

At thirty-six seconds, the crack in the crystal expanded suddenly, and the pale green surface shattered, pieces crumbling smaller and smaller as the pressure continued.

"Stupid *tamade* crystal!" Gwynn said as she shut the chamber down.

She looked up at the clock, and realized she was running late—again. She cursed and saved her data, shutting everything down. Then she jogged to her quarters, which had been conveniently built near her lab.

She had a lot of complaints about the new *Flaxen One* space station that her father spent a small fortune on, but the design was not one of them.

Once in her quarters, Gwynn slipped out of the basic pants and shirt she wore around the lab and grabbed at the dress hanging on the back of her closet door, slipping it on over her head and sealing the back of it by pressing a button in the bodice. She turned on the mirror function of the closet door and swept her longer blonde hair over the patch of shorter purple hair on the right side of her head, a thick stripe that stretched from her temple to just behind her right ear. The blonde covered most of it, and she sprayed it down with a light setting spray, hoping it would hold. Finally, she pulled the white slippers that matched her dress onto her feet and stood up straight to survey the finished product.

Enzo, her father's right-hand man, had told her to dress in the family colors: white and yellow. But the yellow of the Flaxen Moons was a dull, buttery shade that made Gwynn look washed out and sickly. As such, most of the dress was white, with yellow accents contained to a thin sash at her waist and some light beading at the v-neckline. The fit wasn't great—too tight around her hips and butt and too lose in the bodice—but it looked good enough, Gwynn supposed.

She didn't know why she was bothering to even attend the latest of her father's attempts to lure an investor in to help keep Flaxen Moons going. Bertram Flaxenhart was not the business man his father was, and a series of bad decisions, including building an all-new station to house state-of-the-art living quarters and a top-notch lab, all running on a very large and very expensive tuotarium crystal, had left the family on the verge of losing everything. He spent wildly and invested poorly and had absolute faith that somehow Gwynn was going to get the family out of the mess he'd created.

By creating tuotarium crystals. Out of algae.

Gwynn sighed.

It wasn't the science that she minded, which was at least interesting. It was the very idea of the task of creating crystals at all. There were hundreds of thousands of strains of algae just on their farm, and another hundred thousand or so that had been discovered on various worlds throughout the galaxy that she didn't have samples of. Sure, it was possible that one of them, under the right pressure conditions, and in the perfect solvent, could create a tuotarium-class crystal as powerful as the one that ran the station. But Gwynn had been working on this project for two years and had barely gone through a fraction of the strains. It could take decades to find the right combination, particularly since they couldn't afford to hire anyone to help Gwynn with the research.

She finished her look with a little makeup, and then headed toward one of the side rooms off the giant clear-domed room in the center of the station. The ballroom was Bertram's pride and joy, hosting balls one of the few parts of his job that he liked. Not that Gwynn blamed him—she didn't enjoy being stuck at Flaxen Moons either, and she hadn't trained to be an artist, like her father had. But after his father was killed in the Genome War and his older brother, Brandon, was killed in the same accident that Gwynn's mother died in, Bertram was left all alone to take on the task of keeping the family legacy going.

At least until Gwynn came of age. But she was still months out from her twenty-fifth birthday and her full rights and responsibilities as heir to Flaxen Moons. Not that this got her out of any of the family functions, but at least once she was of age, she'd have voting rights. Maybe then she could help Enzo and his husband, Myles, try to curtail her father's spending.

Gwynn arrived at the room that the welcoming celebration for the latest would-be investors was in and felt her heart sink. She was much later than she had planned, and the room was already filled with people, most of them wearing some version of green and gold. She guessed those were the corporate colors. She was intrigued when she saw a young person turn and spotted what appeared to be green glittering sparkles across both cheeks, just under the eyes. Gwynn loved to track the fashion trends in other solar systems. But she couldn't let herself get distracted. She spotted Enzo's tall and thin form at the far side of the room and could guess that the bright yellow thing next to him was probably her father. All she had to do was get to them.

Gwynn tried to make her way through the crowd of people as unobtrusively as she could, but there was a rather wide-shouldered man blocking her way, his rich clothes and long tunic in gold and green making it appear as if he was wearing a uniform. Gwyn couldn't tell if he was security or someone higher up. The way his shoulders were filling out the tunic suggested security; he certainly looked foreboding from behind. She looked back to see if she could get around him and go the other way—her father had to be wondering where she was—but a sparkle-cheeked man filled in the gap Gwynn had just left. After standing on her toes and trying to see if there was another way around, Gwynn realized she only had one option left: she was going to have to ask the man to move.

"Excuse me," she said quietly, hoping she wasn't going to have to raise her voice to be heard over the din of the crowd.

The man looked over his shoulder, puzzled.

"How did you get back there?" he asked.

Gwynn gestured over the crowd that filled up the space around them.

"There was an opening, earlier," she explained. "It then filled up. I'm trying to get to the front."

"You've gotten pretty close," the man said, turning fully to face her. She saw then that he wore thick gold chains and had a corporate emblem emblazoned on the front of his tunic that she vaguely recognized. Not security then. He was probably a good ten years older than her, with a thick black beard that was as neatly shaped as his black hair. Light blue eyes looked out from under thick black lashes, proof of a regressive gene, Gwynn thought, if not a genetic modification. They didn't seem to go with his skin color, which was a few shades lighter than his hair and had a warm yellow undertone.

"If I don't make it all the way, my father isn't going to be too pleased with me," Gwynn said, still trying and failing to look past the man.

"You must be Gwynn then," the man said, smiling and reaching out his hand. "Gair Ingram."

Gwynn stared for a moment, taking in the reality of meeting the owner of the TenDek Corporation, one of the richest men in the galaxy. He was younger and better looking than she had imagined him when reading about him on the AltFeed. She shook off her paralysis and offered her own hand, which he took in a firm grip, stepping slightly closer to her as he shook it.

"Your father speaks so often of your brilliance, he seems to have forgotten to mention your beauty," Gair said. Despite being positive that he was just playing the corporate game with his compliment, Gwynn found herself blushing.

"Mr. Ingram, my apologies," she began, willing her face to cool down. "I hadn't realized who we were meeting today."

"Gair," he said. "And I appreciate your honesty. I suppose we are only the most recent in a long-line of suitors. Who wouldn't want to invest in the future of such a place like Flaxen Moons? The history of these algae farms stretches all the way back to the first colony ships. It would be very exciting to get to be part of that legacy."

"It is very exciting indeed," Gwynn said, not sure what else to say. Gair Ingram had a very different reaction to being asked to invest in Flaxen Moons than anyone else Gwynn had spoken with.

"And I have to say, I am very much looking forward to working with you." He smiled warmly at her.

Gwynn tilted her head to the side, as if trying to hear his words differently.

"Your father has mentioned...?" Gair began.

Gwynn's face grew hot again, but this time with anger and not embarrassment. She forced a bright smile anyway.

"Of course," she said, hoping Gair couldn't tell she was lying. "I just hadn't realized that he'd proposed working with you directly."

"Well, not directly," Gair said. "I don't actually do much with the ReDev team. But a project as big as this will definitely be under my oversight."

"Of course," Gwynn said, her mind racing. ReDev was probably what his company called research and development. But a large project? The only large project that Gwynn had been working on was....

"The crystals," she blurted out.

"Your father said that you are already getting results?" Gair asked.

Gwynn took a step back, her eyes searching out some exit from this conversation, from this feeling of being cornered. What had her father done? What had he said?

"I would love to speak more about this," she said, finally spotting an opening to Enzo and her father. "But I really must let my father know I'm here so that we can officially begin things."

"I am very much looking forward to officially beginning things," Gair said with a twinkle in his blue eyes. For a second, Gwynn was distracted by her panic enough to wonder—was he flirting with her?

Corporate game, she reminded herself.

"As am I," she said back, not really paying attention to her own words. "Until then." She gave a small bow of respect, which he returned, and then he moved aside so that she could get past him. She took a direct route to Enzo, in his own white and yellow outfit, her father a slab of butter next to him in head-to-toe yellow. Gwynn tried not to think about if Gair was watching her, and willed herself not to look back, but as she twisted sideways to get past yet another be-sparkled shareholder, she caught Gair's profile in her peripheral. He *had* been watching her.

She ducked her head down a little to hide her face and any emotion that may be crossing it, and then kept her back to him the rest of the way to her father.

"Dad," she said, urgently, so that only Bertram could hear. "What is going on?"

"Oh good, you've made it!" Bertram said, clapping his hands together. "Enzo, go ahead and signal for the others to start moving people into the ballroom." He made a shooing gesture at the older man, which annoyed Gwynn, but Enzo's face remained placid as he did what he was told. "Gwynnie dear-heart, you look lovely," Bertram said, finally looking at his daughter. "So much white though! And are you covering the purple in your hair?"

"Dad!" Gwynn said with more force, grabbing his arm and physically moving him behind one of the many planted palm trees found all around the compound for more privacy. "What have you told them about the crystals?"

"It's just a proposal, dear-heart, don't be so concerned."

But something was nagging at the back of Gwynn's mind, and it clicked as her father tried to turn away.

"He said *will*," she said. "Gair said will—that this project will be under his oversight. Is this really just a proposal?"

Bertram looked uncomfortable under her gaze.

"I didn't have a choice," he said. "The debts we have—we won't make it another lunar cycle without their support. And there was only one thing they wanted."

"It's what everyone wants," she said, panic mingling with anger. "The ability to make tuotarium crystals changes everything."

"Right, and you said you were getting results," Bertram said. "No one is expecting any miracles."

"Making tuotarium crystals from algae would be a miracle," Gwynn retorted. "I've made power crystals, but none of them last longer than a few seconds. I don't know how to do it! I don't even know if it can be done."

Bertram pulled his daughter close then, his voice low and urgent.

"We have nothing. Nothing! I can't sell this place for what I've borrowed against it. If I don't find a way to pay our debts, it's worse than just losing the farms. I'll go to jail. The debtors will go after you as the heir and make you an indentured servant until you pay off your share. And Enzo and Myles—where will they go? They are too old to start over anywhere new.

"We just ran out of time," Bertram said. "With this deal, we buy some more."

"How much more?"

"Until the day after the Hart Ball," Bertram said. "You don't have to make a lot of crystals—just one, just a proof of concept.

Then you hand over your research, and then we get Flaxen Moons back."

He seemed so confident that it was hard for Gwynn to remember just how horrible of a deal this was.

"And if we don't deliver? What does TenDek get then?"

"Everything," Bertram said.

"Dad, this is a horrible deal!"

"Shush now, dear-heart," he said, looking around the room to see who had heard her. "And anyway, it's too late. The deal has been made."

"How did you let it get this bad?" Gwynn asked. "I don't understand. We'd made a deal. You were going to wait until my birthday, let me have a vote."

"We wouldn't have lasted that long," Bertram said sadly. "Flaxen Moons wasn't in great shape when your grandfather died. He kept things going, sure, but he always had a lot of creditors too. This farm thrived during the Genome War, but without soldiers to feed, we lost a lot of business. And with the Alliance a shell of what it was, the trade routes are more dangerous than ever. Only the large corporations like TenDek with the Blue Band and the security they provide can afford to do any large-scale trade. Maybe your uncle Brandon—he might have been able to turn things around without the help of a corporation. He had the head for this stuff. But…."

Gwynn shook her head. She didn't want to think about that.

"You can do it, Gwynnie, I know you can," Bertram said, patting her on the shoulder. "You're the smartest person I ever met, even smarter than…."

Gwynn shrugged her father's hand off.

"Don't say it," she said.

"We have to get the celebration started," he said. "Dear-heart, try to have a little faith. Things will work out, in the end."

Gwynn couldn't think of anything else to say as she watched her father walk to Enzo and help him herd guests into the ballroom where tables had been set up at the center so that the diners could look up and see the stars. Sure, she thought, everything is going to be fine. So long as I can figure out how to make miracles happen.

READ MORE IN THE GLITTER OF GOLD FROM J.M. PHILLIPPE

Galactic Dreams

Volume 1

KAREN HARRIS TULLY
SOLDIER, Princess, REBEL SPY
A SPACE AGE RETELLING OF MULAN

Volume 2

About the Author

Karen Harris Tully creates elaborate worlds for her novels aided by her bachelor's in political science and economics. After growing up in the snowy mountains of Colorado, Karen experienced the traffic nightmare of Seattle before accidentally realizing she's a small-town girl. She happily lives in Raymond, WA, singing karaoke with her amazingly supportive husband, two beautiful children, and one hyper feline.

Find out more at:
KarenHarrisTully.com

Other Works by Karen Harris Tully

THE FAARIAN CHRONICLES

Exile*

Inheritance

Extinction

GALACTIC DREAMS VOLUME 1

Soldier, Princess, Rebel Spy

*2017 Kindle Book Awards Finalist

Connect with Karen for more information on upcoming books:

» *karenharristully.com*

» *facebook.com/KarenHarrisTully*

» *karenharristully.tumblr.com*

» *instagram: @KHTully*

Made in the USA
Monee, IL
24 May 2021

68499737R00164